MY FRIEND, SEDIKI

Myfanwy Johns

Cover picture is of a Date Farmer

Myfanwy Johns © Copyright 2007

British Library Cataloguing In Publication Data
A Record of this Publication is available
from the British Library

ISBN 978-1-84685-641-9

First Published 2007 by
Exposure Publishing,
an imprint of
Diggory Press Ltd
Three Rivers, Minions, Liskeard, Cornwall, PL14 5LE, UK
and of Diggory Press, Inc.,
Goodyear, Arizona, 85338, USA
WWW.DIGGORYPRESS.COM

*To Reba, who has been so
enthusiastic and supportive*

1

IT WAS late afternoon, and the sun was starting to sink towards the horizon, a large orange ball giving out its last monstrous heat before the cool relief of evening. Abdullah Aziz crossroads was jammed with vehicles trying to cross to the only filling station for miles. Mercedes, Chevrolets, Toyota pickups and Fords all jostled with each other to be first at the pumps. Under the dirty canopy small Arab boys scuttled around the drivers, collecting money and pressing the notes into the hands of an older man leaning against a greasy pillar in a state of apathy. The smell of hot oil and sweat hung in the still air undisturbed by the revving engines and the abominable noise. Horns were sounded, arguments broke out and passengers alighted to shout at each other in raucous voices, Abdullah Aziz crossroads was always the last straw on a long hot day.

Standing on a small dais of concrete observing the melee was an elderly man in a stained dish dash, a long shirt like robe, he wiped his lined face with the edge of his guttrah and spat decisively into the sand. In whichever direction he turned there was desert, a hot scrubby wilderness of thorn bushes and stoney sand, but he was not aware of it for the moment, his attention was fixed on the human scramble in front of him. In this lonely place he might have waited all day for such activity, and he would surely understand the need to be back on the road, for no matter in which direction the vehicles were headed, there was no destination for two hundred miles.

The man in the green Mercedes handed his money to a small boy, mopped at his forehead yet again, replaced his dark glasses and drove back onto the road. Before him lay the last leg of his journey home, a drive of some three hundred miles, which he estimated was as far as the eye could see, for the road ran straight and flat across the desert into the horizon.

"Now for the Whacky Races." he mumbled to himself, and as he pulled out onto the narrow ribbon of asphalt, others did the same and raced each other in order to be first in the convoy. Gradually as speed picked up gaps appeared between them and the traffic evened out and settled down to a steady pace.

The Mercedes cruised along at over a hundred miles an hour, too fast for some, too slow for others. Eddie Miller had learned long ago how to make a space around himself on the road. The journey to the capital, where he lived, was an ordeal he faced at the end of every week, an ordeal in trying to stay awake.

Tired after a week of hard selling in small towns all over the country, tired of the heat and the thousands of miles driving, the last part of his journey home was the most difficult. There was no help from the scenery, no landmarks, nothing of interest to catch the eye or interest the mind, merely an interminable stream of traffic in both directions. To keep awake he would look out for the latest casualties along the road, vehicles left there after their accidents as a warning to others, so it was said. Wreckage of every description lined the road at the edge of the sand. Rusting hulks, brand new cars, overturned pickups, all obscene carcasses, for they had been stripped of their wheels and anything that could be carried away almost as soon as the accident had occurred. Of course the grotesque warnings had largely been ignored, for every time Eddie passed along the road, new heaps of metal had been wedged into place. It was a small exercise, spotting the new ones, but it helped to pass the time.

The Englishman bent forward and fiddled with the radio, a blast of Arab music assailed his ears and he switched it off in disgust, chose a cassette by touch out of a box by his side and sat back to the sound of Country Music. He was a restless man, and very soon he was mopping his forehead again and trying to turn up the air conditioning. It was already to the limit, but the air around him still seemed to be packed with cotton wool. Eddie scratched at the sweat trickling down his leg and wished he were in shorts. He snorted to himself when he remembered that there were no drinks left in the cold box.

"Bad management, old chum." he murmured aloud and then had a thought, his son sometimes left a can of Coke in the pocket of the back seat. Screwing his body around carefully without taking his eyes off the road, he felt with his left hand

and smiled gratefully as he touched the smooth metal. The liquid would be warm and far too sweet, but at least it would do until he reached his flat and the blessed relief of a large G & T- with loads of ice. He smiled to himself again at the thought of the luxury and grimaced at the can of Coke which only served to tease his thirst. Irritably he switched off the tape and the car fell into silence until the hum of the engine became too much for him and he turned it on again.

The man's restlessness was a characteristic that had been built into every part of his make up, and contributed to his career success. Always on the move, ready with a laugh and a word for everybody, he had become a popular figure amongst his customers as well as his peers. In the hot soaking atmosphere of Hamra no one could keep up with him, his energy was boundless and his enthusiasm for his job made him a top salesman for his company.

Success for Eddie Miller was more than money in the bank, however, it was victory over his lack of education as a boy. He had played truant from school more often than he had attended it, only to discover at the age of sixteen that he had no knowledge that could help him earn a living. His personality was the only asset he knew he possessed and with great good sense and a big helping of desperation, he turned it to his advantage. He learned what every good salesman has always known, that to sell a product you first have to sell yourself. After that first realisation Eddie could have sold anything to anybody.

The Englishman was not at all handsome, he was too short and had a thick chunky body with shoulders sloping directly up into his head as though he had no neck at all, his thatch of sandy hair was on occasions at odds with his florid skin which threatened to become purple when he was angry. His one redeeming feature was his smile, it was positively angelic, and when he beamed it was enough to have everyone beam back at him. He had enormous brown eyes which reflected his moods and whether bulging or beaming they acted as a weather vane to his associates. His wife called him 'bullfrog' to herself when she was annoyed with him, but she had never said it to his face.

The sun had gone now and the sky was slashed with colour. Within a short time the heavens would be a dark blue and finally at a blink it would be night and the cool moon would be out. Suddenly the pickup in front gathered speed, the heads of the camels it was transporting lurched over the tailboard towards the Mercedes like sea monsters. Eddie looked about him for the reason suspecting an accident, instead he saw a spiral of wind whipping up the sand at the side of the road into twisters.

"God, no!" he breathed "that's all I need." he increased his speed accordingly in the hope that the wind was heading in the opposite direction. The last thing he wanted at this stage of his journey was a sandstorm that would bring him to a standstill for hours

He breathed a sigh of relief when he saw the small twisters lean in the direction from which he had just come and his spirits lifted as he saw ten minutes later the one landmark that announced his arrival at the outskirts of the capital, a giant advertisement for Coca Cola. Not for the first time he cursed the powers that be that allowed such cruelty, for to see a picture of enticing liquids at a point where most travellers had run out of liquid altogether was just torture.

The man's thoughts instantly turned to the bottle of Gin in his briefcase. It had reached him through many hands and much negotiation and had cost him the best part of £100, but it was worth it to him and he began to relish the anticipation of that first drink almost as much as he would relish the drink itself.

He picked up the empty can of Coke from the floor and crushed it in his large hand, throwing it onto the back seat in disgust. His tongue was about to cleave to the roof of his mouth with the sweetness of the drink, and his thoughts of cool clear gin were making the situation worse. With an effort he turned his thoughts to showering away the dust and grime of the journey, but then in his mind's eye the water was as enticing as the Gin. He could see it cascading and sparkling and his thoughts were back to his thirst again. It was a good thing that there were only a few more miles to go.

In a last burst of enthusiasm the traffic surged forward into the suburbs of the capital, where pavements started as soon as the sand ended. In the distance Eddie could see the tower cranes and half finished buildings lit wih spot lights so that the work need not stop, and within minutes he was driving through the main streets.

Avoiding the traffic which always crawled along the main shopping thoroughfares, the Englishman took several turnings into the back streets, down sandy alley ways bordering unfinished villas and pulled up outside a block of flats.

2

THE capital of Hamra the kingdom, was in fact the original site of Hamra the campsite. Long ago it was a desert Sheikdom ruled by a benign old man who made his living and that of his tribe from trading with the Bedu and smuggling contraband across his neighbours' borders. At one point his fort, situated in what could only be called an encampment, was stacked from dirt floor to the rafters with sunglasses and binoculars. The neighbouring Sheikdom, for some reason known only to themselves, had banned the use of them. In no time at all the stocks in the fort had dwindled to nothing and the money belts were full. On other occasions the old man had imported cameras in order to supply another State which had been smitten with a Muslim conscience and decreed that no photos or likenesses of the human face were to be allowed. The old man had lived on his wits and provided the means whereby his people could supplement their meagre existence and dependence on their goats with goods also from over his borders. The Sheikh had spent many hours sitting on the steps of his fort talking and debating with his contemporaries, looking so much like them that visiting dignatories had difficulty in picking him our from the goat herders until the old ruler would have to get up and introduce himself

All visitors to the small Sheikdom of Hamra whether political, salesmen or Pilots from the mail plane that flew in once a month, had to sleep in a dusty room in the fort and often all in the same room. There was nowhere else except the rickety structures of baked clay topped with a thatch of barrusti or dried palm leaves. That had been the original Hamra, another world of seventy years ago, with a Sheik living amongst his goat herders, only a little more settled than the Bedu themselves. Since those days things had changed so much that only the old could remember how things had really been. They told their families and anyone else who would listen that they blamed old Yusef, the Sheik for sending his sons to the West to be educated. Things were never to be the same again.

A far seeing British government spotting in this small place a future friend, took the boys under its wing. They were educated in Public School and lived with appointed guardians, only returning to Hamra when their University education had been completed.

The four sons were in their twenties when they returned to Hamra and their father's fort. What they found there was enough to alienate them from the old man for good; one solid building in a desert of hundreds of miles and an economy funded by goats and smuggling. They were determined to change it, and they did once and for all. Within a month Yusef was dead and the four brothers had started empire building.

It was obvious to the brothers that without land there would be no power, no development, no money. So they went out and took it. They swooped on their neighbours carrying off the Rulers and sometimes their daughters, who they took and married in order to prevent retaliation. They issued threats to encourage others to surrender to them or carried off their heirs and left them in the desert to die. Gradually they accumulated many possessions and land and the Hamra borders were extended for thousands of miles, until there was enough of the country and the spoils to share between them. The rest of their lives was spent in acquiring yet more land and possessions and guarding them against those who would have rebelled against them, but in one curious way they were all failures, not one of them could produce a son.

Year upon year saw only the birth of daughters. Wives were divorced, new wives married and many children born, but they were all girls. It was a thorn in their flesh and the one reason why the brothers still ruled the country equally, for they were all in a weak position until one of them produced an heir. The descendents of the goat herders told each other that it was a curse from their dead father Yusef, and it certainly must have crossed the minds of the brothers more than once. In time, age and accident overtook the brothers until only the youngest was left alive. In one last desperate attempt to produce a son, the old man married yet again and to everyone's amazement at last produced the heir he had waited for most of his life. The rejoicing amongst the family was of such dimensions that it must have stimulated the old man to greater efforts, for he fathered two more sons before he died.

11

The last of the four brothers had watched his sons grow into childhood with a great deal of delight mixed with apprehension, for he knew that he would not be alive to have the directing of their minds and the protection of their bodies. On his death bed he called a distant cousin to his side. To this man he entrusted the three boys, their health and their education. They were to be brought up as princes, he was told, and the strict instructions included an order to resist the interference from the many women in the family, who had plagued the rulers of Hamra for years.

It was soon noticed that the world press had begun to describe the Sheikdom as a Kingdom. After all, they reasoned if the boys were Princes, then their father must have been a King. To match their new titles and to honour the promise given to their father, the boys were indeed brought up like Royalty, being given the best education in Europe and being housed in the most lavish palaces that could be built for them.

Their education complete, the three princes returned to their kingdom and learned how to rule their country and how to squeeze as much aid out of the West as was possible. The West on their part looked with a kindly eye on yet another small country emerging from its chrysalis into the twentieth century. They provided investment, schools, advisers and sent in supervisors to oversee the enormous development programme that had already started. Hamra the desert State had become Hamra, the capital of Hamra.

To the outside world the princes were exceptional rulers, they enforced the strict Muslim law and controlled their people without appearing to be resented by any of them. Once again they ruled between them, just as their father and uncles had in the past, and once again no son had been born to any of them. The countries of the West, not realising the significance of their joint rule often wished their own politicians could agree to work together in such harmony.

It was the media, however that had taken the young men to their hearts and front pages, finding romance in the somewhat mundane story of a developing nation. It was their good looks that kept the cameras rolling, and their habit of keeping their mouths shut and assuming an air of mystery. Good looks, flowing robes, camel coats with gold embroidery and black shiny beards, all set against a deep blue sky and pale, pale yellow sand, was more than enough for at least one journalist to go overboard in his reports and compare Hamra and it's building site to 'The Desert Song' and later to the Turkish Delight advert. Even hard bitten political reporters seemed enchanted by the princes, ambassadors fawned on them and sycophants of every nation attended their Majlis and presented them with gifts. All at once Hamra was the place to be, overnight it had become fashionable.

To those who simply came on contract to the country and worked on development projects, it was just another desert kingdom emerging from the Middle Ages. They were there to work, sweat and collect their pay. If there was any time left they met up with acquaintances of their own kind and went in search of alcohol, there was always a party going on at someone's villa. For a time they would feel secure amongst friends and the more alcohol they could find, the more secure they felt, even though under Islamic law, the country was as dry as its desert.

It was generally agreed that the only way to survive the heat and the stress while working through their contracts was in this way. They met in each other's houses with drawn curtains, assuming that because they were hidden away, the police, if they knew, would turn a blind eye. For the most part they did, but there were occasions when stag parties got out of hand and erupted into the street, then large numbers of the ex pat community found themselves in jail with the promise of a Muslim punishment to come. Eddie Miller was privileged for he had his wife with him in Hamra, but he was unaware of how much a privilege it was. There were very few visas made available for women., the female sex had never been regarded very highly in the country, since so many had been born to the ruling family. The salesman had been puzzled at the time it had taken to receive the visa and because he was completely ignorant of the history of the country, put it down to Arab inefficiency.

All that was forgotten now, however, and the trials and tribulations of the ruling family left him supremely disinterested. His only concern was that his needs would be met as soon as he set foot in his flat. His leisure and work ran along preordained lines and they did not include anything that did not contribute to his creature comforts and his bank account. He thought of nothing else.

The salesman opened the car door and stretched his legs, reaching behind him for his briefcase which contained his best order yet and his precious bottle of gin. He handled it lovingly, keeping it away from the dust and sand that covered the paintwork of the Mercedes. He gave the car a pat and made a mental note to have it washed the next day, then as the humidity drew sweat from his forehead, he made a dash for the front door. His thoughts were first and foremost on that first drink he had been yearning for during the last hundred miles or so. He grinned to himself as he put the key into the lock of the main door. "Wonderful." he breathed to himself. He was home at last and had no need to go out into the desert until Saturday, the first day of the week.

3

JENNY MILLER had been expecting her husband for some hours, this was his day for homecoming and she knew what was expected of her. Ice bucket primed, glasses on a tray, fresh towels in the bathroom and fresh as fresh clean clothes. Cool clean sheets on the bed, a tasty meal and the air conditioning turned up as high as it would go.

Bobby, their son had tidied his room in a frenzy, dreading the first step on the staircase of the amazing man who came home every weekend and caused havoc, noise and general untidiness, then disappeared again for another week.

At ten years of age, Bobby had developed a deep inferiority complex and the fact that he was an only child did nothing to alleviate it. He had no brother to match up to, there was only his father, and he learned long ago that he would never match up to him. The boy regarded his father with a mixture of admiration and deep hatred. When he was home, his mother had very little time for him and after the first greeting, his father had none at all. If the truth were told, Eddie was constantly disappointed in his son. Bobby was so much like his mother, small framed and thin with blonde hair. His palor was pasty with a skin that gave it a translucent texture, but whereas those pale looks were enhanced in his wife, in a young boy they made him look simply fragile and weak.

He thought he ought to have been able to father a stocky red blooded child who enjoyed fighting and football and of course having something of his own bouncy personality. The more he saw of the child the more disgusted he became until Bobby, utterly disappointed with himself made up his mind that life was considerably more comfortable in his bedroom when his father was home

Jenny gave herself unsparingly to both of them, but to Eddie first. She waited on him hand and foot, creating a comfortable world for him to occupy on the couple of days a week he happened to be with her. For her son she did much the same thing when his father was absent. It was, she felt, her role in life and she accomplished it with conscientiousness.

The young woman had never questioned her way of life, and because she rarely looked inward beyond her role as wife and mother, she failed to recognise that she was a mature adult and an individual. This in turn blinded her to the fact that her son was anything other than a small boy to be fed and looked after, and her husband, the breadwinner and provider, for whom she cooked, cleaned and allowed access to her body. Not for her pleasure but for his, hers was the duty. Eddie was naturally happy with his wife for she never interfered with his decisions or challenged his leadership. It was just as well for there was no room in his life for a woman with ideas of her own, he had to have them all.

There was a hollow clatter of shoes on the terrazo staircase outside the flat, a dropping of something bulky, a curse and then a key in the door. Bobby ran to his mother and she put an arm round his shoulders.

"Your father." she said unnecessarily, and the two of them stood in the centre of the room with their eyes on the door.

The way in which people enter a room can speak volumes about them. Some walk straight in holding the door at arm's length and pause, some peer round a door clinging to the handle to reassure themselves that it is safe to enter, others almost run into a room and slam the door behind them in defiance. Eddie burst into rooms, sometimes dropping his parcels, his key or anything he might be carrying and often falling over his feet in his eagerness to greet the people on the other side.

"Jenny!" he yelled laughing, picking up his key and stuffing it into his pocket. He threw his briefcase onto the couch and then remembered the gin and picked it up again to make sure it was intact. Dropping it again he raced over to his son and picked him up playfully and threw him over his shoulder.

"Bobby!" he shook the boy roughly "How are you son?"

There was no reply, just a mute acceptance of the horseplay, Eddie was already regretting picking up the child, he could feel the thin frail body and it repelled him. He dropped him hurriedly, making for Jenny with his arms outstretched, he caught her to him in a bear hug.

"Jenny, I'm home, I'm home." he yelled dancing her around the room.

16

"Yes, I know." she managed to gasp, laughing and clutching her chest.

Leaving her stranded in the middle of the room gasping, Eddie swiftly went to his briefcase.

"Look!-gin." he said handing it over to her.

"Real gin?" she laughed. "trust you."

"Yep, moved heaven and earth to get it. Pour a double there's a girl."

Eddie threw himself into the couch and tore off his shoes and socks. At once he was on his feet again, pointing his toes and stretching his feet pretending to dance. He winced as he caught his shin against a table, his eyes closing, but at the chink of ice they opened like shutters and he grabbed the glass Jenny offered him. She stood patiently while her husband, standing like a chunk of granite, his feet placed firmly apart; one hand in his pocket and the other holding the glass, gulped down his first drink.

"Ahh!" he groaned in enjoyment "that was Grrrrreat." he shouted gesturing with the glass at his wife who was already on her way to the kitchen "Grrrreat," he yelled again, "what was it?"

"Great." she called over her shoulder, the standard response.

"Have one with me and let's watch the cartoons." Eddie bawled to her and sat down with a thump. Jenny had no need to answer, she knew that he would never notice whether she had a drink or not, or even if she were there at all. Quietly she got on with the dinner.

At some point in the exchange between his parents, Bobby had disappeared into his room and they had not noticed. The salesman absorbed in Tom and Jerry slapped his knee in enjoyment and made regular trips to the gin bottle on the sideboard. The Master was home.

It was Thursday morning and the strong light of day was already penetrating the double thickness of curtains at six a.m. There was no best time of day in Hamra, it was always hot, always humid. Sweat streamed down faces at the slightest attempt at exercise. In heavily air-conditioned flats and villas, male design had omitted that vital piece of equipment in kitchens, and unless servants were employed the mistress of

17

the household spent many hours literally sweating over a hot stove.

In the flats where the Millers lived, the aroma of sausages and eggs drifted up appetisingly from the ground floor on the lazy air. Beef sausage of course, no pork found its way into Hamra.

After a glance at his watch, Eddie lay as still as he could looking at his wife asleep beside him, her golden lashes curling against her cheek like a child. At moments like this he felt at his most comfortable, he warmed to his wife with a tender feeling he would have called love, and others would have called affection. He was debating whether to wake her up so that he could have breakfast, or to launch himself at her for the third time in ten hours and make what passed for love between them. The decision was made for him, a scratching at the bedroom door announced the fact that Bobby was up and about and looking for his mother.

The man watched the door open slowly and saw the pale face hang in the gap. On seeing his father awake, the boy silently withdrew and shut the door,

"Tch!" Eddie tossed his head disgustedly "always scared to death."

It would have to be breakfast now, the warm comfortable feeling had gone and the usual resentment had taken its place.

"How on earth had Jenny produced such a wimp?" he murmured.

Jenny stirred and stretched, not looking at her husband she immediately swung her feet out of bed and into her slippers. Eddie noticed with a grin that the nightdress he persistently tore off her as his passion mounted was always replaced by the following morning. 'She's a modest woman,' he told himself. 'No bad thing out here, too many men.' he went on, 'but there, that wasn't a problem in our marriage, Jenny so quiet and orderly' he might have added 'so tame.'

"Sausages and eggs is it?" he said to her back as she went through the door.

"If you like." she answered mildly over her shoulder.

"I'll be going in this morning."

"Alright."

His mood altered again and he scratched his heel against the sheets until they rumpled up into a heap.

He felt almost joyful, remembering the order he had brought back with him the night before. That would make the so and so's sit up and take notice, he wasn't the best salesman they had for nothing.

He closed his eyes and imagined the whole world, that is Eddie's world looking at him in admiration, laughing with him, slapping him on the back

"Grrrrreat!" he shouted out aloud "what is it?----Grrrrreat!" he answered himself. "must have a shower." He scrambled out of the untidy bed with nothing on, he nearly always slept in the nude.

"Bobby!" he bawled through the open door "where are you boy?" He felt good, everyone should feel as good as he did, he would bestow his cheerfulness and good nature on the world in general, even Bobby. He felt even better at this unwarranted show of geniality, he would let Bobby scrub his back.

Eddie pounded into the bathroom, scarcely noticing the clothes laid out for him. The fresh sweet smelling towels lined up exclusively for him, only if they had been missing would he have noticed.

"Come on boy, you shall have the privilege of scrubbing my back, good exercise for you." he chortled, laughing out loud in his happy mood.

The man would never learn, as quickly as he changed moods and adapted himself to them, he was slow ro realise that others were unable to do the same. So many people responded to him, his moods, his laughter, he confidently expected that each time he tried, his son would respond also. It was never to be and it surprised him every time he noticed it, but he never gave up trying.

Bobby sidled into the bathroom, his father's mood warning him that he had better do what was required of him quickly and efficiently if it was not to change. The young boy hated washing his father's back, not just because he hated his father, but because he hated his father's body. Eddie was proud of his physique and showed himself off blatantly, he had none of the short man's inferiority complex, but neither did he show signs of the superiority with which small men normally compensate for their size. Whenever he could he would walk around the flat naked, not for any other reason than that he was not ashamed of his body, and he was more comfortable that way.

Bobby stood by the door looking at the large chunky body under the shower. He felt that he would have been happy to sink his teeth into his father's buttocks. He looked at the man's legs, hairy with sandy coloured strands streaked by the water. He knew that when dry those same hairs would be curled, where the shorts he wore stopped, and short and straight to the crotch. The broad smooth brown back looked as strong as it was, the backbone nestling like a long dimple. The boy watched his father throw water and suds over his head and then his fierce washing of the short wide neck.

"He's like a bull." Bobby thought dispassionately, "like a great orange bull."

He grinned to himself feeling clever, and at that moment his father turned.

Bobby instantly looked at the floor, this was the worst part. He simply could not imagine how his father could stand there and show off his genitals with a complete lack of shame. They were so big, so lumpy. Compared wirh himself he thought an adult was ugly, very ugly, he could not bear to look.

"Hey," Eddie stopped lathering himself and saw the downcast look of his son. "No need to be shy, my boy, when you have something like this to offer."

He flicked at his penis and laughed uproariously and began to lather his shoulders. Bobby looked up and directed his gaze at the frosted windows beyond the shower. From the front he knew that his father was ugly even when he had his shorts on, his hairy chest was course and curled over the top of his collar. Somewhere the child had read 'Thou shalt not look upon thy father's nakedness' It was no surprise to him at all, no one should look on nakedness when it was that ugly.

The boy's thoughts did not register on his face, from long practice he had learned to hide behind a mask of indifference. Unfortunately whereas in Jenny the mask she assumed gave her the appearance of mystery and seduction, in Bobby it merely produced a look of vacancy.

"Oh for goodness sake, come and give me a scrub." Eddie's voice was betraying his already changing mood. He might have known that being in the same room as his son for more than five minutes would produce nothing but irritation for him.

The child grasped the sponge and stood on the bathroom chair. Water splashed down all over him until his hair was soaked and his shorts limp, but that was no concern of his father. Peering through the teeming water he handed the boy a nailbrush.

"Come on, scrub." he ordered "I'm no softy like some I could mention, scrub- hard!"

Bobby scrubbed and scraped until the broad back was almost bleeding, but a false sense of pride prevented the man from giving in and he waited for the boy to weaken first.

"That's enough." he said eventually "you must be getting tired now, better go and have a rest." he said spitefully and the child thankfully scuttled out of the door.

Eddie looked at his back in the mirror and decided to put some ointment on the raw patches. "Good scrub." he said to himself. He would not have admitted even to himself that he had gone too far, was always apt to go too far, and eventually might have to pay for it.

4

THURSDAY was reporting in day for the company salesmen who had been scattered over thousands of miles for a week. It was also a day to look forward to, for being the equivalent of a Saturday with a holiday the following day, parties and get togathers were arranged and the prospect of a lie in bed in the morning was a treat

The company Eddie worked for had their offices in the centre of the city in a small block of flats. Leaving home a little later than usual, he drove as fast as the law would allow, lost his way around a new detour that had appeared since the previous week and arrived at the office with a screech of tyres. He dived out of the car, bumping his briefcase against the strengthened glass of the main door and swept into the foyer.

However irritated Eddie had become on his journey into the city centre, his mood had not changed, he loved Thursdays and he was going to enjoy this morning. Raising his briefcase over his head in salute, he greeted the Pakistanis sitting in the reception area.

"Salaam you lot." he yelled in chummy fashion and they grinned back. He knew that the papers they were shuffling from one to the other would still be circulating by the end of the day. Pakistani clerks had that one great talent, they skilfully produced at least half a dozen papers when one would do, and in the process created extra jobs for their relations.

"Aleikum Salaam." they all murmured shyly to the chunky salesman and Eddie passed through the connecting doors into the passage and up to the Sales Offices.

Eddie sauntered into the chief's office dropping his case on the floor and wiped the sweat from the back of his neck with a spotless white handkerchief.

"Phew! when's winter then?" he said in greeting to the group of men sitting around the large desk.

Murmurs of "Here, here." and "You can say that again." and laughter came from the garishly dressed circle. Thursday meant no canvassing, therefore they could relax and wear anything they wished to within reason, coloured shirts, shorts, T.shirts and jeans. Reggie Mycroft by contrast was always immaculate in crisp white shirt and black trousers, the managers' uniform.

"Morning Eddie." he grinned at the newcomer "just in time this week, no hangovers?"

General sniggering around the group produced a brotherly feeling, a warm camaraderie, he shook his head.

"Can't guarantee to-morrow folks, having a party to-night, everybody coming?" There was general assent.

Eddie sat down next to his friend. "You'll be there won't you old chap couldn't have a party without you."

Don turned his round pink face towards him suspiciously "Why not?"

"Well, when the dancing starts, if you are there, we can't get any complaints from the floor below can we?"

The general hoot of laughter was in response to to the look on his fat friend's face.

"Oh, don't worry, I'll be there and I'll bring Martha as well, then you can make as much noise as you like." he retorted good naturedly.

"Well gentlemen" the chief cut in "let's look at our figures for this week, sooner we start sooner we'll finish.".

Eddie reached for his briefcase and savoured the moment. This was what it was all about, good orders, best figures, plenty of commission and the agreement of his peers, that he was indeed the best. Life was very sweet at Thursday briefings.

As a rule he was one of the first to leave the meeting, his restlessness not allowing him to stay long in one place, but to-day he had some business of his own to attend to.

"See you later." the chief called to the salesmen as they left the office. "shut the door Reilly, will you?"

Eddie finished replacing his papers in his briefcase and looked over his shoulder to be sure the door was securely closed.

"Right, chief, have you got it?"

"Yes, no problem, it's in the staff lavatory."

The salesman laughed, a short bark

"That's terrific. The last time it was in the tank on the roof, at least we are getting nearer to earth. Don't tell anybody for goodness sake, no one will fancy it if they know where it has come from."

Reggie tidied some papers on the desk,

"Don't worry Eddie my boy, they'd drink the stuff it it was pouring out of the cistern, and well you know it."

"How much Squire?" Eddie made a flourish of taking his wallet out of his back pocket.

"Twenty."

"Phew! That's a bit steep old man."

The chief sat back in his chair and placed his hands behind his head in order to shield his bald spot from the cold blast of the air conditioner.

"Sorry, but it's the best, and even after you cut it, it'll be strong enough to fell an ox."

"Oh well, if it's the best." he thought of the money he had paid out for his comparatively small bottle of gin and gave in.

"O.K., got to have it anyway, down to our last 20 bottles of wine." he opened his wallet and selected some notes.

"Sterling."

Eddie dropped his hands

"Aw, come on Reggie old man." he protested.

"It has to be that way at the moment I'm afraid." the chief dropped his hands and leaned forward. "I don't think you understand what risks these chaps are taking to produce his stuff."

"But they've produced Sediki for years in Hamra, before Europeans came along, they must know how to protect themselves surely?"

"Oh yes they do, by moving around all the time, trouble is they keep getting caught and the supply is starting to dry up, unless you are really in the know."

Eddie pursed his lips.

"Getting dangerous?" he asked thinking of the party.

"Three last week." Reggie drew his index finger across his throat.

Eddie looked alarmed

" No problem for us though eh?"

"No problem as long as we are careful." Reggie sat back

abruptly, catching his bald spot in the draught again. "Go on then, get your booze and I'll see you to-night.

The salesman silently handed over the notes and started towards the door.

"By the way, where do you keep your wine?" the chief asked innocently "must be a problem in a flat."

Eddie grinned cheerfully

"You are not wrong Squire." he answered "it's buried in a friend's garden, but I'm not telling whose."

"All right, you can keep your secret." Reggie laughed. "send Shafique in will you, I have a message for him."

Striding through the foyer on the way to the staff conveniences, Eddie called "Shafique! You're wanted."

Inside the staff toilets Eddie located a large box under the towels in the cupboard, inside was a gallon demijohn. Carefully resealing the lid, he placed it under his arm and made his way to the car. The warm air hit him as the call to prayer sounded from the mosque opposite, it was followed immediately by a succession of mosques calling raucously "Allah Akbah!" Balancing the box and the briefcase on the bonnet, he fumbled with his keys. Out of the corner of his eye he saw the faithful gather into long rows inside the building. The windows were wide open to allow in any stray whiff of breeze. At the entrance, rows and rows of shoes and sandals laid neatly side by side, had the appearance of a market stall As he scrambled into his car, the long row of worshippers knelt down and bent forward, touching their heads to the ground like branches before the wind. The grace and solemn moment was lost on the Englishman.

"Bottoms up!" he said irreverently and forgot about them instantly

Eddie took his sun glasses out of his pocket and placed the cold frames on his nose. There was always a moment or two to wait while the condensation dried, before he could see through them. In that first moment he thought that someone was looking at him. He pushed the glasses down his nose and looked over the top, but the glare produced a haze of it's own, he pushed them back again. As his vision cleared he was certain that someone was watching him. He looked intently across to the door of the mosque, he squirmed for a moment when he saw a tall Arab looking directly at him.

25

It was not unusual for Arabs to idly watch passers by, but this one was not idly looking in the Englishman's direction, he seemed to be watching intently. Eddie squirmed again and took a quick look at the box by his side. Secret Police? The box looked innocuous enough, there were no markings on it and it indicated nothing. He looked up again and the Arab had gone. For a moment Eddie felt the hairs rising on the back of his neck, perhaps someone knew what he had in the car. He slid the car into the mainstream of the traffic and started to relax, he managed a short laugh to himself. How could anyone possibly know what he had in the box? Guilty conscience that's all, he convinced himself. Nevertheless it had been a distinctive Arab, and he *had* been looking directly at him or his car. Eddie thought about it as he manoeuvred yet another detour around unfinished buildings and the cranes parked in the middle of the road.

"There's one thing about it" he said to himself "I shall know him if I see him again."

As a salesman, Eddie made a fetish of remembering faces. It had stood him in good stead many times when others were hesitating over names and trying to remember customers. He made it his business to fit every face to a name,. So that wherever he met the person again he would know him. He made a mental note of the Arab, concentrating his picture memory on every detail he could remember about his appearance.

The dish dash he wore had been no different from millions of others, the camel coat, although elaborate in gold decoration was hardly unique, the white headress and band, the guttrah was again unremarkable. The man had played with the same sort of worry beads as any other Arab, flicking them backwards and forwards across the back of his hand. Eddie was searching for something different about the man. A glint of sunlight catching his watch strap solved the problem. "Gold" he said " those worry beads were solid gold." he saw in his mind the glint of sunlight on the beads, the rich glow against the brown hands. "Gold worry beads." He whistled. "money!" he affirmed to himself. "Right, so far so good, what else?"

He thought of the face of the man, wrinkling his brow in

concentration. A small boy knocked at his window while he was stopped at the lights and asked him for alms and Eddie exasperated at being interrupted waved him away, his eyes wide with impatience. He could see the face of the Arab, yes, very dark, cultured? Not necessarily so. Nose? Hooked- yes definitely hooked and very hooked as well he remembered now, and those eyes. Yes, it was the eyes that had drawn his interest in the first place he realised. Dark piercing eyes over a hooked nose. Right, that was it. He knew him now, he was satisfied he would know him again even if he met him in England. The face was noted, docketed and filed away in his mind. Eddie would know him anywhere, the only thing that was missing was his name.

Picking up speed he had already dismissed the Arab out of his thoughts and was concentrating on the preparations for his party. Jenny would have all the right food, she could always be depended on. His responsibility was the drinks and that would only take a short time to arrange.

'Maybe a shower and a nap until the sun went down' he thought, it was very inviting.

5

FOR Jenny, Thursday had a routine of its own. While the super salesman was at the office, she would put to rights the muddle and mess of the previous evening. The neat flat would have been turned into an untidy bachelor pad. Glasses were stuck to tables, cushions on the floor on top of shoes and socks, papers strewn all over the place by means of a careless throw followed by a cascade onto the floor. The bathroom would be littered with wet towels and a light sprinkling of talcum powder would cover every surface. The bedroom was in a similar state and the sheets so smoothly cool and inviting the night before would now be rumpled and in a heap. Later she would have to prepare for the party.

Jenny sighed, but she really minded very little, for she accepted it as her job, after all it made her feel needed and not only that, she enjoyed putting things to rights. The lounge was finished and she had begun on the bathroom when the doorbell rang.

"Damn!" she muttered "I bet that's Martha."

Wiping her hands and tossing a stray wisp of hair out of her eyes, she opened the door.

"Morning! Doing the clean up after the boss has hit it routine?"

Her friend was standing on the threshold and by her side was a tall man.

She turned to him

"Same every week for us wives. Hubby comes home turns the little palace into a tip and goes off to the office. Then we have to clean the place up all over again."

The man grinned and shifted his feet.

"Brought you a fella." Martha grinned up at the man who held his hand out to Jenny.

"Jolly, Bill Jolly"

"I'm Jenny, do come in, I'll put the coffee on." she turned into the room.

"No time, sorry." Martha pointed down the stairs "Still got my bomb site to sort out, I'll leave Bill with you though, he's got problems with his curtains or something, told him you're the one to help- OK?"

Bill Jolly followed Jenny into the room, she rubbed her hands together nervously wondering what to say.

"Oh do sit down-" she said in a rush "I can't imagine why Martha thought I'd be any good to you, but I'll try if you like." She glanced over her shoulder "um"

"I think I've come at the wrong time " Bill Jolly offered seeing quite plainly that the young woman had her thoughts elsewhere.

"No-well, I do have a little time before Eddie comes home. You're new I presume?"

She sat down opposite him and looking at him properly she was struck by his face, it was very kindly, the eyes were warm.

For an answer he stretched out his arms and hitched up his trouser legs, they were stark white.

They both laughed easily.

"I'll tell you what the problem is and be on my way." the man offered.

"Would you like coffee?" Jenny had resented the interruption, now she felt of a sudden that she would not mind sitting down for a moment or two.

"No, not now."

"It's the curtains?" Jenny cut in.

"Well, it's everything really, the place is terrible, unbearable colours, ghastly looking furniture, most things seem to be broken, holes in the carpet, you name it, it's unlivable."

"Oh boy!" Jenny pulled a face at his expression. "Where is this place?"

Bill waved his hand in the direction of the door "Over the road in that monstrous block of flats. I'm sure the rest of the world lives there as well, it must be the noisiest place I've ever lived in. There are people passing my door all day and the terrazo floor echoes. It sounds as though a herd of elephants are learning tap dancing out there."

Bill caught sight of her hiding a smile behind her hand

"I'm moaning aren't I?" he grinned at her "I know I am, but it's the first chance I've had to have a good moan and you really are listening aren't you?"

"Yes, yes of course." Jenny said politely.

"There are so few people in this world that listen."

"Really?" she had no idea of the response required of her. She glanced at her watch

"I can see you are on tenterhooks to get on, why don't I come back another time now I have met you.?"

"Well, I don't want to appear inhospitable, but we have a party tonight, and there's so much to do---- why not come to the party?" she was pleased at the thought. "we could have a proper talk then." Jenny was suddenly anxious for him to say yes, it would be nice to have a fresh guest, a change from the usual people that circulated constantly from one party to another.

Bill stood up and looked down over her fair head,

"Not much for parties I'm afraid. Anti social you know." he teased.

"Oh go on!" everyone will be delighted to meet you.

"Never mind about everyone, what about you?" he flirted, beaming down on her confused face.

Jenny swallowed hard.

"I didn't get you that coffee." she said eventually "Do sit down, I shall have to make some anyway."

There was a noise at the door, a customary fumbling with keys and a dropped briefcase, a scuffle with the door and Edward Miller burst into the room balancing the box containing the Sediki precariously while he retrieved the key from his teeth.

"Jenny!" he bawled and strode across the room to the kitchen. In passing he placed the box on the dining room table and only then caught sight of the man on the couch.

"Sorry old man, didn't see----- " he looked at his wife through the dining hatch, she was filling a kettle.

"Bill is new to the company, just out." she told him.

"Great stuff!" Eddie beamed at the man and extended his hand walking towards him, his head stuck out as though about to attack. "Eddie Miller." he said, his 5'6" looking up into Bill's 6' 3". as Bill Jolly stood up.

"Hell! You are tall." he exclaimed in wonder.

Bill smiled patiently

"Bill Jolly---- yes it is cooler up here and yes I could have been a policeman but my feet were too flat.---OK?"

"Yeah." Eddie cast his large brown eyes to the ceiling and back again. "Point taken squire, shan't meansh again."

The salesman threw himself into an easy chair

"Sit down." he ordered and looked over his shoulder towards the kitchen. "Jenny!" he bawled "drinks."

"No really," Bill said quickly "Not for me, your wife is making coffee."

"Wha-?" Eddie was shocked, he could not remember the last time someone had refused a drink in Hamra. He took a long look at the visitor.

"Bit early isn't it?" Bill tried to soften the refusal feeling the change in atmosphere.

"Not really." Eddie said flatly and stood up again and strode to the sideboard." always the right time for a drink, you'll get to know that if you are out here long".

"Yes, yes of course." Bill murmured taking a cup of coffee from Jenny and balancing it on his bony knees. For some reason he felt in the wrong and wished he had gone before this ginger haired man had come home.

Eddie carried his glass over to the easy chair and bounced into the cushions the ice clattering noisily. He took a long drink and opened his eyes wide to the ceiling.

"Grrreat!" he shouted. "What is it?"

"Great" Jenny answered automatically and then caught Bill's eye and felt silly.

"What's the job?" Eddie asked abruptly.

"System analyst" Bill answered pleasantly, feeling obligated to cajole this wild personality.

Not wanting a drink and being a System Analyst made some kind of sense to Eddie.

"Mmm." he commented. He had already started to look impatient and without knowing why, Jenny had begun to feel as embarrassed for Eddie as she was for Bill.

"Bill wants me to help him sort his flat out." she explained "new curtains and things like that."

"Oh yes." Eddie said without looking at his visitor. He took another gulp of his drink and chewed on a piece of ice.

Bill finished his coffee quickly, the homely atmosphere of the room had changed into a charged battle ground, he felt that he was somehow at fault, and must get out of there as soon as possible. He stood and thanked Jenny for the coffee.

"Cheers!" he said to Eddie, it was the most affable phrase he could manage at that moment.

Eddie's eyes bulged as he looked up at the man in front of him, he made a last effort to overcome his distaste

"Got a party tonight, friends, some company people, like to come?" he stood up and advanced towards the gin bottle.

The newcomer had already revised his intentions of attending the party, he had no desire to spend his time with someone whose sole aim was to put him down.

"Very busy I'm afraid, still moving in." he replied regretfully. "had to ask for help with the flat, that's why I was here, Jenny said she would try."

His mood changing instantly, Eddie beamed at him.

"Oh yes, Jenny very good sort, help out certainly."

'Me Tarzan, you Jane.' Bill thought to himself and smothered a grin.

"Can't work all the time you know." Eddie was calling to him as he stuffed ice into his glass." Parties are important, plenty of chat and drinks and all that."

"Well, it's very good of you, but--------"

"Please yourself." Eddie cut in rudely and picking up his box from the table with one hand and carrying a glass in the other he stormed into the kitchen. Jenny walked to the door with her visitor.

"Eddie is very boisterous when he's going to have a party." she said apologetically.

"Do come, we haven't sorted anything out yet." she looked up at Bill and he could see that she was sincere. Feeling that during the last fifteen minutes he had been on a roller coaster where some kind of battle had ensued, he suddenly made up his mind about the party.

"For you, I'll be there." he said smiling "we have a lot to say to each other."

The young woman watched as Bill Jolly loped easily down the stairs, she had surprised herself. The housework was unfinished, the party catering not even thought about and all she could do was wish that her visitor had stayed. She wanted to know so much more about him. Yes, there was a lot to talk about. Grinning to herself she thought 'I do like him.'

6

JENNY stood for a while looking out of the lounge window. There on the sky line were hundreds of flats like her own. Some finished, some with gaping holes for windows. The traffic snarled and diverted then jammed in every street. Through the darkened glass of the window she could see the sun beating down relentlessly, casting black shadows in corners and glaring blindness along the streets. The central air conditioning hummed contentedly sending cool air gently across the room and she was glad that she had no need to go out that day

"What a place!" she said aloud "nothing to see, nowhere to go and always sweaty." she pulled herself together, it was time for lunch, time to see what kind of a mess Eddie was making in the kitchen. Picking up the coffee cups and straightening the cushions she returned there, to her headquarters.

Eddie was cutting the Sediki, he had decanted half of the clear liquid into another demijohn and was filling both with water.

"Right twit, that one." he commented.

"Mm." she answered noncommittally.

"You wonder where they come from, those toffee nosed wimps." he poured a small amount of liquor into a tumbler and tasted it. "Good God!" he exclaimed, and then "Bloody good stuff Jenny!"

"Good." she said dutifully.

Eddie filled his old empty gin bottles one by one and took them into the lounge. He checked the mixer drinks, cigarettes and cigars, then his duties were finished.

When lunch was over, Bobby who had dashed in and out again returned downstairs to play with Georgie, Don's son, he was not missed.

"Now then." Eddie rubbed his hands together, "A nice shower, a little bit of nookie and a zizz." he said crudely.

Jenny sighed heavily, she should have been happy that her husband was home, she should have been happy that everything was in order and in place, but she was disturbed.

For the first time in Hamra she had seen her husband through someone else's eyes, and realised what a child he was.

The bustle of the day had subsided. The last Salah, prayer time, was over and night had fallen. A sweet smell of Oleander travelled along the streets from the villa gardens on the warm night air. Small Arab shops, still open for business shed their light onto gloomy pavements scattered with building rubble. Where contractors had finished for the week, barricades had been erected with the usual diversion signs pointing in every direction at once, so that if anyone had taken any notice of them, they would end up travelling in circles. Bedu returning into the desert had already taken the flashing warning lights that had been placed near dangerous pot holes and the unwary were in danger of twisting an ankle or even breaking their neck.

Men of all nationalities sauntered along the main thoroughfares watching other men, there were few women out after dark. There was almost nothing for the single man to do and nowhere for them to go except cafes and supermarkets. Most would return to their flat, portacabin or compound and read a book, or get drunk on illicit liquor and risk being caught by the Religious Police. Others would catch up on their sleep and hope to remain comatose through Friday, waking only to start work again on Saturday. It was a barren life in a barren place and no one seemed to care about anyone else. Even friends were only acquaintances and once the contract was finished, the contact was broken.

Eddie, though, was happy, he felt comfortable again. He looked around his home with affection, it was clean, comfortable, bright and welcoming. The glasses twinkled on the sideboard and the bottles glowed pink and green. He had recovered the last bottles of wine from inside the air conditioning system, and grinned to himself when he remembered telling Reggie that he had buried them in a garden. It was always wise not to let anyone know where you hid your booze. He barked a short laugh as in his mind's eye he saw Reggie with a spade, drunk as a lord, digging up the nearest villa garden. It wouldn't be the first time someone had done that, he reflected.

He glanced at his wristwatch and then at the table, Jenny had excelled herself with the buffet as usual, everything was ready.

"Are you ready Jenny?" he called through the closed bedroom door. "First guests won't be long."

"Coming." she answered and opened the door, patting her hair.

Eddies eyes bulged like humbugs and he beamed "You look Grrreat!---" what do you look like?"

"Great." she said with a smile. Although his compliments were rare, when he did pay one it was like basking in the sun.

"Everything looks terrific" he went on "done a fine job." he said encouraging his troops before battle. "Drink?"

"No Captain." Jenny responded.

"What?"

"No, its all right, not yet, there's something I want to ask you." her husband's mood would not be so accommodating again that evening.

"Ask away old girl." he said over his shoulder, busy with a bottle.

"Can we go down the Souk to-morrow?" she asked.

"In the morning?"

"No other time to go to the market." she said "you did promise Bobby last week."

"Oh Bobby!" he said disgustedly.

"Go on Eddie, it's such a long time since we all went out together" she touched his arm looking at him appealingly as her son had to her earlier in the day.

"Oh heck Jenny, I'm not going to be fit for anything in the morning." he protested. "just as I was looking forward to getting as high as a kite." he looked like a small child deprived of a treat.

Jenny was in turn annoyed

"Good heavens! Eddie, there are parties every week, you could stretch a point."

"*We* don't have a party every week" he said petulantly.

She snorted in derision

"You always say Bobby is a baby, but you act just like one yourself sometimes." she turned away and fiddled with the napkins on the table.

Her husband watched her for a moment scowling, but nothing could dent his happy mood for long. He swallowed what was in his glass and gave in.

"All right, we'll go down the Souk in the morning, and I hope you enjoy it," he said adding under his breath " because I won't."

"Baby!" Jenny said to him. Playfully he caught her hand "Stop fiddling around with those things and give me a kiss." he ordered swinging her around and catching her in his arms. She fended him off.

"Stop it!, your guests are coming I can hear them on the stairs."

"All right, but you just wait until later." he threatened good naturedly.

"OK. I'll wait." she laughed.

"Where is Bobby anyway?" Eddie was only interested in case the child would be a nuisance that evening.

"Downstairs with Georgie, staying the night there."

Eddie rubbed his hands together pleased.

"Shafique baby sitting?"

"Yes, they both like him, he tells fortunes."

"Does he now?" Eddie had a thought "maybe he'd come up and tell a few for us."

Jenny was alarmed

"Of course not." she said quickly. "Poor old Shafique would hate it."

"Would he?" Eddie was surprised.

At that moment the bell rang and Eddie bounced over to the door.

Some wit had previously described Martha and Don as a couple of Kellies at the bottom of a budgie's cage. It was insulting but anyone could see what was meant. The couple were both small and fat, both of them had a high colouring and both of them were as homely as anyone you could wish to meet. Martha moving towards middle age had taken on a new lease of life, Hamra was her first tour abroad and she was taking to the social life like a duck to water. Don, a good solid salesman, never contributing heart stopping figures to the chart in the office, brought in consistent steady orders. He enjoyed the social life as much as his wife and everyone seemed to like them.

"Hello Jenny." Martha came into the room jauntily. "like my new dress?" she gave a twirl. Jenny was startled at the gaudy shades of orange and red, the huge flowers with purple centres. She attempted to smile.

"Yes, of course, very nice." she finally managed.

"Drinks you two? Eddie fled to the sideboard with Don close behind.

"Told her not to wear that thing." Don said behind his hand in Eddie's ear.

Eddie grinned and screwed his eyes up, shaking his head

"Never mind old chum, at least you can't lose her." the two men spluttered with laughter.

"Drink Martha?" Eddie's eyes twinkled at her. Absentmindedly she held out her hand, her own eyes on the table.

"Good grief! What a spread!" she exclaimed " I must have a taste of everything, I knew we were right not to eat before coming, you always put on such a good feast." she turned to Jenny "Cheers!"

"She'll never get used to eating as much as she wants to." Don was saying to Eddie. "Since she went on that starvation diet I've had to keep an eye on the cat's dinner when it's been on the floor too long." he laughed uproariously at his humour and his pink face became suffused with colour, his eyes stood out and sweat beaded on his forehead.

"Hey! Steady on old chum." Eddie admonished. "go on like this and you'll never last the night out."

Gradually the room filled with guests, drinks were placed in open hands, small groups of friends formed, old enemies separated to opposite ends of the lounge. It was all routine, and the noise level rose along with the level of alcohol in the blood. Martha, almost as red in the face as her rotund husband, was enjoying herself immensely. She was laughing louder and louder at her husband's jokes and they became sillier as the evening lengthened. She caught Jenny's hand when she was passing with a plate of chicken legs.

"Jenny!" she yelled in her ear "Who on earth are those people in the corner?"

Jenny looked across to the other side of the room where Eddie was holding forth on how to sell engines to the Arabs. It was easy to pick him out in the crush, for his voice boomed out in higher decibels than any other, and he was in such good humour that he wanted everyone to hear him. A tall spindly man with blonde hair drooped over her husband staring blankly into his face, beside him a short Lebanese hung on every word.

"Don't really know Martha, Eddie did say something about Embassy people."

"That'll be it." her friend said triumphantly. "that fair one looks a real droopy drawers." She turned to the small crowd around her.

"Have you noticed that about Embassy people? They always seem to be wet and wishy washy, and they never speak to you, stuck up lot."

She looked over her shoulder at the men again

"You mark my words, they won't speak to anyone else while they're here, we wouldn't be good enough for them".

At that moment Eddie decided that he had said all there was to say on the subject of salesmanship and grabbing a bottle went round topping up glasses. The room became unbearably hot, and although the air conditioning was set at full, the atmosphere was heavy and humid, the cigarette smoke hanging in great whispy clouds in the crowded room. The ginger haired man took his handkerchief out of his pocket, feeling the heat for the first time and dabbed at his brow. He sat on a dining chair near the fan brought in from the kitchen, he was well content. The party was a success, everyone was laughing and talking, there were no false attempts at conversation, no awkward wallflowers, there was still plenty to drink and the food had all but been consumed, a compliment in itself.

He looked round once more, noticing how everyone was chatting and laughing together. No- not quite- there was one girl, he had only just noticed her.

"Strange." he thought " I don't remember her coming in. Gate crasher?"

He watched the girl sitting like a statue on the couch near the window, apart from other guests. Her head was bent over a magazine, her long hair, black and straight as a horse's tail dropped forward to hide her face. She had on a pink dress of some fine material that wafted gently in the breeze from the air conditioning. Eddie was at once struck with her demeanour as well as the stark contrast of her jet black hair against the pink stuff of her dress.

For some reason he was diffident in his approach to her. She looked up as he came near, her eyes black in a white face. Eddie checked his step, why she was ugly, he thought and then, no! almost beautiful. She was beautiful, she was terrific. He stood over her and said conversationally

"Enjoying the party?"

"No". the girl said flatly looking him directly in the eye.

"Oh!" the man was non plussed, wondering how you answered that.

"Er, who did you come with?" he tried.

There was no answer.

Eddie stood shifting one foot and then the other, acutely embarrassed, he thought her extremely rude, and his immediate reaction was to leave her alone.

'Damn it, its my flat, my party.' he thought.

"I'm Eddie Miller." he extended his hand in a new attempt at a response "your host." he added and let his exasperation show a little. She stared back, not a muscle in her face altered. He was about to give up when she appeared to make up her mind about something. The girl replaced the magazine on the coffee table, stood up and shook Eddie's hand

"Corinth." she said simply and her voice was deep, then she walked over to the wall and looked closely at a painting. The man followed eagerly at her heels.

"It was nice of you to come." he burbled "how did you get here?"

The dark haired girl leaned forward to examine the signature in the corner of the painting. "In a car of course."

"Oh you know what I mean." Eddie once again almost turned away in exasperation.

Corinth straightened and looked him directly in the eye, they were of equal height.

"No, I do not know what you mean, you talk nonsense mostly."

He could detect a foreign accent, but that was not the problem he was sure, why on earth was she so rude and prickly? Why had she come and who had brought her, but the biggest question in his mind was why he was bothering with her at all. Perhaps he should chuck her out and risk offending whoever she had come with. Damn it, she was spoiling his party.

'Someone must know who the girl is 'he thought 'I'll ask Martha, she's bound to know.' He half turned, fed up with trying to be polite when he felt a small hand on his arm.

"All right Mr Eddie Miller, I will tell you what you want to know."

He held up his hand

"Hang on there, I'm not grilling you, you don't have to tell me anything, I was merely trying to make you feel welcome."

"Yes, I agree that was what you were trying to do. The fact that you were failing means that I shall have to rescue you." her face remained impassive, only her black eyes twinkled as though she were finding the situation amusing.

Eddie's mouth was hanging open in astonishment, he felt both angry and insulted that someone should talk to him in that way. He began to think that she might not be all there.

The girl stood with her head thrust out a little to emphasise what she had to say.

"My name is Corinth, a stupid name, but my parents were archaeologists and I happened to be born there. They were very good at their job, but unfortunately they lacked imagination. I came here in a car with David and I shall go home in the car with him.. I was introduced to you when I arrived and you forgot about me immediately, which I do not find very flattering." Eddie opened his mouth to speak but she went on.

"Your party is just the same as any other party, loud, boozy and full of uninteresting people. I don't like it, I only came because David asked me to and I hope we go again very quickly."

Eddie could find nothing at all to say to this speech, David was the lanky chap he had met at the Embassy and he had no intention of upsetting him. He stood for a moment awkwardly and then turned on heel and walked over to his other guests who apparently had noticed nothing.

"Come on lads and lassies." he bounced over to the bottles. Let's top up those glasses."

To reassure himself that his party was still the success he had thought it, he started telling his salesman jokes.

His friends had all heard them before, but they were willing to laugh at anything by now. He moved to another circle and told most of them all over again to renewed laughter.

"Hey, Eddie, tell us that one about--- about---" Don, his face bright red, beads of sweat standing on his forehead and his eyes popping, was near the stage where sentences could not be finished. The crowd laughed with glee.

"Go on," Reilly goaded him, "have another go."

"No." Reggie said "have another Sediki and you won't want to remember what you were going to say." The men had begun to giggle at each other a sure sign of inebriation. The women for the most part had fallen silent and were gradually sitting down throughout the room.

Martha had elected to sit on the floor and seemed to be talking to herself. Jenny placed

Reggie's wife in front of the fan and waved the air into her face. Eddie was pleased they were all having a good time, and then realised that he was stone cold sober.

'What a thing' he said to himself, 'I'm at a party and I'm not even tiddly. He felt that he ought to remedy the fact straight away and poured a neat drink for himself. Against his better judgement he peered over the top of his glass to where he had left Corinth. She had gone. He looked over the heads of the partygoers and pushed past one or two, but there was no sign of her. The mystery girl had disappeared. At that moment Jenny came over to him.

"We'll have to get Reggie's wife home or into bed soon, she isn't too good."

"Never mind that." Eddie said brusquely "have you seen that queer dark haired girl anywhere?"

"The one with the pink dress?" she looked round the room.

"Yes, yes.!" he said impatiently "the one with the black eyes and sulky face."

Jenny looked at her husband in surprise

"Not lately I haven't, I wouldn't have thought you would remember her."

"What's that supposed to mean?" he said crossly. He pushed her to one side carefully and took a sip of his drink. "I hope you hid the gin." he added, watching David and the Lebanese empty one of the bottles of Sediki into their glasses.

"Oh yes, don't worry." Jenny sounded weary. She hardly had time to speak to Bill Jolly on his own and she knew it was too late to start now.

Eddie walked over to David and his companions, they were deep in conversation and broke off as he approached.

"Super party, Eddie old boy!" David said in his smooth voice.

"Yes, very enjoyable." The Lebanese echoed. "your wife is a very good cook."

Charm was restored to Eddie, he accepted their compliments and smiled amiably.

"Glad you enjoyed yourselves, tell me, where is Corinth?"

"Corinth?" David seemed surprised by the question. "Oh yes, Corinth." He got up from his perch on the small bookcase and stretched looking over all the heads. "Was here somewhere just now."

"I know, I was talking to her."

"She'll be around, no need to worry, probably in the loo." Eddie could not have admitted that he had already looked in that room so he said no more. Instead he asked

"Who is she David? I've never seen her anywhere before."

"Not likely to, old man, you are honoured to have her here tonight." Eddie had no such feelings "very unsociable don't you know". David went on, she can't stand parties really, but I begged her to come to this one, I did really think she would enjoy it, I told her all about you, she does so like Macho men."

Eddie was at once complimented and dismayed. If he was supposed to have been a Macho man, she was obviously disappointed, her response to him told him that. Eddie could almost feel the dent in his ego Eddie cleared his throat noisily

"Er- I suppose that's why I haven't seen her before, that is if she doesn't like parties, I mean."

"Hates them old man, not a good word to say for 'em. Of course, as you know I love parties, go to all of them, plenty of drinks, laughs and all that, nothing quite like it."

"That's why they do their own thing."

"Eh?"

"That's what you call it isn't it David?" The Lebanese was saying scratching at his curls. The lanky man nodded and sank his nose into his glass. "Yes, they do their own thing. Good relationship, they hardly see each other at all." The small dark man went into peals of laughter ending with a silly giggle, when David swept his eyes over him.

"He's right of course," the fair headed man leaned once more against the bookcase "works wonderfully, I do what I want to do and so does she, and there's never a cross word"

"Sounds wonderful." Eddie said uncertainly.

David flicked his head back taking the lank blonde hair out of his eyes.

"Have to go soon, old sport, police will have us going home if we're not careful, never do." he said shaking his head lugubriously. "got a position to keep, what say you Aziz, old buddy?" he turned to the Lebanese who nodded vigorously his dark eyes crinkled into a permanent smile. The salesman looked at the two unlikely friends. All the old chums and sports and the old Yuppy tone that David constantly produced seemed a trifle forced even to his ears. How did they manage to be friends? However in a country where the oddest people team up together he supposed it was not so unusual.

The party was breaking up, half the guests had by now staggered to the door and said their farewells as best they could. Hardly any of them were sober, and most of them incapable of distinct speech. Wives helped husbands negotiate the one inch step onto the landing, husbands helped wives to find the contents of handbags. It was a merry sight and a compliment to their host who had provided so thoughtfully for their hangovers in the morning.

The noise was alarming. Giggles, brash laughter, short screams and mock alarms coupled with high pitched farewells, would have brought an army of police down on them if it had carried on into the street. As it was, the moment the main door opened, the noise subsided into smothered giggles and a great deal of shushing. They had all had long practice of getting home as silently as possible.

David and Aziz were the last to leave, they offered their hands and shook Eddie's warmly, neither of them betraying the fact that they had taken even one drink that evening, they were as sober as their host.

"Must come and have some mother's ruin with us one evening, old boy." David said "found a source, damned expensive, but keep it for special friends."

Eddie greatly flattered managed a nonchalant "Love to."

The door was about to close on them when he opened it again.

"What about Corinth?" he asked frowning. "she can't have gone home on her own."

"Probably sitting in the car, old sport." The answer came up the stairs, "always ends up that way." and the footsteps faded.

"Right!" Eddie called to the empty landing and closed the door. He leaned his back on it and took in the chaos in the flat.

7

HAMRA SOUK differed only slightly from any other Souk, It was larger. Small paths wide enough for one donkey led into larger alleyways where four people could walk side by side. The larger thoroughfares were shaded by Barrusti, dried palm leaves woven into matting, and the smaller ones by the height of the shack like buildings.

Elegantly adorned gateways leading into vast private courtyards were interspersed with mean Arab houses with lock up stores. These were built three feet above ground level and reached by stone steps, so that the dusty alley served as a canal when the rain did eventually come. The water coursing through the Souk might only last one day a year, but it came in tremendous quantities, and they were prepared for it.

The Gold and Silver Souks were at the heart of the trading area, and here Arab women gathered together in large groups, their black Abbayas and veils flitting in and out of one store after another looking for all the world like a family of crows. They were there to exchange their gold, their dowry, which remained theirs all their life. It seemed to be a hobby of theirs bringing in some jewellery and taking something quite different home with them. They spent a good part of the day trying on and taking off gold, jewels, silver and anything else expensive that took their eye. Jenny loved the Souk for its colour and smell. All stores selling the same merchandise traded next door to each other, so that each alleyway could be relied on to have the same goods throughout. One might have ironmongery, cheap Chinese saucepans, trays, some electric kettles and camel halters, another would have nothing but material of all kinds. A little further away the aroma of the spice sellers stores would entice the curious. Pungent smells of perfumes, aromatic herbs, incense and spices of all kinds were displayed the length of the alley outside the stores in wicker baskets, the warmth of the air drawing out the aromas.

Jenny picked up a piece of black rock that looked like a sticky piece of coal.

"Look, Bobby" she sniffed at it "do you know what this is?" Bobby shook his head and looked at his father.

"Don't look at me, young feller, I don't know either." he shrugged his shoulders

"It's Frankincense" she held the piece of gum out to the boy "here, smell it."

"Yuch!" Bobby pulled a face and drew back.

"Oh, it's nice, I like it."

Jenny replaced it in the basket and smiled at the Arab sitting in his chair at the doorway. He grinned back pleasantly nodding his head.

Bobby picked up a piece of white marbelled rock like substance from another basket.

He put it to his nose

"No smell on this one, Mum." he held it out to her.

She took it and at the same time caught the Arab's eye, he grinned broadly and started to laugh and shake his head. She looked at Eddie, "what do you think it is?" she asked him sniffing at it determinedly.

Eddie said quickly "Put it down Jenny, you're being laughed at." The Arab had leaned back into the doorway and was shouting at someone inside who in turn started to laugh. She replaced the piece of rock in the basket quickly.

"Probably an aphrodisiac or something." Eddie said moving off. The storekeeper stood up and placed his hands over his stomach, rubbing it hard and rolling his eyes as though in extreme pain.

"Oh!" Jenny laughed and called to her husband "it must be for constipation." she giggled at the man who sat down smiling.

"All right, all right" Eddie said crossly "don't make a spectacle of yourself." he grabbed his son's hand and they walked down a short path between the old buildings and into the part of the Souk where the restaurants were.

Here the smell of the spices was overlaid by a more pungent one of curry. The cafes and eating places all seemed to be run by Pakistanis, and although no curry was offered for sale, somewhere in the depths of the solid walled buildings, the women of the households were busy preparing the familys' food. All the eating places were full and at one place they watched while Arabs of all ages were choosing their meat and having it barbecued on smoky grills. Colourful kebabs and plastic fruit decorated the counter against which a procession of men, their headdresses hanging forward, watched intently as the meat sizzled and gave off wondrous odours, Eddie felt himself getting hungry.

Amongst the cafes there were juice sellers. These were a one man business in a small room, they had a counter, and an electrical juice extractor. With one of these, a pile of oranges and one or two tables and chairs, the proprietor managed to keep body and soul together.

Eddie led the way into one of these businesses and ordered three glasses. he sat down thankfully and hoped that the morning was nearly over. There was nothing about Arabia that fascinated him. The Souk was merely a trading place and as a salesman he found it wanting in every particular. The picturesque market to him was merely a dirty smelly way to make money for charlatans, he would never have gone there if he had not promised Jenny the night before. At least there was some compensation for it, they were to lunch at one of the best hotels in Hamra.

The juice was cold and delicious, and Bobby wanted another one, but Eddie had looked at his watch and decided that the time had come for lunch. They had risen from their small table and were making their way to the door, when it opened and a tall Arab walked in. With unusual good manners to a European woman, he held the door open for Jenny. The family walked through and Eddie turned to speak, but the words never came for he was staring into the man's face The beard, the nose, but above all the eyes were very familiar and he knew immediately where he had seen them before, outside the mosque opposite his office. It was the same man undoubtedly, this time at closer quarters and this time he spoke.

"Good morning!" he said in a perfect English accent and then closed the door behind them.

Eddie was annoyed, he felt distinctly rattled and he did not know why. Why did the fact that he had just met a man he recognised make him feel that way? During the long walk back to the Mercedes he was silent, seeing in his mind's eye the face of the tall gaunt Arab. he could not make it out, but the man made him feel that he had been waylaid, almost as though he knew the Miller family would be there "Crazy!" he said to himself "coincidence obviously." but he felt the need to convince himself.

The uneasy feeling lasted until he was sitting in the dining room of the hotel, surveying the buffet meal laid out down one side of the room. A man to enjoy every physical experience to the full, Eddie brushed aside his misgivings and applied himself to the supremely enjoyable task of eating.

"Come on Bobby! You can eat as much as you like and go back for more.." his father pushed at his shoulder.

"You mean *you* can, you know what will happen, he will hardly have anything on his plate and say he isn't hungry."

"No I won't" Bobby was cut by her disloyalty.

"Come on then old chap, let's see."

The child tried because he wanted his father to stay jovial, but he truly had little appetite. Eddie for his part had a slice of everything and a spoonful of everything else. Curry, kebabs, cold meats, salads, hot vegetables, creamed fish, baked fish, chicken in aspic and then all the side dishes. His plate was overloaded. He was not alone, however, it was Friday, the day to pass time for the ex pat community. It took time to ponder on what to eat and then devour it and in a world where there was nothing to do and nowhere to go, eating was a very agreeable way of spending the afternoon.

Most ex pats had a favourite hotel for lunch and because they liked to gather where they could meet people they knew, they stuck to the same one most Fridays. It was a pleasure for Eddie to be able to wave a lazy arm in the direction of one party or another in greeting, he was more than happy to grace the dining room where there were so many people who called out to him by name. he glowed and felt important, he loved it all.

The salesman had been eating with his usual enthusiasm for some time when the door opened across the room and he sat up with a jerk, entering were David and Corinth and they were not alone. They were with a party of people unknown to him and they stood for a moment by the head waiter chatting and laughing Eddie was intrigued to see that Corinth was smiling quite normally.

"Almost as though she's human." he thought to himself.

"Here, Jenny" he said aloud, look who's here."

She looked up and caught David's eye, he waved languidly in their direction and spoke to Corinth. The face she turned in their direction was expressionless.

Eddie was half onto his feet, and threw his napkin onto the table. "I'll ask them to join us." he said quickly, but Jenny caught his hand

"No, please don't ask them over, let's just be by ourselves today, I've had enough of ----" she was about to say 'party people' but it was too late, Eddie was barging into other chairs and apologising to their occupants as he filed through the tables to the door.

Bobby watched his father wishing the floor would open and swallow him up. The loud voice full of bonhomie was circling back to them over the heads of other diners. he saw sympathetic glances and grins between the people who had greeted them on entering and fancied that they were laughing at his father, he cringed and slithered down into his chair so that only the top of his head showed. "What does he have to go and do that for?" he asked his mother despairingly.

"I don't know, I really don't know." Jenny said from between clenched teeth. Bobby looked at her, a kindred spirit for the time being and took her hand. Jenny looked startled and then read the understanding in the boy's face. She patted his hand "Eat up Bobby, we'll be going soon."

Happily for Bobby only David and Corinth returned with his father to their table and within moments the rest of the room had resumed their conversations

"Here we are then," Eddie said unnecessarily "you know Jenny, and that's my son Bobby."

"Of course." Corinth said frostily as she slid her cream silk skirt under her fine legs.

"Hello Jenny!" David patted her on the back and sat beside her "lovely to see you again, must say thank you for a lovely party last night."

"You're welcome." she murmured shyly.

"Yes, always come here after a party y'know, makes the weekend I think." David laid a limp hand on his lank hair and flicked a strand out of his eyes.

"That's just what I say, great place to finish up." Eddie nodded violently.

"What's the fish like old chap?" he looked into Eddie's plate curiously.

"Marvellous Dave old man, marvellous!" Jenny winced at the look on her son's face, maybe she was not the only one that could see how ridiculous his father could be.

"Got to have some right now," David said "absolutely starving, stomach thinks the throat's cut y'know." he laughed and guffawed and untangled his thin frame from the table.

"Hang on squire! Come with you- refill and all that." Eddie scrambled upright catching his napkin up with his plate and tripping over Jenny's handbag.

"Are you eating?" Jenny asked Corinth to cover her confusion.

"I might." the girl answered shortly and turned to Bobby "is the Coke cold?"

"Of course!" Bobby answered, his tone mocking her. Corinth's eyes kindled and Jenny smothered a grin.

"Well, I am going to have a Coke, would you like another one?"

"Of course." Bobby was nonchalant, the girl held no terrors for him. Corinth snapped her fingers to the waiter.

"You should say 'Two Hamra champagne' the boy said to her cheekily.

"Bobby!" his mother checked him.

"Leave him alone.!" Corinth raised an imperious hand and Jenny stared at her in amazement. "I have a brother like him and just as cheeky." she explained turning to the waiter. "I want two Hamra champagne." the man grinned and went to fetch them

"Who calls them that?" she asked the boy.

"Daddy does." Bobby answered scornfully as though everyone knew that.

"Naturally." Corinth said under her breath.

After the two men had returned to the table, Jenny was able to leave the conversation to them, noting with irritation how Corinth would chip in with her comments and then withdraw again, engaging their attention as soon as she felt it was fading. She said nothing herself and no remarks were addressed to her, so she was able to let her thoughts drift over their heads. Through a haze of cigar smoke, she picked out the extraordinary décor of that lovely room. Several steel rods strung with great coloured glass balls from floor to ceiling, provided pockets of privacy throughout that vast room. The turquoise velvet curtains held in place by sashes of gold trimmed brocade brushed the carpet that glowed with tiny needles of yellow and white in an ornate design. A shaft of sunlight like a laser, beamed across the room onto the oak counter where Arabic coffee was made in golden brass pots. She loved the room, at times she could imagine that it was completely out of this world. The only thing that spoiled it, she thought sourly, was the hum of conversation overlaid with her husband's boisterous laughter.

It was still a wonder to her that she had married such a man. Her inclination had always been for solitude, her thoughts totally private and she lived inside herself. Eddie, on the other hand, needed people around him and thinking was not a great activity for him. What was in his head was more often than not on his lips before he could do anything about it, and that needed an audience. Solitude would have been a particular kind of hell for him.

Bobby had taken a liking to Corinth, perhaps he could see beyond her rudeness or perhaps even at his young age, he was aware of her feline attraction. Whatever it was he had gradually inched his way to her side until he was standing holding her unresisting hand. She had not rejected the advance, merely ignored it and carried on sipping her Cola, or offering a short comment on the subjects the men were chatting about.

Eddie, only too aware of Corinth, tried to stop himself from staring at the girl. She sat in her chair like a queen, her back straight, her long lustrous black hair lying on her cream silk blouse, a stark contrast to her white face and coal black eyes. For his part he leaned so far into the table that his chin was almost on his plate. He told loud jokes and threw himself about in the chair laughing at them, he made fatuous comments and generally tried too hard to appear normal. If he had any nerves, they were twanging.

Suddenly Corinth stood up and dropping Bobby's hand she announced flatly "It is time to go."

The boy looked at his rejected hand and sat down quickly.

"But you've only just come." Eddie protested.

"Nonsense." she answered briskly.

"But you haven't eaten." he persisted.

"No."

David placed his napkin on the table and stood up.

"Time to go is it, old thing?" he said to her, she made no reply but picked up her bag. "right you are then, must fly dear boy." he said to Eddie. "Cheerio!" then "Oh, while I think on" the thin man leaned over the table and looked directly into the salesman's eyes "Got a stag party next Thursday, want you to come, meet some people and all that." his tone was confidential, smooth.

Eddie's face lit up "Love to old chap, what time?"

"Oh, about nineish." David stood upright "don't forget, particularly want you there, old man, devastated otherwise.

"Oh quite!" Eddie was enormously flattered and cast a quick look in Jenny's direction. "don't worry, I'll be there."

"Cheerio now." the tall man waved a soft hand and tickled the air "bye Jenny."

"Did you hear that?" Eddie burst out after they had gone "they want me to go to their party, what do you think of that?" the chunky man ran a hand through his curls in amazement. "It's climbing the ladder old girl, just think- Embassy people."

Jenny looked at him wondering what all the fuss was about. "They came to your party, what's so great about going to theirs?"

"Jenny!" he was exasperated "you don't understand these things do you?" he went on "Embassy people, contacts, the right ones, orders, spondulux." he rubbed his first finger and thumb together and kissed them enthusiastically.

"Oh money!" she said in a flat voice.

Her husband swung his great head round to look at her, he was instantly angry.

"What the hell do you mean 'Oh money?' What do you think we are out here for, eh?" his face flared with colour "you can only treat money with contempt my girl, when you have plenty of it and we haven't."

People were turning and looking at them and Jenny knew that her husband's voice had travelled as usual beyond the boundaries of their table. "Sh!" she laid a hand on his arm, "everyone's looking." Eddie shrugged off her hand and clamped his eyes up and down, took a deep breath and stood up.

"Come on, let's go." he snapped and just then caught sight of Don and Martha at a distant table. His anger was gone at once and he beamed from ear to ear, shouting over to them and waving his hand. "See you tomorrow." he bellowed drawing the attention of all the diners.

Don lifted his glass to him "Bottoms up" he called.

"Only if she'll let me." Eddie said in a stage whisper looking at Jenny and grinning. Blushing, she left the room as quickly as she could with Bobby scuttling at her side and Eddie barging after them.

It was prayer time, Salah, when they emerged from the hotel and the streets were full.

Men were leaning, strolling, sitting on the kerb, all waiting the regulation 20 minutes to return to their stores and businesses. It was a full time job for any driver at such a time to manoeuvre between the pedestrians and the traffic.

The religious police armed with batons, pulled out in front of the Mercedes and shouted into their megaphones. Everyone knew what they had to say and paid no attention. They had already obeyed the law by ceasing trading. No money would change hands during Salah, and if it did they all knew the punishment. After the walls of their stores had been beaten down, and they had been beaten up, there would be very little left of business for them to attend to.

The Millers sat in a traffic jam watching the multinational crowd hover around shop windows and form groups here and there for a chat. It was a dull picture, the only colour to be seen was from one or two Sikh turbans that bobbed along the street.

"Quite something isn't it?" Eddie was still thinking of his invitation.

"Why?" Jenny was indignant, she hated being shown up by Eddie's temper.

He turned to her and patted her hand "Aw come on Jenny, you know why we are out here, money is what we are after isn't it? and anything that will get it for us is what we have to go for."

She allowed herself to be placated, no one could be annoyed with Eddie for long "I can see that, but I still say that if you invited them, then it's only right that they invite you."

"Ah, but that doesn't always happen with those sort of people, they accept invitations all right, but you can't always get one from them."

"You mean that it's a privilege to have them to your place and that's enough?"

"Something like that." he answered and saw an opportunity for pulling out of the traffic and driving through a side street.

"I've just thought of something," Jenny said suddenly "You're away all next week."

"'Fraid so old girl, the other side of the country, can't be helped, plenty of new customers over there need sounding out."

"Well, it's just that if you are off to this stag party on Thursday night we shan't see much of you shall we." she sounded quite happy about it and Eddie gave her a quick glance. "it's just that it will give me plenty of time to see to Bill's flat."

It struck Eddie, that she should have been more disappointed that he would not be home. It made him feel uneasy for a moment. Then he remembered Bill Jolly and his quiet way and smiled to himself. No danger there, let the little woman enjoy herself.

"Yes," he said jovially "you enjoy yourself, after all there'll be another party the following week for us to go to."

"Oh yes! there'll always be another party, Eddie." she sighed heavily, but he was oblivious to her meaning.

8

EDDIE had barely left on his week's trip when Bill Jolly presented himself at the flat door. Jenny was pleased to see him, although she would have preferred to have finished her work first. Cleaning up after Eddie's weekends was like clearing up after a hurricane. On top of that Bobby was home from school, some sort of teacher conference he told her.

With a pile of sheets in her arms, Jenny gestured with her head for the man to come in.

"Oh, I know, I'm far too early aren't I?" he half turned to the door "I'll go back and come later."

Jenny dropped her load of sheets and towels onto the floor and shook her head furiously. "No, of course not, stay now you're here. Good excuse for putting the coffee on, do sit down."

Scooping up the laundry again she made for the kitchen and looking over her shoulder she saw that Bobby had started to talk to their guest. Jenny put the clothes in the washing machine and started the coffee. By the time it was ready she was surprised to see that Bobby was still chatting to Bill and had sat down and made himself comfortable.

"You two seem to have a lot to talk about." she remarked happily as she poured the aromatic liquid into mugs

"Mm, that smells good." Bill murmured and he took his drink and a biscuit and leaned back looking completely relaxed.

"He collects stamps, Mum." Bobby said enthusiastically "and he paints."

"Oh, that sounds good, Bill, is it your hobby?"

"A very new one I must say, time weighs very heavily on your hands out here and I thought to fill some of it, so I've started to paint. Not very good at it, but I enjoy it.."

Bobby had slipped away to his room and Jenny thought that he would probably stay there for the rest of the morning, but just as she turned to Bill again, Bobby came out of his room carrying an enormous sketch pad that was almost as big as he was.

"Where on earth did that come from?" Jenny asked curiously, "I haven't seen that before."

Bobby laid it on the carpet and started to turn the pages. On each one were sketches of people, old young, Arab, Western, Asian, children, adults. It was quite a brilliant display and Jenny was amazed by it, she had no idea her son could draw.

"Well," Bill Jolly sighed dramatically "I thought to take up painting as a hobby, after seeing this lot, I don't think I have a chance!"

"Do you like them?" Bobby asked timidly.

"Of course I like them, I think they are really, really good, Bobby, you are a talented artist."

"An artist." Bobby repeated in wonder "yes, I like that, I'm an artist."

With that he closed the sketch pad and heaved it off the floor, he took it back into his room and was gone for a time.

Bill Jolly looked at Jenny with concern" You didn't know your son could draw did you?"

"I had no idea, he's never shown us anything like that before, it really is quite amazing."

"You'll have to bring him over to my flat---- when it's looking better, and we'll have a painting session. I'd enjoy that."

"I'm sure Bobby would as well, which reminds me—your flat."

"Yes, I did come to ask if you had remembered that you were going to help me, and then I sort of got tied up with coffee, stamps and sketches!" the lanky man laughed and sorted his legs out and stood up, "are you still on?"

"Yes, of course, I'll come over now."

"What about your clearing up?"

"Let it go hang, it won't matter for once."

Jenny felt a strange feeling of liberation, she looked around her messy flat and sniffed. "Too bad." she said aloud, "there's always tomorrow."

Bobby was already drawing again, so they left him in his bedroom and walked across the road to try and do something about Bill Jolly's flat.

Flat no1. was in an abysmal state. It had been occupied by bachelors for months and everything was stained, broken or badly worn.

Jenny caught her breath as she took in the small lounge "How could they possibly have put you in here without tidying the place up a bit first?" she looked around and wobbled a broken table with her hand "it's dreadful."

Bill took a clean cloth and spread it on the settee. "There, sit on that, keep your clothes clean.

"I can see why you were moaning now," Jenny laughed "no one could blame you, where on earth are you going to start?"

He came and sat next to her and gestured with his hands. "I don't really want to spend money on the place, they did promise me that I should have a better place after three months."

"The probationary period."

"Right."---- but that's a long time and I know I'll be positively suicidal by the time that's up if I don't do something."

Jenny stared around the room in fascination, the cream paintwork was yellowing, as it always does, the holes in the brown carpet were caked around the edges with dirt, the side tables were rickety with chips of wood and splinters sticking out of the legs, and all the lamp shades were dented or torn.

"A zoo." she said finally.

"A what?"

"A zoo." she laughed "that's what its been used for."

"You mean that the previous occupants were animals?" he grinned.

"Definitely, and savage with it." she looked the curtains over and wiped her hands on her handkerchief. "Actually the curtains aren't bad, they can be washed, I think they are the best thing you have really."

"Well," Bill shrugged his shoulders "it seemed to be the one thing I could change in here to improve matters, but really it all needs burning doesn't it?"

"Pity! we can't do that, you don't want to spend much money, so where do we start?"

During the next hour or so they talked and planned and sorted. Jenny looked through the ornaments and pictures Bill had brought out with him, and with ingenuity and camouflage and more than a little detergent, they had planned between them how to change the little flat into something more like home.

The calls from the mosque prompted the young woman to look at her watch,

"I shall have to go I'm afraid."

"Let me make coffee." Bill urged, springing up and striding into the kitchen.

"I should go." Jenny called out hesitatingly. She stood up and smoothed her dress, following him into the tiny room. "it is rather late--- and I have quite a lot to do." she faltered as he turned to look at her.

"Look it's ready, just a cup."

She was happy to be persuaded "Well, all right, but I shall have to go after." she warned.

Bill carried the tray into the lounge. "It's been a marvellous day for me, you know, I've enjoyed having you here so much." he added " not just because of the curtains."

Jenny sipped her coffee hardly knowing how to reply. she had never played games with men and could rarely summon up clever repartee, so when she did answer him it was the truth.

"I've enjoyed it as well Bill, it's been fun."

The man's face lit up for a moment and then he thought. "This won't be the last time will it?" he asked anxiously "you will come again won't you? I mean you will have to come and see that I'm dong what we planned and sorting it out properly won't you?" he added slyly.

Jenny was relieved that he was asking her to return, she had been afraid all along that having sorted out his problems, he would forget all about her.

She beamed up at him." Of course I will, I shall have to come and supervise won't I, you may need some help."

For an instant she regretted showing her feelings for the man so obviously but then almost immediately she felt that liberated feeling again, daring.

"Definitely." he took her hand "I think I may need you." there was no mistaking his meaning and she blushed, rose from the settee and made for the door.

"I must go, Bobby will be looking for me."

Bill watched her cross the road from his window and

congratulated himself on finding such a lovely creature in that city of men.

"You little smasher!" he said to her through the glass "Hamra's turning out to be very exciting."

Eddie came home on Wednesday evening and once again the flat seemed reduced in size when filled with his personality. He whooped and bounced in and out of rooms, pulled Bobby's leg and teased his wife. For a short while she was relieved to see him home again, and not for the first time fell into the trap of thinking she could sit down and have a chat with him.

"Missed me?" he asked drinking his gin, a thirsty man straight from the desert. he handed her the glass before she could reply "What have you been up to then?" he threw himself onto the settee, the soft cushions belching up on either side of him. Jenny handed him his second drink and made to answer, but he leaned forward and turned the television on. Eddie immediately turned it off again on seeing Bedu girls throwing their long hair backwards and forwards in their ritual dance.

"You would have been proud of me." he said naively gazing at the blank screen "topped my own sales record." he looked up at her Isn't that Grrreat?" he rolled the word off his tongue. "What was it?"

"Great." Jenny said obediently. She made no further attempt to speak and turned away to finish cooking the dinner, but Eddie grabbed her hand.

"Here, here, come on, what have you been up to wifey of mine." he said fatuously and dragged her down onto the settee. Once again she made an attempt to answer but he forestalled her by giving her a resounding kiss, and did it with such gusto that it left a red mark on her cheek. She protested and struggled to rise, but he grabbed her again and held her tight to his box like chest.

"Time for the horse feed." he said looking at her with familiar lust.

"What's that? she managed to gasp.

"Oats my darling, not had my oats for a few days now, off to bed with us." And so saying he grasped her hand and dragged her to the bedroom. This time she dug in her heels and struggled out of his grasp.

"For goodness sake, Eddie!" she put a hand to her dishevelled hair her face red with annoyance.

Her husband held out his hand "What's the matter?" he asked innocently.

"I'm getting the dinner and Bobby's in his room." she made the excuses.

"What's the matter with that?" he moved to hold her again but she sidestepped.

"Come on, keep the dinner hot, Bobby will stay in his room, he always does" he looked bewildered at her response to him.

"That's just it isn't it," Jenny answered walking quickly into the kitchen, Eddie following close behind. "Bobby's always in his room, it isn't right you don't bother with him at all."

With the mention of their son, Eddie's ardour seemed to cool. "Where's the gin?" he looked around the kitchen and started groping inside a cupboard.

"No, don't listen will you?" she stared angrily at him from the cooker. "it's a good thing that Bill understands him." Jenny instantly bit her lip knowing she had said the wrong thing, and started busying herself with the gravy.

Eddie turned his large head in her direction, his eyes round like humbugs

"Bill?"

"Oh! you heard me that time." she retorted.

"I heard you." he confirmed "who do you mean exactly?"

"Oh, it's only that Bill Jolly seems able to bring Bobby out more than------er, we can" she finished lamely. It was not the way she had wanted to bring the subject up. "Damn Eddie, always putting me in the wrong." she thought.

Jenny kept her eyes on the gravy and poured it into a boat. "Come on, dinner."

"Never mind the dinner." Eddie's voice was dangerous, he had taken an instant dislike to the tall man the moment he had met him. "how did old Jolly Jolly get to know our son so well? He must have been here again, was he?"

Jenny nodded.

"When was he here?" Eddie was suddenly suspicious.

"Why, Monday I think- yes Monday."

"Oh yes." The chunky Englishman's voice was so low it was almost growling. "those bloody curtains."

Jenny looked at her husband in surprise "What's wrong with that?"

"Oh nothing at all." he said sarcastically "a complete stranger waylays my wife, gets her involved in his curtains and sorts my son out. I like that, I like that very much." he emptied the last part of a bottle of gin into his glass and drank it neat. "all right let's eat. Where's our darling son, let's see what he thinks of Mr Curtain bloody Jolly."

The man marched over to the boy's room and barged inside. The child was sitting on his window sill staring down into Bill's flat. To his father there was something unnatural in the fact that a small boy of ten could sit in a dark room, gazing out of the window with such intensity that he was oblivious to everything else.

"Bobby!" Eddie snapped, and his son wheeled round "dinner!" and the man turned swiftly and just as quickly sat himself down at the polished table.

Bobby guaging his father's mood accurately moved quickly to close his door and sidled into his seat watching apprehensively as the man poured more neat gin from a new bottle. His mother looked at him and gave him an encouraging nod.

"Eat up Bobby, it's your favourite."

Eddie swung his bull like head in his direction.

"Mr Jolly." he stated abruptly "Well?"

Bobby looked down at his plate not understanding.

"Bill Jolly, what he say to you, eh?" Eddie's eyes were becoming watery from the gin and his son sighed a breath of relief when he saw it, he knew that the more his father drank, the more genial he would become.

"He's nice." Bobby managed to say as he munched on his steak "he talks to me."

"Oh! How wonderful!" Eddie's voice boomed the sarcasm round the walls.

He opened his mouth to say something else but the aroma from the plate in front of him caught his attention and he plunged into his meal. He enjoyed the first mouthful and the next, and as the pleasure of eating overtook events he forgot what he had been going to say to his son and became mellow. He looked up and grinned at his wife and now the bad moments were over she smiled back relieved, hoping there was little encouragement in it for her husband to sweep her off her feet and take her to bed.

There was no need to worry, after dinner the English programmes were beamed to the television and Eddie, all anger and distaste forgotten, sat with his arms stretched across the back of the settee and chortled into his gin at intervals slapping his knee and enjoying himself. Even Bobby sat by his side for a while, hoping to have some notice taken of him, but he crept away later realising that his father was not aware that he was there at all.

Jenny, sitting in the armchair she had adopted as hers, watched from under her lashes and surprised herself by thinking what a nice evening she could have had if Bill had been sitting on the settee instead of Eddie. The fact that it was possible to sit and chat to a man was still a novelty to her. There had never been a chance to chat to Eddie, he simply did not chat, or at least not to her.

She had come to realise that Bill had drawn her out and made her feel at ease, as though her opinions were important. She found that she was able to communicate with him in a way that had never been possible with any man before. It was a new experience and she enjoyed it, but knew it would never work with her husband. For a moment the thought struck her that Eddie might not have anything to say. She grinned and opened a book, there was a thought for you!

9

THE sun had set, the street lights switched on and the evening call to prayer was over by the time Eddie made his way to Abdul Aziz Street on Thursday night. It was a warm and remarkably spicy evening, a gentle breeze blowing off the desert wafted the perfume of flowers over the residential district near the Summer Palace. Here large villas encased in high walls, had beautiful gardens. Palms, banana trees and bougainvillea formed a border along the walls, shielding the tenuous grass and border flowers from direct sunlight. Lillies, Hibiscus and Oleander waved gently in the evening breeze throwing their perfume high into the air and over the walls.

Here and there between the grand villas, small wooden kiosks were being used to sell the fast foods of Arabia. Falaffal, Shwamis and Kebabs sizzled and smoked, creating pungent odours down the length of the street. By Hamra standards it was a cool evening and there were many strollers about.

Eddie felt a warm glow run through his body as he caught sight of the exclusive villas, here he was successful in all he did, earned good money, was invited to the best houses and able to walk in an open necked shirt and light weight trousers at nine o'clock at night. At that moment he came as near as he could to loving Hamra.

He stopped before the heavily ornate gate and looked up at the small stone coffee pots perched on the supporting columns. he thought them very attractive and shading his eyes from the strong glare of the gateway light, he managed to pick out more coffee pots on the roof. The whole roof could be seen from the street, but not one window, and if it had not been for light filtering up through the Palms and Bougainvillea trailing along the wall, he would have said that there was no one at home.

The man took a deeply perfumed laden breath and walked to the large gate. It opened as though he had been watched and a Pakistani in a pink shiva kamis stepped forward and asked his name, he then walked into his watchman's hut and picked up a phone and returned at once.

"Go in." he said peremptorily pointing to a polished oak door at the end of the flower lined path. As soon as he placed a foot on the first step of the porch the door swung open.

"Eddie! my old chum, come on in, good to see you." David in a bright yellow open necked shirt and sandles grasped the salesman's arm, shutting the door behind them swiftly.

The hall was Arabic, a large square room with upholstered benches lining the walls. There was a small fountain pouring into a copper dish and a Kuwaiti chest bound with brass. The carpet was Persian and for a moment Eddie felt he ought to remove his shoes, knowing how priceless it was. David, however, not waiting a moment ushered him into the reception room beyond.

At first it appeared to Eddie that there was very little difference between this gathering and a posse of salesmen at a promotion party. The room was packed to overflowing, all were talking and laughing as loudly and as fast as they could, drinking heavily and telling dirty jokes. He felt at home immediately, but because of his small stature he found that he was looking at the backs of men's heads and apart from a tall mirror that extended presumably from floor to ceiling and the large candelabra he could see little else.

"Hey Aziz!" David waved over the tops of a few heads "Eddie's here."

Giving the salesman a nudge he indicated a crush in the corner of the room. Aziz appeared from the middle of it holding a bottle, Eddie recognised the Lebanese who had accompanied David to his party.

"Eddie, good to see you." the dark haired man said, shaking his curls and beaming good naturedly "what to drink?" he led the way to a small bar replacing the bottle and holding up another "gin?"

"Great." Eddie breathed " is it the real thing?"

Aziz laughed, "As real as you'll get anywhere, my friend."

"G & T then" Eddie said happily. he looked around to speak to David, but the host had plunged back into the crowd and been swallowed up.

Aziz acknowledged his look " He'll be back in a moment, too many guests this evening."

Leaning in a comfortable way with his elbow on the bar,

the salesman turned to look into the crowd " No problem, no problem." he said over his shoulder and drank deeply "this is great" he drank again " quite a party isn't it? I don't think I've recognised anyone here at all." he said.

"No." the Lebanese looked around the room vaguely. "business acquaintances mostly." he said.

"Oh quite!" Eddie nodded and held his glass out "any chance of another?"

Aziz's brown eyes crinkled and his smile was broad "Of course, it is my pleasure."

Eddie looked at him curiously and the man added quickly "I have instructions to make you have a good time."

"Oh!"

The hum of conversation and the odd bursts of laughter continued for some time before the Englishman began to feel abandoned. He had been invited especially to meet these guests and he knew for certain that he wanted to meet *them*. Who knew what it might lead to. Might even get a better job when they got chatting with him, some of the men looked like directors, he thought, or captains of industry, the clipped well heeled accents said it all.

At first he thought that they might all have come from the embassy, but then he knew that there were not so many staff there.

Aziz had been silent for some time, after a short chat he had busied himself with glasses and bottles and placing trays of drinks for the Indian servants to serve. he was behaving almost like a servant himself, it puzzled Eddie. The Englishman was becoming impatient, he was in two minds whether to introduce himself to the nearest bunch of men, if he had been in any other place he would not have hesitated. However he had begun to have the feeling that whatever contribution he could make, would not be welcome.

It was not in his nature to be so diffident, but as the evening wore on the feeling became worse until in exasperation he turned to Aziz

"Look here, old chum. David said he wanted me to meet some people and he's disappeared on me altogether. I can't stay here propping up the bar all night, it's getting embarrassing. He placed his glass on the bar and stretched, trying to see over the heads of the people.

65

Aziz was all concern "Just a minute, Eddie, don't worry about it, I'll go and see"----- and with his sentence trailing off he walked quickly through a door and into another part of the house.

The guests from time to time had cast curious glances at the man standing by himself at the bar, but assuming that he was enjoying a good drink and talking to the Lebanese, they had left him to himself. One man, ready to meet someone new was about to remedy the situation when Aziz returned, his eyes crinkled and he smiled happily.

"Time to go." he said holding out his hand.

"Uh?"

"Someone wants to meet you." Aziz explained "in the library."

Eddie took out his handkerchief and mopped at his forehead, the room had become very stuffy. he put it away again and yanked at his trousers before following Aziz behind the bar and through the door.

The hall leading into the back of the house was dark with only one copper lamp shedding light at the end of it. Opposite the light the Lebanese pointed to a panelled door "In there, I have to get back, the guests"----- and before Eddie could protest, he was gone.

Eddie cursed finding himself in such a situation. he was accustomed to being in control wherever he found himself, but during the last few hours he had been feeling distinctly uncertain of himself. Now he was faced with a closed door, no one about, and someone who wished to meet him, goodness knows who, on the other side. Where were all the introductions and good manners he had expected? Momentarily he was angry and thought of stepping back inside the reception room and going home, he resented being treated this way. In spite of himself though, his curiosity was aroused "What was going on?" he asked himself, "I'm here now, may as well see what's on the other side of the door, say hello and go back for a last gin."

With that plan in his head, he mopped at his forehead again and reached for the handle. The heavy door swung open silently, and unusually for the man, Eddie stepped inside cautiously. The first impression was that the room had no lights, everything was dark and shadowy, then as his head came round the door he stepped back in astonishment. There on a pink rug in a pool of light from a small lamp sat Corinth.

The girl was dressed in a garment that moved restlessly in the draught from the air conditioner. It appeared to be gossamer as it shifted, hung in the air and dropped gently to the rug. Corinth's arm was draped across the seat of an armchair and was clothed in the same material. her black hair lay motionless on her breast and in her white hand she held a book.

For the first time since Eddie had met Corinth, she smiled at him.

"Shut the door." her voice was soft and light, he felt mesmerised and did as she bade. "come over here to me." she extended her arm and as in a dream the man obeyed. "I have something to say to you." she went on placing her book beside her feet and he noticed that they were bare. He had no time to gaze at her small toes and tiny ankles for she was telling him to sit down opposite her. Still hypnotised by the situation he sat on the edge of the seat and gazed at her, his large brown eyes wide.

"Eddie," Corinth spoke softly "I want to say I'm very sorry."

"Sorry?" his voice exploded in the silence.

"Sorry," she repeated "I've been extremely rude to you and I'm sorry. will you accept my apology?"

"Why—yes, of course, but"

Corinth laughed, a delicate feminine laugh he noticed, "stop gaping, you should not be so surprised you know."

"Surprised?" the man had no resources to call on, he felt that he was behaving in a ridiculous manner, but then he had never had to deal with such a situation before.

The girl got up from the rug, gracefully stood before the imitation fireplace draping one arm along the high mantelshelf.

"You are a man of the world, yes?"

"Yes." he agreed with alacrity.

"Then you understand women." she went on "all men of the world understand women."

"Of course." Eddie rubbed the back of his neck and inched his way backwards into the armchair, endeavouring to look relaxed, he was wary.

"Of course." Corinth smiled. For a moment Eddie suspected her of sending him up, but one look at her glowing eyes and he dismissed the idea.

"So you can understand why I have been so nasty to you, can't you?"

Corinth began to walk towards the small table within the boundary of the light where there were glasses and a decanter. "Er"—he opened his mouth and then shut it again. What the hell was all this about. A flash of anger instantly dissipated as she brought him a glass, smiled deeply into his eyes and touched his fingers with her own.

"You know that I have been attracted to you, it has been a struggle for me to fight it." she said withdrawing from him. From a glass jug she poured what appeared to be water into another glass and held it up to him. "to friendship!" she said and sipped.

Eddie was unsure whether he wanted the drink or the apology more, but he accepted both happily and smothered his astonishment at her declaration.

There had been nothing that was normal about this evening, and now the latest surprise which should have knocked him for six, following on the rest merely set him back in the chair looking stunned.

Once again he told himself "She's almost beautiful, no damn it, she is beautiful, she's great." Automatically he held out his glass and Corinth refilled it at once. He sat and sipped and tried to collect his thoughts, the girl went over to the music centre and pressed a button, Sittar music blended into the shadows, emphasising the unreality of Eddie's situation. Everything had been alien about this evening, but he was not uncomfortable anymore, he was beginning to enjoy himself. The gin and Corinth had been very effective, he was warming to the girl.

Even though it had always been an accepted joke about commercial travellers, Eddie had never been a womaniser. he had been too busy, too anxious to get on. Apart from one or two associations, Jenny had been the only one for him. Flirtation and coquetry had left him cold he simply did not understand it. It was his view that if you wanted something you got on with it, no need for all those stupid games people talked about. Now here he was, the object of such a game and he found it exciting. he could only be sorry that he had never learned the rules. There had been occasions in the past when women had made their interest plain concerning him, and as his friends would say, he had seen it coming on, but not with Corinth. Eddie had totally failed to read the signs with her. He was extremely flattered by what she had said and not for a moment did he disbelieve her, modesty was not in his character. It was the effect it had on him that amazed him most, he really did enjoy the game, he was excited by this approach and then he realised that he was entirely smitten by the girl.

Corinth tucked her legs under her and sat down on the rug, leaning her back against Eddie's chair. Without any effort, he thought he would be able to touch her hair, her shoulders. She turned her body so that he could see her face.

"Say something Eddie, don't leave me stranded in mid air." there was no response, he was desperately trying to think of the right thing to say. "Don't tell me that I have hurt you too much." she pleaded, her voice soft and her hand on his knee.

"You're lovely." he managed to croak, knowing it to be inadequate "I think you are------wonderful." she looked up at the man her face expressionless

It was the matter of a moment's decision and Eddie bent to kiss her. Not an aggressive kiss with his usual gusto, which left the mouth and skin bruised, but a kiss as reverent as a boy's first. A pang shot through his body and he looked down at her in amazement. "I think I'm in love." he said in astonishment. "Yes, I am! I'm in love! and he bundled her in his arms and kissed her face, her hair, her shoulders. He stopped when he felt her struggling.

"No, no Eddie!" she broke free and stood up, her face pink. "Not here, not now." she smoothed her hair agitatedly.

For the first time since he had set foot in the room, Eddie was brought back to the present. Here he was in his friend's house, kissing his friend's wife, while a party was going on next door. At any moment someone might come in. Sweat broke out over his forehead at the thought.

"No, of course not." he agreed hurriedly and laughed." I'd forgotten for a moment that we were in Hamra." he laughed again and said fatuously "you had taken me up to heaven." it

69

was a good thing that he looked away from his beloved's face as he said it.

Corinth picked up her glass and replaced it on the table.

"What's to be done?" she said eventually looking up, Eddie's eyes widened eagerly. "You travel a lot out of Hamra don't you?"

"All the time." his expression fell, what chance was there going to be to get to know each other better.

"I'm afraid I'm not here much."

"Right then," Corinth laughed at his face. She flicked at his shoulder with a pink fimger nail. "where are you this week?"

"Al Jalawi, Khofar, border towns."

"I shall meet you." she said decisively.

"How?"

"Oh, I have a driver, he takes me everywhere and keeps his mouth shut."

Eddie looked uncertain. "What about David?"

"What about Jenny? she countered.

"That's different!" he said brushing the thought aside.

"No it isn't!"

"Don't worry about Jenny." he assured her dismissing the uncomfortable thought. Eddie touched her arm and she moved away out of his reach.

"Then don't worry about David."

"Alright, all right, which town?"

"The best hotel is at Jalawi, I like the décor." Corinth mused inconsequently,

"The food's good too." Eddie blurted out.

She looked at him in surprise and teased him. "Are we going there just to eat then?"

Eddie laughed aloud placing his hands in his pockets, he was feeling very much at home at last, the Game was going to be very enjoyable.

"The Phoenician, at Al Jalawi on Saturday, all right?" he moved towards the decanter. Corinth caught his intention and hurriedly moved towards him.

"You must go now."

"Already?"

"Yes, I'm afraid you must, David will be coming soon, the party must be over by now."

"God! I'd forgotten the party." the man slapped his forehead.

"Yes, you'd better go."

"Darling." Eddie caught the girl by her arm "please let me kiss you goodnight, it's such a long time until Saturday." The girl complied in silence, presenting her cheek for a moment. It was all he could expect in the circumstances.

"Goodnight Eddie." she said softly opening the door for him.

"Goodnight my darling." he whispered back and the door closed on him.

Behind the library door Cointh wiped her cheek with the back of her hand, throwing out a gossamer covered arm, she whispered in dramatic tones "Goodnight sweet prince." and then she jumped onto a carved chair, flung her arms wide and shouted "Parting is such sweet sorrow, it's a long time till Saturday. Yuch!" and then the dark haired girl jumped down, rescued her shoes from under a cabinet, switched on all the lights and settled down to a good read.

The reception room was empty and the lights turned down when Eddie slipped back through the door. Glasses and ashtrays had been cleared and the house boys were dusting furniture. Eddie glanced at his watch, only midnight, not a late hour for a party to break up. Puzzled he walked into the Hall and was greatly comforted to see a smattering of guests sitting around the walls on the upholstered benches.

"Eddie old man, come and meet some friends of mine" David, the genial host as sober as ever patted the seat beside him.

"Everyone gone?" Eddie asked accepting a glass.

"Only the extras, dear boy" his friend assured him "here you see the real guests, my intimate friends." he gave the word intimate a roguish emphasis.

The rest of the night became a blur of introductions and gossip. Eddie was quickly bored by it, he was unable to enter into the spirit of it at all. He had no acquaintances known to them and in any case his thoughts kept turning to his meeting with Corinth.

His ears pricked up though at the word 'selling'. It seemed that David supplied the Palace with something or other, he was being congratulated for pulling off a lucrative deal.

"Have to walk carefully though, old man, like a cat on

71

electric wires." guffawed David, "still, good business all the same," he conceded.

"What's this to do with the Embassy?" Eddie asked curiously.

"What Embassy?" David asked frowning.

"Ours, the one you work for."

"I don't work for the Embassy, Eddie boy." laughed David, "where did you get that preposterous idea?"

The salesman wanted to point to his accent, his clothes, his education, his large villa in the right part of town, his way of handling himself, which in any place could open doors that would remain firmly closed to the likes of Eddie. Instead he said "I met you at the Embassy."

"Yes, but only visiting, old chap. Have to visit the commercial section every now and again to know what's going on you know."

"My mistake." Eddie barked a short laugh "what is it you do then?"

"Clearing and forwarding, lucrative business in this day and age in Hamra. Import, export- good business." he finished his drink "Now then boys, how about a hand of poker?" he stood up looking around the few remaining guests. "No need to get up to-morrow until luncheon." David looked at Eddie. "How about you Eddie, old chum?"

Eddie shook his head hurriedly, he had never been a gambler and had avoided all recruiting drives to make him one. He swallowed his drink and set the glass down on a brass table.

"Sorry squire, but I don't gamble, no fun in it for me, but you go ahead, it's time I was off anyway."

"Well, if you're sure." David mumbled politely, not seeming in any way put out.

"Lovely party David, thanks again." Eddie turned on the step. "must come to my next one."

"Shall do old man, shall do. Goodnight!" and the door closed.

Eddie had negotiated the flower bordered path, the iron gates and said goodnight to the watchman before he remembered that David had not even asked him where he had been until joining him in the Entrance Hall. Eddie shook his head to clear it in the night air. It had been a most peculiar evening, the oddest party he had ever been to and the strangest girl had agreed to meet him in Al Jalawi on Saturday. Shaking his head this time in wonder, he walked to the car and drove home.

Jenny was asleep when her husband returned that night. Thankfully Eddie undressed and got into bed quietly so as not to disturb her. Since returning from the North on Wednesday evening, Jenny had managed to keep him at arm's length, for with the Thursday sales meeting, the snooze in the afternoon and the party, Eddie had been kept busy. In spite of that, now he only wished to lie and think back over the last few hours. Settling down into his pillow, and placing his arms behind his head he thought of Corinth, the large villa, the well heeled occupants and David, strange fellow. He felt that David must have known where he had been all that time, he could not have assumed that he had been in the toilet!

That Corinth! he had fallen for her, he knew himself to be curiously excited by her and realised with rare perception that if she had been as nice to him from the first, as she had been that evening, he might never have given her a second thought. He grinned to himself in the dark. She had been very clever to gain his attention by playing such a game. She had aimed a blow at his vanity, no male or female had ever ignored him before. The more he thought about it, the more he admired her ploy. Now, because of it, he had more than rice and chicken to look forward to in Jalawi next week, he could hardly wait.

About his wife lying by his side, breathing gently and evenly in her sleep, he thought not at all. After all, most men needed an extra something during the long haul of marriage and he felt that he had been very good up to now. Jenny would know nothing about it and he had no need to feel guilty, for whatever he was starting would be far away from the capital and no one except Corinth and himself need ever know. He turned over still smiling and drew the sheet up to his chin to shield himself from the chill of the air conditioner. Friday tomorrow, lunch at the Intercon.

"I wonder if Corinth will be there?" he asked himself as he drifted into untroubled sleep.

10

JENNY found her husband's attitude distinctly odd that Friday morning. He made no demands on her, ate an enormous breakfast in almost complete silence and mooched about the flat, hands in pockets staring out of the window. He seemed to spend longer than usual about packing his case for the following day, and spoke to Bobby as though he actually liked the boy.

Although she was happy to get on with her chores uninterrupted, Jenny had the perverse desire to wish that Eddie would bounce a bit more, laugh a little or even turn the place upside down with his usual demands on her. At first she thought he had a hangover, and asked about the party. He was strangely reticent about the evening, and she took that to mean that it had not lived up to what he expected. Later in the morning she handed him some aspirin, which he glared at uncomprehending.

'No, he did not have a headache, yes he felt extremely well, no, there was nothing wrong with him.'

Eventually she left him alone, then she began to feel guilty. Maybe he was still thinking about Bill, maybe he was jealous. That gave her a flash of pleasure, it would be a new departure for him. Then she thought that Martha might have waylaid him on the stairs and told him that Bill had come visiting last night. That would be dreadful after the row they had almost had, but it could explain why he was behaving so peculiarly this morning.

"It isn't Bill Jolly is it?" she asked tentatively.

"What isn't?" he was holding the velvet curtains back and staring down into the street.

"Well, you were pretty angry about him on Wednesday."

Eddie looked up mildly surprised. "Was I?" The stocky man sauntered over to the telephone and played with the buttons pressing each one in rhythm.

"Eddie!" Jenny said sharply.

"Mmm?" he murmured putting his hands back into his pockets. He let out a long breath. "Oh no, don't worry, Bill

Jolly's all right, no problem." and he looked at his watch "ready?"

"Ready for what?"

"Luncheon."

"Luncheon? What's that supposed to be?" she asked him a little wildly.

Eddied giggled foolishly "That's what David, old bean, old man etc etc calls it."

Jenny was becoming impatient with him. "If you mean are we ready to go to lunch, then I'll be ready in thirty minutes, it's far too early to go yet." she walked to the door, "I'll have to go and get Bobby from---from"---

Her husband had not noticed her hesitation and as the door closed behind her he made his way to the sideboard, fumbled behind a pile of plates and brought out a bottle of Sediki.

He shook his head at it. "Not exactly what one would expect after last night but the best I can manage."

Friday lunch was early for the Millers that day, Jenny could not understand why Eddie insisted on going so early, and finally after sitting over three coffees, why he wished to stay so long. Corinth and David were nowhere to be seen and apart from Martha and Don at the next table, continually arguing with each other, nothing happened out of the norm at all.

Returning to the flat, Eddie announced that he was going out for the afternoon and left Jenny to ponder on what was really going on in his mind. She assumed he would be off to see one of his salesman friends and felt more than a little annoyed that he was out of the door before she could ask to go with him. Then she thought that perhaps Bill might be at home and before she had taken a second thought, Bobby and Jenny were moving over the road and knocking on Bill's door. He had spent the morning trying out a new set of oil paints and Bobby was going to try his hand at a canvas. Now Jenny, delighted to try her hand also was given her own brushes and canvas and they spent the rest of the afternoon experimenting. They were a thoroughly contented threesome.

Eddie had no desire to meet anyone, he drove round and round the empty streets of Hamra for more than a hour. During the suffocatingly hot afternoon, most sensible people were resting or sleeping. One or two women dressed from head to toe in a black abbaya and veil, glided from one building to another. The stores, padlocked and shuttered gave the capital a deserted air. Small stalls that would be surrounded with customers later, had polythene sheets draped over them and stools perched upside down on the overhanging barrusti roof. Small piles of sand, restless in the hot desert wind, piled up in corners and of a sudden rippled across the pavement. Here and there goats were chewing their way through large piles of refuse, leaving only polished tins gleaming in the sun. In an alley, narrow between leaning Arab houses, a donkey stood patiently at the end of a short rope, waiting for the time when the water seller would require him to carry an full oil drum through the Souk.

By four thirty the supermarkets were open again and Eddie, for want of something to do, parked the car and entered the cool interior of one of the larger stores. Inside there were many men like himself with very little to do and nowhere to go. Few seemed to want to purchase anything, they simply looked around. Goods from all over the world were picked up, examined and replaced. Two men with heavy Northern English accents were examining with delight a tin of hot pot made in York. Americans picked up jars of marshmallow, tins of pork and black eyed peas. Italians were having a debate about pasta, rejecting any that had not come from their own country. It was a measure of homesickness and it made Eddie sad for a moment. A bleak feeling passed over him as though he too had no one to care for him in this lonely place where hardly any man had a woman, but he had two. 'Just think of that Eddie, old man!' he told himself 'that can't be bad.'

The thought gave him a measure of superiority and abandoning the store in a spasm of impatience with himself, he jumped into the car and drove home. Shafique, the office clerk, was waiting for him outside the front door when he arrived.

"Sir, they would not let me in." he announced aggrieved. "they say it Sunday and therefore no work, but I know and you know too, it is Friday only and sometimes there's work, they play with me."

Eddie slapped the thin man on the back "Just their little game, Shafique, come on." The Pakistani followed him up the stairs. "What's the problem?"

"Have message from Mr Mycroft."

"The chief?" Eddie was surprised "What does he want on a day of rest?"

"Have a letter Mr Miller." Shafique handed an envelope to the salesman who gestured him into the flat.

"Drink?" he offered.

The Pakistani shook his head "Water please."

Eddie smiled at the frail looking man "All right, you're still a good Muslim then?" Shafique grinned and nodded "not been corrupted by all the salesmen?"

The man shook his head again. That reminded Eddie that he would need some more Sediki.

"By the way, shall need another jar of the special next week, I'll be back on Thursday as usual, can you manage it?"

For a moment Shafique hesitated and making up his mind nodded vigorously "Yes Mr Miller, but price will be up this time."

"It was last time."

"I know but it keep going up, because very risky, very risky." the man repeated shaking his head sadly.

"Oh well, hang on, let me read this." Eddie tore the envelope open as he went to the kitchen for the water.

The message from the Sales Manager was to the effect that Mr Miller was to pop into the office in the morning. It was not an unusual memo, there were often papers to sign, contracts to be confirmed and other matters to see to before he made his journey into the rest of the country for the week, but this week it had come at the wrong time. Eddie wanted to be away, to feel free to be able to prepare for and meet Corinth. Now he might be delayed and the horror of it struck him, what if he was unable to get to Al Jalawi by tomorrow night? If he failed to meet her how would he be able to get in contact with Corinth again without everyone knowing about it? He started to panic. His first thought was to ignore the message, but then even for the dark haired girl he refused to lose orders and commission. He would have to go and trust to luck that he would be able to get away and make up for lost time on the road. It spoiled his evening though, he was apprehensive about the time it would take to start on his journey. It would take at least twelve hours to get there, and then he would be tired, maybe not too tired, but not as fresh as he would have liked to be for action, he told himself crudely. "Damn! Trust Reggie to go and spoil things."

Happily for Eddie, his chief only kept him a short time. Notes about new opportunities for sales, a few names and addresses handed over and the top salesman was on his way.

He seemed more aware of his surroundings that morning, it was a result of his excitement. The road, though busy, held no frustrations for him, the traffic flowed smoothly. The desert wind was soft and playful in the morning air, the sun hot, but still cool enough to enjoy behind his shaded windscreen. The landmarks swiftly passed by, there were no accidents and before midday the Mercedes had moved into the zone where the aerial could pick up English broadcasts from neighbouring states.

Nearer to Al Jalawi the desert became more populated, and he passed small clumps of houses with Barrusti roofs, shacks with a petrol pump outside and other shacks with great mounds of spent tyres leaning precariously against the walls. By sunset he was near to his destination and looking forward to a long shower and a decent meal, his cold box was empty and he was getting thirsty. It had been dark for two hours when he pulled up outside the Phoenician in Al Jalawi.

Eddie always felt a great deal of pleasure in booking into Hamra hotels, not one of which he would be able to afford back home. The true luxury of them overwhelmed him constantly, and the sheer boredom of his journeys and the frustrations of his job were more than offset by the manner in which he accomplished them. He walked through the ice cold entrance hall to the desk, and shivered a little now that the moment had come to meet Corinth, he surprised himself with a spasm of nerves.

"Bit cold." he nodded to the receptionist.

"There is a message for you, Mr Miller." the clerk said reading the signature from the booking card.

Eddie's heart sank. he knew it would be from Corinth and almost certainly he was convinced that it would be a 'thank you but no thank you.' kind of message.

The clerk handed him a slip of paper, a telephone message then. It was short and simple. It said 'Tomorrow night instead.'

Eddie breathed again. "Might be better at that." he thought "plenty of rest."

Cheerfully he bounced over to the high speed lift, silently it deposited him on the top floor and he quickly examined the room he had been given. He knew from past visits that it was a replica of every other room in the hotel, the only difference was the view in the morning and he thought the paintings were quite decent. He wanted everything to be right for Corinth. He grinned ruefully at himself in the mirror, surprised by his concern. Everything about this relationship was new, even his own reactions were new, he felt as though he were turning over a new leaf. A shower and a change of clothes was enough to freshen him up for dinner, and taking another look at Corinth's message he stuffed it into his pocket and went down to the dining room.

The food, though excellent, lacked what Eddie would have liked most, a bottle of wine, it was the only thing that marred his pleasure at the wonderful hotels of Hamra. However, his mind's eye on the Sediki nestling in the air conditioning system back at his flat went some way to compensate for the lack of table wine.

The one or two European women dining with male escorts were afforded every concern and interest by the entire male staff and guests, they were stared at in various degrees of fantasy. Only in restaurants were women forced to put up with such attention, they were unable to move away from it.

In one dark corner an Arab woman in full Abbaya and veil fed herself with a spoon, lifting her veil from her face at intervals and threading the spoon upwards into her mouth. It was a delicate operation and accomplished without fuss. She must have been the only comfortable woman in the room, because there was nothing to see, no one bothered to look at her.

Checking at the reception desk later. Eddie discovered that there was no booking for Corinth, but he thought nothing of it, he was expecting her to share his room anyway, checking had merely given him something to do. If her name had been in the book, it would have made him feel closer to her and sent him to sleep comforted. As it was he had no need of comfort, the long drive and the many thoughts tumbling over each other had quite worn him out and he slept deeply until dawn.

The morning was beautiful. The pale sun pierced through the desert mist as it gradually rose over the town. From the top floor, Eddie could see over the garden of palm trees and Oleander to the opposite side of the road where there was a small mosque. Its minaret soared like a pencil into the morning sky, reflecting the sun on its loud speakers. It sat pearly pink in a cushion of brown textured sand. Everything around it seemed clean and spotless as though washed daily. Eddie, ever the realist, knew differently however. He knew, almost as though he had made the trip over the road to see, that the mosque would be in need of a repaint, the sand in front would be scattered with refuse and cardboard boxes half eaten by goats; the sand dune would be shielding a tyre shop, black and greasy with dirt and noisy with a compressor. The scene held no charm for him, he had seen, too often on his travels, a beautiful picture book scene dissolve into dirt and chaos on closer inspection.

It was Sunday and even the thought of having to visit a long list of customers and receive countless glasses of tea did little to dampen his spirits. A good morning's work, a zizz in the afternoon and then--- Corinth would be here. Or would she be here by the afternoon? Or even in the morning? For a man with so much reason, Eddie had to admit that when he thought about Corinth it completely left him. If he thought about it, to expect her by the afternoon she would have had to be on the road during the right. No, he would expect her at about dinner time, that much was reasonable. he promised himself to forget all about her until after he had finished his rounds. His work was still too important, emotional entanglements would never replace the attention he gave to it. Jenny had never come before his work, not for a moment. It would have meant more than a change of heart for Corinth to have done so.

By midday Eddie was in a frenzy of impatience. The calls were taking too long and liable to spill over into the afternoon and maybe later than that. His prospective customers all pressed their hospitality on him, he was introduced to distant relatives of eager tradesmen drank numerous glasses of sweet perfumed tea, and taken time, too much time, over the opening gambits. Arabs enjoy meeting new acquaintances, take time over introductions, talk about anything except the business in hand for quite some time, but this morning it seemed that they would never give him the opportunity to get going with the sales talk.

Mohamed Noor, a big burly Bedu with a dirty dish dash, had given him an order on his previous visit and now took a proprietry interest in the salesman, insisting on him greeting all his friends, offering him lunch, coffee, tea, anything so that he would stay a little longer. It took enormous tact and good humour to extricate himself from the situation, but as soon as he entered another office, another shack, there would be Mohamed Noor claiming him for his friend and confidant. Finally in desperation Eddie consented to eat with the man, and before he could understand what was happening, he found himself sitting cross legged under some palm trees with about a dozen others, dipping into a great metal tray of rice and chicken in front of him. They were all so pleased to see him that one by one, they dug into the white mound speckled with cloves and spices and extracted succulent pieces of chicken, laying them in front of him. Rather like a cat presenting its owner with a mouse, Eddie thought bleakly. He had no option but to eat, and eat and amidst protestations to eat again, until he felt that movement of any kind would see him splitting up the seams. At last they were satisfied, they could see that he was red in the face and completely overfed, he had behaved correctly as a guest. There had to be more time allotted to peeling apples and oranges, swallowing beakers of water, which he hoped had come straight from the well and not an oil drum. Then a sleepy conversation about Hamra affairs and he was allowed to leave. Abruptly they all stood up and quickly shook hands, and Eddie felt as though he had been keeping them against their will, but he knew it was only their way, and he scrambled ungracefully to his feet.

Now his only thought was to sleep. The sun was rampant, the heat unbearable. His shirt was soaked the moment he stepped outside the shade of the palm trees, the rice and chicken were having some kind of effect and Eddie's head began to ache. He caught sight of his red face in the rear view mirror and grimaced. At that moment he was feeling far from well. For the rest of the afternoon he slept the enormous meal away. The sun set, the desert cooled, little sounds of hotel occupancy floated up from below and still he slept. When at last he woke, he had forgotten where he was. Refreshed, he stretched out the full length of the bed shuddering slightly in the cooled room. His head was pleasantly empty of thoughts and he gazed out of the darkened window. Then------ he remembered.

"My God!" he yelled.

He leaped from the bed and switched on the light, blinking at his watch. "eight o'clock. Damn!"

Hurriedly he showered and changed, he had intended to look his best for this meeting and here he was, all the time in the world gone and he had to rush. Slapping after shave over his chin and emptying some down the hairs of his chest, he grabbed his room key and ran for the lift.

11

REACHING the foyer, Eddie looked around eagerly. A procession of men and women were walking in and out of the lounge, Indian women trailing transparent material in gaudy colours walked side by side with Arab women in black abbayas. Tall stately Arab men in camel coats nodded in conversation with each other, their gold trimmed collares glinting in the myriads of tiny lights that lit up the ceiling like stars. In the corner of the large room a fountain played, its water gushing with refreshing sound over many coloured lights, a group of Europeans and their wives laughed and chatted, but Corinth was not among them.

Eddie was too anxious to look casual and he rushed at his usual speed from room to alcove and from lobby to coffee shop. His sharp eyes took in all the black haired women that were present. Corinth was not among them. He went to the desk and asked the receptionist whether there had been any more messages and his hopes rose when the Pakistani handed him a letter. They plummeted again when he read the ill formed letter from Mohammad Noor. He had been invited to meet his family on the following day. At that moment Eddie brushed aside the compliment he had been paid as just another obstacle in a string of obstacles that seemed designed to keep him from Corinth. He knew well that it was rare indeed that any male, whether Arab or not, was invited to meet female members of a family. The fact that they would stand and acknowledge a greeting and then disappear was not to belittle the honour. Muslim fathers or husbands never allowed a male stranger to even look at his female relations, they were a possession exclusively his

Eddie put the invitation to the back of his mind, later he would feel flattered by it, for this moment he was plunged into gloom. The dining room was the last place to look and if the dark haired girl was not there, she had not come---yet. he added to himself hopefully. He hesitated for a moment to set foot in the large glittering room, and then deciding to find out once and for all, he entered.

Hotel guests for the most part had either already eaten or were not yet ready, the tables were sparsely filled, each diner seemingly on an island with empty tables all round him.

It took only a glance to see that there were no women at all in the room. Eddie chose a table out of the glare of the main lights which formed a pattern around a blue décor. He faced the door, his back to the wall in the corner. His despondency found new levels when he realised that he was not hungry.

'That wretched lunch,' he thought to himself 'I have to sit in one of the best hotels and only have an omelette or something.' It was too bad, the trip was becoming a hopeless disaster after it had started out with such high hopes. He was glad that the tables next to him were empty and childishly wished that the rest of the tables would empty and leave him to his miserable self.

"Sir?" A waiter handed him a menu. The Englishman took it and looked for something to stimulate his appetite.

"How are you sir?" the waiter stood over him smiling.

"Mm" Eddie grunted

"You remember me sir, I told you about my interiors."

The salesman looked up at the waiter and took stock of him, his face broke into a smile "Oh yes! Mr Drop isn't it?"

"Droop Sir!"

"That's it, great! well, how are your interiors this week?" the man was cheered by a friendly face.

"Well sir, I paid a visit to the local doctor here in Al Jalawi and he gave me some pink pills."

"Mm?" Eddie encouraged him.

"But you know sir, these Indian doctors don't know anything."

The salesman looked at the waiter in surprise. "But you are Indian aren't you?"

"Oh yes! Not from the same part of the country you see, this doctor he was very ignorant."

Eddie found it hard not to smile, he asked seriously " Didn't the pills do you any good then?"

"For a little while only, and then it started all over again."

"I'm sorry to hear that Mr Droop, never mind, I'm sure they'll work in the end." he said and then smothered a laugh, if the problem was constipation, then he'd just made rather a good joke, he thought.

"Here get me a Spanish Omelette will you and a glass of Hamra champagne.

Mr Droop took the menu and smiled obsequiously. "You remember what I asked you last time, sir?" he urged "about the job?"

Eddie felt a spark of anger and looked at the man sharply.

"Yes I remember, and I remember telling you that there were no jobs in our firm at the moment, and I can say that there still are no jobs with our firm. O.K?"

"Yes sir, thank you sir, but---"

"I know, if I hear of anything."

"Thank you sir." the waiter, bowing slightly moved away

'Damned people!' Eddie thought explosively, 'can't be pleasant to anyone without asking for something, and it's always another job never satisfied with the one they've got. What was it Don called it? The white man's burden.' Eddie's eyes crinkled into a smile,' he had it right, everywhere a white man goes there's a little dark one asking to get him a job'.

Eddie had finished his omelette and started on some ice cream when he decided that nothing was going to happen that night. Corinth was not coming, he may as well make up his mind to it. Periodically he had watched the door, and apart from a colourful array of Indian Saris, no females had appeared or entered. Feeling a little lost in his disappointment, he pulled out of his pocket a crumpled magazine he had picked up in the foyer, and began to read.

The waiter returned to bring his coffee and as he stirred the liquid, he was aware of a man in a dark suit approaching the door. He thought nothing of it except that he hoped he would choose a table as far away from him as possible. Eddie was therefore astounded when the chair opposite to him was pulled back and the newcomer sat down. Eddie frowned at the page in front of him, refusing to look up or acknowledge the man's presence. 'With all the empty tables in the room to choose from and he has to sit here,' he thought 'I shan't speak to him. he can go and talk to someone else.' Eddie said to himself childishly.

The starched napkin was taken from the table by a brown hand and spread on the lap opposite. he saw with a shock that it was someone he knew. It was Aziz.

"Good Evening!" the merry little man said and bowed his head in greeting

"Good God!" Eddie exclaimed, "what on earth are you doing here?"

"Just a moment." the Lebanese said taking a menu from Mr Droop. "Take this plate away, it is greasy." he handed the plate to the waiter, who with many apologies returned with another.

"I will have baked Hamour with limes. Make a good green salad and allow me to pour the dressing." Aziz handed the menu back to Mr Droop who scuttled away to the kitchen in obvious deference to a master.

"Well?"

Aziz poured a glass of water for himself, coughed slightly and grinned at his companion. "I've come to see you."

"What?"

"I also have a message for you." he brought out an envelope from his jacket pocket and handed it to Eddie. "look, it is sealed."

Sure enough the envelope had been sealed with wax and a design had been pressed into it. Eddie turned the envelope over and studied the writing. Mr Edward Miller, Al Jalawi, it read. His heart was thumping, he had no idea what Corinth's handwriting looked like, but it was a fair guess that the letter was from her.

"Go on, open it."

"Who's it from then?" Eddie asked slyly wondering how much the Lebanese knew.

"With that handwriting, probably from Corinth." he answered lightly. The salesman glanced at him sharply. "well didn't you have some business or other with her the night of the party, something to do with your wife and redecorating your flat?" Aziz asked innocently.

"Oh yes! Yes, that's right." Eddie grasped at the straw and held on.

"It's probably about that, go on open it."

There was no way he could avoid it, so Eddie took a knife and sliced the paper, inside was a short note..

'Dear Eddie,' it ran, 'Aziz knows nothing, I cannot meet you this time, my father has arrived unexpectedly. There will be another day. Make sure the seal on this letter is unbroken, I do not trust Aziz to keep his mouth shut. Corinth.'

It was little enough after all, and a deep sense of loss crept over the man. No Corinth, and how on earth was he to renew their acquaintance if she hated parties where everyone met? He brightened at the thought that she had promised to come another day. Somehow he was going to have to get in touch with her again.

"All right?" Aziz was enquiring.

Eddie looked up startled, he had forgotten the little man was there.

"Oh fine, yes, fine old chap" perhaps if he kept in touch with Aziz there might be a way round the problem, he thought, one way of trying anyway.

"She's a good interior decorator you know, learned it in Europe, has a flair for those things."

"Yes, quite." Eddie was puzzled at the way Aziz mentioned Europe as though it were foreign to her.

"What nationality is she then?" the salesman asked pushing the letter into his pocket and picking up a spoon absentmindedly.

The Lebanese seemed taken aback by the question and appeared to be thinking.

"Do you know, I'm not too sure." he answered slowly "I know she has spent most of her life out here, although she was educated in London., but I'm not sure of her pedigree." he laughed " that's what you call it isn't it? Pedigree?"

Eddie smiled politely and nodded, suddenly wishing he could go to bed.

"You didn't come all this way to give me that letter did you?" Eddie asked curiously.

"Certainly not, I have come to offer you a proposition." the smart little man leaned back in his chair and adjusted his napkin as the young waiter placed his fish in front of him, and the salad to the side. He offered a basket of rolls and Aziz waved his hand to indicate that he wished to be left alone. The Lebanese waited until Mr Droop had walked away to station himself beside a pillar, and picked up his knife and fork.

"Proposition?" Eddie prompted.

Aziz bent forward as though examining his fish minutely. "Can you hear me?" his voice was low. The Englishman leaned forward to catch his words and responded quietly.

"Yes, what's the secret?"

"An Arab I know wants a partner for his business."

Eddie leaned back in his chair and laughed "Is that all?" he said scornfully. "good God, it's not the first time someone has told me that, I suppose you want me to oblige."

Aziz glanced up at the salesman in annoyance and cast a quick look around the room.

"Quiet! This is highly confidential, please bend forward and listen, there are so many ears about even when you don't expect it."

Eddie leaned forward with a patronising smirk "Go on then, but I'm not really interested.

Aziz poked at the Hamour with his fork, pierced a slice and covered it with melted butter

"You will be when you hear my proposition."

"What's the business?"

"Booze" Aziz whispered back and took a mouthful of lettuce.

"What?" Eddie nearly leapt out of the chair, his voice exploding around the nearly empty room.

The Lebanese looked around him again. One or two diners looked at the two men, but seeing nothing unusual returned to their conversation or their thoughts.

The Englishman lowered his voice and glared down at the dark head "You have simply got to be joking, Aziz, my old buddy."

"No," he assured him continuing to eat daintily until he placed his knife and fork side by side and signalled the waiter.

"Two coffees." he ordered, and then while Droop was walking to the kitchen "no, I'm not joking, I'm very serious and when you hear the proposition I think you will be interested."

Eddie leaned back in his seat. "Forget it!" he snarled.

"Wait, there is much to talk about."

The waiter placed the two coffees on the table and presented the bills to be signed.

"Not for me there isn't." Eddie growled under his breath, scrawling his name on the paper.

"Now leave us alone, we wish to talk." Mr Droop was ordered and he returned to his conversation with the other idle waiters.

"Now then." Aziz wiped his mouth on his napkin and started spooning brown sugar into his coffee. "I will tell you all about it." he held his hand up as his companion was starting to speak. "Let me tell you first and then you can say what you want to."

Eddie subsided and instead sipped at the scalding coffee.

"First of all the business, the real business is not legitimate, you will appreciate that of course, but the covering one is. My Hamran wants to sell bathroom equipment, you know the kind of thing, bathroom suites, medicine cabinets, soap holders, nice large items and lots of small ones that will display nicely for the customs. He wants to import this equipment, customs will inspect and see all that is as it should be. The goods will then pass to a warehouse, from where a salesman will sell the goods." the brown eyes crinkled into a smile as he nodded his head towards Eddie at the word 'salesman'. "The salesman of course will be the partner and will make quite a lot of money from the sales and profits, but somewhere in the consignment there will be goods, other goods, not offered for inspection to the customs. They will disappear like lightening the moment they reach the warehouse and the salesman, still only selling bathroom equipment"- he pushed his head forward to emphasise his words "will gain also from the profits and sales of these items."Eddie's face had worn an expression of complete unconcern at the beginning of the dark man's tale, now he began to show interest. Aziz glanced up at his face and knew he was saying all the right words. "So you can see that the amount of money involved is a very large one." he went on. He dropped his voice to a whisper again "How much did you pay for your last bottle of gin?"

"Two fifty sterling." Eddie whispered back, his head bobbing forward again.

"If you know that each bottle is imported for £5, you will see what profit is involved.

"How many boxes in the consignment?"

Aziz shrugged "Could be fifty, could be a hundred, depends."

"Phew!" Eddie's head was computing figures like lightening, his mind already organised to exploit the sales of bathroom equipment. The money was big, he was already anxious to get his hands on it. The market for bathrooms and accessories alone was extensive with such a building programme going on in the country, and the profits should be vast.

The Lebanese waited for his companion to to think the implications through, watching his face very carefully. He sipped his coffee and deliberately remained quiet, then seeing questions begin to form he went on.

"You would not need to leave your job, in fact you could sell your product and bathroom suites at the same time, isn't that what you do in your country?"

"Yes, it's done sometimes." Eddie absently pulled at his lip.

"All you would need to do would be to sign a document making you the business partner, therefore the importer, and the rest is easy.

Late diners were starting to come into the room and the buzz of conversation was getting louder. Tables on either side of them were filling up and for a short time neither of them noticed, so engrossed were they.

Eddie was still thinking through the whole idea, his mind was muddled, there was so much to get straight. One bad move and this kind of operation could mean nothing but serious trouble.

"Here, let's have another coffee in the lounge, it should be quieter there and we can take our time." Aziz signalled the waiter.

12

THE lounge was quite empty when the two men entered, it was a large dimly lit room full of overstuffed settees and brass tables. Table lamps with large brown shades poured light over their immediate areas and left the rest outside their perimeter in a soft suede textured glow. It was a room for conversation and relaxation and the two men sank into the cushions in a far corner thankfully.

"This is better." Eddie said stretching his legs out under the oblong table in front of them.

"OK. we'll go on before someone comes."

"Tell me first, who is the Arab, the Hamran?"

Aziz scratched at his curls and ran his finely manicured hand through them.

"Sorry, but I cannot tell you, he wants to remain---- how you say it?—secret."

"I think you mean incognito, no one to know who he is?"

"That's right, secret."

"Oh-ho! I knew there'd be some drawbacks" laughed Eddie "small print at the bottom of the contract eh?"

"Well" Aziz tried to reason "the money is so good and the conditions of labour so small, that you must expect some conditions, and there aren't many in any case."

"Conditions of labour?" the salesman's eyes opened wide.

"Yes, that is what they call it isn't it? What you have to do."

"What would I have to do?"

"I've told you, sell bathroom equipment and accessories and sign a contract to say you are a legal partner."

"Is that really all?"

"Yes, of course now and again you would have to check up at the warehouse for reordering----- bathroom things that is." he added quickly " someone would think it strange if the owner never went there at all."

"What about the Arab?" Eddie asked slightly mollified.

"Silent partner." Aziz answered definitely "Does not want to know anything until the money is in his hands."

"Just a minute though, there are going to be times when I have to meet him surely? Anyway why does he want to keep the thing a secret? Too much danger?"

"Not at all."Aziz bristled "he has his own reasons for keeping his identity secret, it isn't the first time this has happened in Hamra."

Eddie sat and gazed at his shoes, pursing his lips. It sounded too good to be true, but to be fair he had heard of other Ex Pats becoming partners and making thousands for themselves. In a new country where business know- how was in its infancy, there were many Arabs with money to burn, and they liked to do business at a distance.

The idea of becoming a business partner was not the problem, it was the goods to be marketed. The idea of them turned his stomach into knots at the thought.

"What happens if I'm caught?" he turned to the Lebanese "don't tell me!" and he passed an index finger across his throat.

"For selling bathroom equipment? Aziz asked innocently.

"Listen buddy boy, it is just possible that the customs will find exactly what you don't want them to find one day, isn't it? and then where will Uncle Eddie be eh?"

"Won't happen." Aziz said airily and went on " if you agree to this proposition I'll show you why and how, just be assured that it will not happen."

"All right, all right, let's suppose for the sake of argument it's as safe as houses." he broke off "where the hell's the coffee?"

"There's plenty of time, he'll be busy I expect, go on." The Lebanese fumbled in his pocket and brought out a lacquered cigarette case and offered it to Eddie.

"I'd have to get permission from my company." Eddie said pursuing his thoughts "visas etc, you know the kind of thing."

"No problem."

"What if they say no?"

"They won't."

Eddie thumped his cushion "How the hell do you know that, you don't even know my company." he said angrily.

Aziz smiled slyly at his companion. "I know because if you put your mind to it you can sell them the idea without any trouble at all."

"Slimy bastard!" the salesman meant it as a compliment

"Thank you." the small man narrowed his eyes momentarily "I'll take that for a compliment."

"Take it anyway you like, old chap." he answered easily "anyway, why me?"

The question had only just occurred to him

"You are the best salesman with the best record in Hamra." Aziz said simply.

Eddie smiled his pleasure and said flattered "Am I? Well, yes, I suppose I could be." then he frowned "how do you know?"

"There are ways of finding these things out. You don't think we just picked you out of the telephone book do you?"

Eddie stubbed his cigarette out and threw himself back into the cushions.

"Gosh!" he said in wonder. "what a proposition!"

The waiter bearing a brass tray with a coffee pot and cups and saucers came at last.

"Where the hell have you been, Droop?" the Englishman said beligerantly.

"Sorry sir, but very busy in the dining room, I come as soon as possible."

"Alright, I'll come and sign the bill after we have finished." Aziz waved his hand to indicate the man's dismissal. Eddie stared at the waiter's receding back.

"Has he been onto you about his interiors?" he asked with a laugh.

"Frequently" Aziz replied "in fact for a boy of his age, it would seem that he does not have much of a future." he threw back his curls and laughed loudly at his own humour.

"You said 'we' just now who is we?" Eddie returned to the subject in hand.

The Lebanese poured steaming coffee into the cups "The Arab and myself of course."

"Of course, but where do you come in?"

"I'm his agent."

"Oh!" Eddie sipped at the hot liquid and had another thought. "What about the paperwork? I'm not much good at accounts and things like that, just about fill in an order form and work my bank balance out."

93

"No problem, the paperwork will be done by the clerks, you will only have to sign the finished result for the auditors, all the hard work will be done for you." the man grinned "I told you it would be easy."

Guests were filtering into the lounge by now and the two men leaned forward facing each other, their voices low.

"Come on Aziz, you could have got anyone to do this couldn't you?"

"No, unfortunately there doesn't seem to be a choice, you are right for the partnership from all sides of the question. I want you to think very seriously about it--- and quickly."

"Eddie looked at the man sharply. "Quickly?"

"Yes, the first container has been ordered and will be arriving soon. We have to have a definite answer."

"When?"

"Next Saturday is the limit." Aziz drew the cigarette case out of his pocket again.

"No, have one of mine." Eddie said absently offering his packet. He brightened "Here! Any perks with the job?"

His companion understood perfectly, he grinned his eyes crinkling "You mean free samples?" he asked.

"Yeah" Eddie nodded heartily.

"If you agree to become a partner, then there's no reason why you shouldn't have as much as you like within reason. That's already understood." Aziz was very serious.

Later. Eddie knew that it was the promise of the free samples that had clinched it. He would go home that week on air, a prospective partner in with the promise of unlimited money and unlimited booze.a lucrative business. 'Who could ask for more?' he asked himself.

The two men sat back and relaxed each thinking their own thoughts. Eddie's mind was seething with activity, Aziz was contented that he had won the man over and was already thinking of the next step. Guests came and went through the glass doors, an Arab sitting in the shadows of the far wall stood up and adjusted his camel coat, the brown transparent garment floating out behind him as the breeze from the air conditioning caught it.

Eddie looked up vaguely in the man's direction and then with more attention. The man seemed familiar, for a moment he half expected his new friend Mohammad Noor to walk over to him, but then suddenly he knew who the man was. The tall figure, the goatee beard, the piercing eyes, but most of all those heavy gold worry beads. The man from outside the mosque. Eddie's large eyes opened as wide as they would go, he glanced at Aziz who seemed to be behaving oddly.

The Lebanese was trying to make himself as small as possible, he had picked up a magazine and was hiding behind it, sunk into the cushions. The salesman looked up at the Arab approaching, he was gliding towards them and for some reason he began to feel panicky. It was as though that gaunt figure was following him. He seemed to be everywhere he went, he wished he knew what he was up to.

Eddie had assured himself that on previous occasions when they had met it had been coincidence, but taking one look into the man's startling eyes, the Englishman was beginning to think otherwise. He looked at the salesman as though he knew him, wanted something from him or was maybe watching him. It unnerved the sandy haired man and he turned to Aziz. Before he could speak, however, the Arab had gained the table, his gold beads flicked once or twice across the back of his hand, then bowing to the two men bade them a

"Good evening!"

Eddie muttered a good evening in response, Aziz said nothing, hidden behind his magazine, and then the tall man glided away and out of the room Immediately Aziz threw down the magazine and sat bolt upright.

"Well, Eddie," he said in false good humour "have to go now, leave it to you to think about." and the small man leaped up from the settee.

"Here! Just a minute," Eddie reached a hand out to him "what's all this about. I've seen him before and what was that act with the mag?"

The Lebanese was agitated and his black curls bobbed up and down as he looked over his shoulder towards the door.

"Yes, I know, don't worry, no problem, have to go now, tell you all about it next week." and without another word he escaped through the glass doors and was swallowed up in the groups of guests standing in the foyer.

The salesman left alone with his coffee, sat back and tried to sort things out in his mind. Obviously there was a connection between the Arab and the Lebanese, he seemed terrified of the man. Who could he be? Secret police? He discarded that thought almost immediately, he had seen the so called secret police. Dressed to kill in European clothes and infiltrating parties and peeping over compound walls. The Secret police never wore Arab clothes, and certainly not upper class Arab clothes, which was indicated by expensive gold trimmed camel coats. In any case his Arab had a superior air about him rather as though he came from a noble family. A Sheikh perhaps? It would explain the beads.

Aziz must be involved with many deals, all Lebanese seemed to be, perhaps he had done something in the past that was dodgy and the Arab knew it. It was all a bit hair raising. Eddie thought about Aziz and the deal he was trying to make with him, he wondered how safe such a partnership would be if the Lebanese was already involved with other shady deals. Eddie was in two minds about the whole matter. On one hand he desperately wanted the money the partnership would bring him- not forgetting the booze- he reminded himself, and on the other he was in a country where flouting the law was liable to get the culprit

What was the punishment for importing liquor? Not the chop surely? Not for a European! He shuddered at the thought, "Was it worth the risk?" he asked himself again. Then he remembered all the people selling alcohol. The ones that got caught were the Sediki sellers and distillers, he had never heard of anyone being caught selling the real stuff, There were too many top people who wanted it, and in whose interest others kept silent. He shook his head and stood up, he would sleep on it. Searching out Mr Droop, he signed his bill. He stopped for a moment at the desk to ask what room Aziz was in and then remembered that he had no idea what his surname was, he gave up and went to bed.

13

FOR the rest of the working week, Eddie's mind hovered between fact and fantasy. On one hand he totally rejected the idea of going into a secret partnership with someone who was going to sell alcohol coupled with all the risks that involved, and on the other he mused about the money it would bring him. He saw a life where his bank balance would grow along with his social contacts, his popularity would increase, he would always be the life and soul of every party. He saw a large country house with acres of grounds deep in the heart of the English countryside, and the temptation to accept was becoming overwhelming.

Thinking back on all that had happened to him, his change of friends, his expectations, even his habits, everything was changing. It all had started after he had met Corinth, the progression of events was staggering, at times he was totally bemused. He made his visit to Mohamed Noor the following day, duly greeted his wife and daughter, had another stomach stretching meal sitting on cushions and left Al Jalawi on Monday afternoon

On Tuesday he followed up the new contacts at Khofar on the coast and at a small desert town called Boraida. It was a curious place, depending for its prosperity on herds of goats and a one street Souk. Either the wind had changed its pattern since the small town had been built or there was a particular reason that Eddie did not know about, either way the Souk had been built directly in the path of the worst desert winds. On either side of a wide road, the shops with their wooden shutterlike doors stood open for business in the path of the blowing sand. During the gentle breezes, the grit sidled and eddied into corners and piled up gently in the gutters, but at some time every day the unruly desert would blow itself up the wide street, the Souk acting as a funnel for the deluge of sand. Some storekeepers would wrap their headresses around their faces and sit imobile in their small shops until it was all over, others would hurriedly close their doors. It mattered little either way, for the sand would penetrate every corner and crevice, then for the rest of the working day the storekeepers would spend their time sweeping and dusting until piles of grit stood outside every store in the road. For a time there would be stillness in the town, giving a chance for trade and some kind of relaxastion, but soon the breezes would start again and the piles of sand outside each place of business would start to move away in rivulets and tiny bursts of energy until the grit had once more reached the desert.

There was no suitable hotel in Boraida and so Eddie returned to the coast for the night. Pleased as ever to see the sparkling blue sea, the almost white colour of the sand and the dhows, graceful and ancient far out in the ocean, he happily booked into the best hotel on the seafront.

For a time, Eddie forgot the events of the past week, ate a very good dinner and took himself off for a walk on the Cornische. It was a wide promenade and Hamrans sometimes took their families and even their televisions for picnics during the cooler evenings. There were many Europeans in Khofar and as always Eddie wished his company had been based here and not in the capital. Being on the edge of the Gulf gave him a feeling of freedom, people seeemed more relaxed, they smiled more and had more contact with other Gulf states. Eddie sighed, back to Hamra tomorrow, he sat on one of the stone benches looking out to the now darkened sea. The small lights twinkled from the dhows and the smell of seaweed and the taste of salt in the air was enjoyable. It was cooler here in the evening, although perhaps a little more humid, he felt his shirt coldly clammy against his skin. Muffled sounds from several television sets along the Cornische wafted over to him, a mixture of Arab music and Arab singing. He always found it excrutiating, a melody without harmony repeated over and over again. It was in keeping, however, that night, for the sounds came from a distance and it was palatable.

Once again he began to think about the proposition that had been put to him. He really ought to ask someone about it, take some advice. He knew he had no chance of doing that though, the salesman had not needed to be told that he must keep the whole thing to himself. It was frustrating for the cargo he needed advice about was the secret part. If he were to agree to take the business on, he knew that he could never tell anyone about it, ever. Even if he refused the offer, it could still come out in the future and he would be as suspect as Aziz, having been seen with him in public.

He thought for a moment of confiding in Reggie, after all the chief must have come up against this sort of thing in the past, he might even already be involved in something like it himself. He had a feeling that Reggie would say "Play safe." and "Have nothing to do with it." and that maybe was the best reason for not asking his advice. Deep down inside him Eddie knew he was going to go for it. he wanted the money and he wanted the prestige it would bring him. All he needed to know was that he would not be caught.

Aziz had reassured him, but then he would, he was trying to sell him the idea. Eddie stood up and stretched and began to walk slowly along the Cornische. The answer seemed to be "Yes." no problem, but--- "how can I protect myself and what about those customs?" There were numerous ways to dispose of the booze once it was through customs, that did not bother the man very much, it was the search at customs. That he would have to make sure of before he signed anything. His mind made up on the point, he crossed the road and walked briskly back to the hotel. He had no way of getting in touch with Aziz and the little man had vanished before an arrangement to meet could be made.

"If he wants his answer by Saturday, he'll just have to find me." Eddie muttered to himself as he drifted off to sleep.

It was late when Eddie arrived home, he had been on the road for fourteen hours and he was physically and mentally exhausted. Letting himself into his flat he was irritated to see at once that Jenny was not there.

The lights were out and the flat had an empty feeling to it. He peeped in at Bobby's room and it was empty. He cursed feelingly, he was tired, he wanted a meal, and where were they anyway? Switching on all the lights he was somewhat comforted to find a tray with cold meats and salad on the table and a plate of bread and butter covered with clingfilm.

The salesman sat down without bothering to shower and ate his meal. He looked at his watch, 10 o'clock, where the hell was she? Carelessly he started looking in cupboards and behind crockery, dropping things on the floor and picking them up again. He found the Sediki and looked at his watch again. he decided to go down and ask Don if he had seen his wife. He was on the stairs when the main front door opened and he could hear Bobby chattering to his mother.

"Where the hell have you two been?" he greeted them over the banisters "I've been home ages."

Jenny ran lightly up the stairs, Bobby trailing more slowly behind her, "Hello, you're late this week." she said passing her husband and laying a pile of books down on the sideboard. She was wearing a pale yellow dress, her hair was soft and shiny and her face flushed, she looked very desirable at that moment, but he was not going to let her off the hook.

"Where have you been?" Eddie asked again with annoyance, closing the door behind his son.

"Only over the road." Jenny said smiling. "I kept looking to see if the car was outside, I'd almost given you up for tonight." She bustled about with plates and cutlery and took them into the kitchen. Eddie walked after her quickly and grabbed her arm. She swung round and dropped a knife.

"Where over the road?" he growled suddenly suspicious.

"At Bill's" she said and then put in "we've started a painting class." she picked up the knife and placed the dishes in the sink. "Come on, look I've got some books here." he stepped back to allow her to pass and followed her into the lounge.

"Just a minute, just a minute! I don't want to know anything about painting." he was getting angry, his face started to change and his eyes to bulge. "I've been away all week, working my guts out to keep you and that fine son of yours, and you can't even be here when I get home." Eddie placed his hands on his hips and leaned forward from the waist. "Cold meat and salad, a fine homecoming. Now listen to me Jenny, I won't put up with that sort of treatment, I'm going to have to have a word with Mr Bill sodding Jolly. You are not to go over there again- is that understood?" She opened her mouth to speak, but he held up his hand. "Shut up and listen, I'm not having my wife chasing another man." he yelled into her face thrusting his bull like head forward in emphasis. "No way you're going to make me a laughing stock in the company."

Jenny stared at the man in front of her for a moment and suddenly burst out laughing, a wave of sound he had never heard from her before. Eddie straightened up and looked at her with a shocked expression.

"You looked so funny." she gasped leaning weakly against the dining table. "you ought to see yourself. Bull frog Miller." she pointed at his face.

"What?" Eddie could not believe he was hearing his wife speak to him in this way. "are you ill?" he asked frantically looking for an explanation.

"Not at all," she answered gaily "come on Eddie have some Sediki, make you feel better, make a nicer man of you." Jenny grasped the bottle and poured a hefty measure into a glass, added some orange juice and held it out to him.

Silently he took it and gulped the liquor down as though it were medicine. She took the glass and filled it again.

"There!" My duty done, two glasses filled, one meal prepared, clean towels and clothes in the bathroom awaiting your lordship, only one more thing to do and I've fulfilled my purpose for this week.

Stunned Eddie sank into an easy chair still staring at his wife.

"Are you drunk?" he asked finally.

"Not a bit, not even had a drink. I just feel liberated, that's all Eddie, old man, old chum, old---bull – I –feel—libera----ted." she sang the last words and started to dance in a slow circle, the skirt of her dress swirling out from her. Gradually she danced into the kitchen, where singing to herself she started to wash the dishes.

Eddie, his drink forgotten, rose from his seat and went into his son's room.

"What's wrong with your mother?" he asked the small boy who peeped at him over the sheets.

"Nothing." he answered nervously.

"Oh! You and your nothing!" Eddie said impatiently, and then more quietly hoping to draw the boy out "she seems in a good mood doesn't she?"

Bobby nodded eagerly " Yes." was all he said.

"But why? That's what I'm asking you." Eddie was becoming impatient again.

"She's happy." Bobby said simply and drew the sheet over his head.

"Yes, she is isn't she?" said the man to himself as he closed the door. "But why? what's been going on to make her that happy?"

Eddie was still smarting from his wife's laughter, she had never done that before, never laughed at him to his face like that. Suddenly she was not the person he knew, that behaviour belonged to someone else altogether.

The thought made him feel slightly insecure. It was obvious that Bill Jolly was at the bottom of all this, coming into their lives and starting to wreck his routine, then paying more attention than was healthy towards his wife. Eddie resolved to punch him on the nose the next time he saw him, it was the only response he could think of.

Eddie thought a cold shower might be the best retreat he could manage at that moment and for once locked himself in the bathroom. Jenny, her mood frothy and more than a little rebellious changed into her nightdress and sat on the settee staring into the blank face of the television set.

When her husband emerged from the bathroom he hunted around in his cupboard and unearthed a pair of pyjamas he had not worn since coming to Hamra. There was something odd about Jenny that night and he was already feeling a little insecure, nakedness portrayed confidence and security, clothing was a cover for his insecurity.

"Come and sit down, Eddie." Jenny called from the settee. he came into the lounge and picked up a glass, carefully sitting in the chair opposite.

"Pyjamas Eddie?" she asked playfully.

"Nightdress Jenny?" he answered waspishly.

"You have just had your ego dented haven't you," she grinned "not very nice is it?"

"I don't know what you're talking about, the man responded and jumped up to get another drink.

"Oh yes you do! I've just done to you what you have been doing to me for years and I've decided that you will never do it again. Put me down" she added in case he was confused.

Her husband paused in pouring the Sediki and she went on talking to his back.

"I will do my duty, but no longer am I going to be a puppet."

"Puppet?" he spluttered and looked at her.

"I'm a person in my own right, Eddie,"Jenny was explaining seriously.

"I know that." he said impatiently and threw himself down into the chair.

"No you don't!" she argued " you treat me like a robot, there for your pleasure and there for your use. I want some pleasure out of life as well. I'm entitled to that aren't I?"

"Bill bloody Jolly." he murmured to himself.

"Yes, I've a lot to thank him for." Jenny admitted.

"I'm sure you have." Eddie said dryly. "what have you been up to with him?" he was suspicious.

""Don't be silly, Eddie, we share the same interests, he's lonely, I'm lonely. When you are away we just keep each other company, have lots of chats and develop our hobbies."

"Oh for goodness sake!" Eddie snorted into his glass. He could hardly make head or tail out of what she was saying. He thought for a minute she was going out of her mind.

"Hobbies!" he sneered "I can just imagine what those are."

"No you can't." she answered brightly refusing to get angry, "for instance I've discovered that I can paint quite decently. That's what I was trying to tell you about tonight."

"What does your friend, Martha have to say about all this?" Eddie asked suddenly.

"What's it to do with her?" Jenny asked in surprise.

"Does she know?"

"Does she know what?"

"That you spend all your time over at Bill Jolly's flat?" Eddie set his glass down on the table

"I don't really know," Jenny considered "I don't care really, I'm fed up of spending my time round gossiping women. I'm telling you I'm going to develop my talents and pursue something more worthwhile. If Bill Jolly can help, and I know he can, then I'll take full advantage of it."

She looked at her husband defiantly he looked back at her wondering for a moment if she had always been like this and he had never noticed.

"Mind he isn't the one taking the advantage!" he said nastily, not understanding the change in her. Then "Jenny!" he wailed "don't you love me anymore?" his face was screwed up, he was tired and vulnerable, he felt like a child. He felt unsure whether to give her a good hiding or to appeal to her better nature. However he also felt that nothing he said or did that evening would be right.. Really it was too bad after the problems of the week, to come home and find another one. Jenny stood up abruptly.

"Right, come on Eddie, one more thing to do and my duties will be done for tonight."

"Bugger that for a game of soldiers!" he said aloud. If that was supposed to be a invitation to the delights of the bedroom, it was as enticing as cold porridge, he told himself. Eddie was so tired that he was glad to go to bed and sleep. Gingerly he crept into his side of the bed, turned his back on his wife and closed his eyes. Thankfully Jenny sighed and was fast asleep before him.

14

JENNY had promised herself that she would not go to any more parties. She had always hated them but felt obliged to be there with her husband. Now, having started to become what she called 'her own person' she made a vow that this Thursday would be the last. She had to go to that one, she had promised Martha to help with the buffet. It was Don's turn that week and Martha was fussing.

"You know how he is, I don't expect he's told anyone, I can't find where he's hidden the wine and if I don't remind him he might not even turn up." she said in exasperation.

"Oh, come on Martha! He's not that bad." Jenny said winking at Don hiding his face behind his newspaper.

"Look at him, he's just about the most useless, hopeless, incapable—"

Don coughed politely and turned a page. "What's the use, I can't even find the words to insult him properly." Martha bustled into the kitchen "What do you think about Vol au Vents?" she asked her friend.

"Fine, very nice." Jenny was folding paper napkins and shaping them into flowers.

"Thought I'd have lobster and mushrooms, you know that mix in a sauce, there's a French name for it."

"I know, delicious," Jenny agreed "I'll do it for you if you like."

"Would you, love?" Oh I'm hopeless, I'd never manage all that fiddle."

Don lowered his newspaper and said to no one in particular "She'll manage to eat them all though."

His wife threw a dishcloth at him, it landed on his paper and slithered down into his lap. Mildly he removed it and placed it on the coffee table.

"Oh! what wouldn't I give for a husband like yours occasionally" the middle aged woman said to Jenny. "At least there's some life in him, he does get annoyed sometimes, he can laugh, you can see the man is living can't you." she bustled into the lounge with a plate of crackers.

"Yes, too much sometimes." Jenny said flatly.

"No, Ducky, not too much. Just look at Po face over there."

Jenny threw a glance in Donald Baker's direction. The chubby man's face was expressionless.

"You can see what the game is can't you?" she looked at her friend "he sits there like a sphynx hiding. He hides behind that paper so that whatever I say he can state that he hasn't heard it, because he was reading the paper" Martha leaned her hand on the dining table and looked disgusted. "Shifty, that's what I call it." she said. "Do you know, Jenny when he used to be away so much, I couldn't wait for him to come home. I got everything ready, little treats, drinks in, a sexy nightie, all that sort of thing. Then home he would come, hardly a word said, no surprises for me, or treats for that matter, no conversation, nothing. He would sit down after his dinner and read the blooming paper. Then he would go to bed tired out."

Jenny was embarrassed for the silent listener behind his paper. "Surely not, I can't believe that." she laughed nervously.

"Well, you can love, in fact I'm not sure how Georgie was born at all. it must have been an immaculate conception." and she slapped her friend's shoulder and went into peals of laughter.

Jenny grinned and looked over to Martha's husband. he lowered the paper slowly and winked. "Battleaxe." he said quite distinctly and went back to his newspaper.

Martha looked fixedly at her husband "Did he speak or did the wind blow?" she asked rudely.

The Baker family were renowned for their bickering, or more to the point, Martha was well known for baiting her husband. It was generally held in the firm that Don had given up answering Martha years ago and had surrendered to the relentless battering of words coming out of her mouth. On the face of it an unlikely marriage, but it seemed to work for them, and although neither were ecstatically happy, they were contented enough. As Don had once said to Eddie, "It's a load of horse manure, but it's the only bag I've got."

His friend was never quite sure of the full meaning of that statement, but he caught the drift.

The party was as successful as all the parties were. Another week of the contract gone, even if there were nothing else to celebrate, that would have been enough. There were no outsiders this time and Bill Jolly came along after a pressing invitation from Martha.

"He's a smashing chap isn't he Jenny?" she said pointedly to her friend. "asked him specially for you."

"For me?" Jenny looked at Martha sideways.

"Yes love, I know you two are friends."

"Yes, but not that sort of friends, Martha, I know what your matchmaking is like."

"Give it time, love, give it time." her friend patted her on the arm and walked off.

Eddie in a fair muddle over the turmoil in his life had decided that the solution to it all was to get as drunk as possible. To that end he was sinking Sediki as though it were going out of production. Don resisted his attempt to drink it neat, by filling his glass with ice.

"Phew! I don't know how you can drink that stuff neat like that." he said.

"Never mind, Don my little brandy ball, it's not the smell that counts. Hold your nose and down it goes." and so saying he would empty his glass yet again.

After Bill had arrived and been greeted by everyone, Eddie made a point of following him around. Jenny was apprehensive and tried to head him off, but he was insistent in his befuddled state, he felt he ought to keep an eye on him.

"Been kept busy this week, Bill, old chum?" he asked the tall man, his eyes wide and innocent beginning to bulge and water.

"Fair to middling." Bill gave a safe answer.

"Fair to-----middling?" what kind of answer is that?" Eddie swung his glass out in the direction of Reggie and his wife "D'you here 'at?"

Martha was at his elbow "Come and sit down and taste some of these vol au vents, Eddie, Jenny made them." she tried to push him into a seat.

"Yeah! Goo old Jenny, everybody's helpmate." he said and giggled. Thrusting his head out at Bill, he persisted "True ain't it? Everybody's"----

"Here, Jenny, I don't know what's up with Eddie, but he isn't going to last the course this evening, he'll have to put his head under a shower soon." Don said.

Jenny frowned and looked down at her husband slumped into the seat Martha had been successful in negotiating under him. Sweat was beaded on his forehead, his face was bright red and he was starting to mumble to himself

"Sorry Don, I think I'll take him upstairs before he gets any worse, can you help?"

Between Reggie and Don, Eddie was half carried half dragged up the stairs and into the bedroom. The salesman flopped onto his bed, giggling and muttering to himself.

"Georgie!" Martha reminded Jenny "The boys are up there by themselves with Eddie.

"Don't worry, I'm going myself now, I can't stay here not knowing what Eddie's up to." "It's such a shame," Martha said "it isn't even midnight yet, don't men let you down."

"You can say that again." Jenny was angry. Bill came to her side and said "I'll come up with you." and when she was about to reject the offer he added, "just to make sure things are all right."

Bobby and George were people watching. During the last week, Bobby had timidly introduced his hobby to his friend. The two boys were kneeling on the floor with their chins on the window sill, staring into the windows of the flats opposite. "Look! There's that Lebanese." Bobby laughed "you watch him now." and in flat No 3 the dark haired man of Eddie's acquaintance began to search his room, picking up cushions, removing ornaments and looking underneath, examining his telephone. The boys chortled. "In a minute he'll close rhe curtains and then in about ten minutes I think he'll have a visitor, you can't see too well down there." Bobby was instructing George. "there!" he pointed as the curtains were drawn carefully across the large window.

Jenny was acutely aware of Bill Jolly being in her flat after midnight, her husband unconscious in bed and the two young boys in the bedroom. It was a situation known to everyone in the company and although she was mostly unconcerned, she knew someone would be making something of it.

"You must go now, Bill, you can see everything is all right, Take Georgie with you as well." she instructed.

"If you're sure, what a pity, I was enjoying myself this evening as well." he pulled a mournful face. She smiled and touched his arm There's still time, they won't break up for a while yet

"No good, I shan't enjoy it now." Bill said matter of factly "I only went in the first place because you would be there." He placed his fine slender hands on hers "you know I'm only happy in your company." he added in a low voice, his eyes on the boy's door.

"You mustn't say things like that." involuntarily her eyes went to her bedroom door, almost expecting Eddie to be standing there.

"Why not?" Bill's voice was urgent "I mean it, and you know it. I don't suppose I shall be able to see you now until next week."

Jenny shook her head. It was pleasant to be admired, to be wanted.

"I'll probably be able to come over on Saturday, we could go on with that painting, Bobby really enjoys it."

The tall man leaned over the pale golden head "I don't care what Bobby likes at this moment. It's what you like that matters to me, you must understand that, Jenny."

She looked up at him and impulsively stretched and kissed him quickly. "Goodnight Bill."

He would have caught her to him, but the boys came out of the bedroom.

"Have we got to go now?" George asked.

"Yes, off you go, see you tomorrow." Jenny said gaily.

Her eyes were shining and her face flushed as she said goodnight once more to Bill. It was quite some time before she moved away from the door and set about getting ready for bed.

15

EDDIE had a remarkable capacity for alcohol. He could drink heavily and yet the next morning have recovered almost totally from the assault on his liver. A slight squeamishness and a ravenous appetite was the only sign of an evening spent in over indulgence.

Because of this he was up early the next morning in time to answer the front door bell, much earlier than most people on a Friday morning. It was Aziz.   The dark man ran quickly up the stairs and into the flat "Can't stay long." he said breathlessly "had to tell you about this evening."

"Have a drink or something" Eddie pressed him. "Sit down at least."

Aziz as immaculate as ever in smartly creased trousers and open necked shirt, sat down quickly.

"I want you to see something this evening, are you still interested in my proposition?" he asked.

"Yes," said Eddie carefully "but there are one or two points--."

"Of course, that's why I want to meet you this evening, down the Souk."

"Hamra Souk?" Eddie asked looking over his shoulder at Bobby who had just entered the room. Something in the boy's stance alerted Aziz and irritated Eddie.

"What's the matter with you?" he asked the boy. Bobby's eyes were wide.

"Nothing." he answered sullenly but still looking at Aziz.

"Go and get your breakfast then," his father dismissed him. "my son" he said to the Lebanese as an afterthought.

"Ah yes!"

"Whereabouts in the Souk?"

"Last week you went down the Souk with your wife and son."

"Yes?" Eddie looked startled.

"You went into a juice seller "Aziz went on "do you remember which one?"

"Ye-es I think so, but how the hell did you know that?" Eddie sat down with a thump. "hell, Aziz, you terrify me with your shifty ways."

The man smiled in his oily way "Do not worry my friend, I have to know these things, it is all part of the business."

"Some business."

"Yes, it is some business, I can promise you that."

"OK, I remember the place, Is that where we meet?"

"Quite correct, I shall meet you there at 5 o'clock."

"Drink?"

"No. no, I have to go now." and the curly head bounded up, " you are still interested, yes?"

"Yes, but as I say, there are one or two points."

"We'll discuss them tonight, and remember not a word to anyone."

"Of course not, what do you think I am?"

"Hello!" Jenny caught sight of the visitor. She entered the room wearing an emerald skirt overlaid with colourful flowers. Her shining hair lay softly across her shoulders and she looked lovely. Eddie caught his breath as he looked at her and Aziz was lost in admiration."

"Your wife." he said and bounded across the room.

"This is Aziz, remember he came with David to our party?"

"Ah yes, I remember, Good morning." she touched his hand briefly "would you like some coffee?"

Aziz seemed to waver for a moment, then recovered himself

"Er-no thank you Mrs Miller."

"Oh Jenny please."

"Jenny then, I'm afraid I have to hurry."

After the man had made his departure, Bobby came in and stood beside his mother whispering.

"What are you whispering about now?" Eddie asked him impatiently.

"He says that he's seen Aziz over the road."

"What, where?" his father was interested.

"He says that he lives in a flat over the road."

"Did he really have to whisper like that?" Eddie was irritated by his son's timidity, "surely he could have managed to say that out aloud?" he glared at Bobby. "How do you know that?"

"I've seen him," the boy said defiantly, "he's always looking under cushions and things."

Eddie guffawed "What's he talking about?" he asked his wife.

"He does, he's always looking under his cushions And picking up things and then he has a good look at his telephone." the boy stepped towards his father, anxious to be believed.

"What on earth for?" his father was intrigued.

"I don't know." the boy said and then with spirit "Georgie has seen him too."

Suddenly Eddie realised how Aziz knew so much about his family's movements. The searching around his room might suggest that he was suspicious that someone had been there and put something in say the telephone- a microphone perhaps, or something to incriminate him? Eddie was impressed that Aziz was so cautious. Perhaps he was a spy, Eddie grinned at that, he really did not think so.

After the outburst from Jenny the day before, Eddie was a little apologetic when he told her he was going out again without her. Neither of them had referred to the previous evening, or Jenny's peculiar behaviour on his return home. Somehow Eddie thought that by not mentioning it, the whole episode could be forgotten. It was a pity therefore that he had to leave her again.

"Don't worry about me, I'll do some painting." Jenny said lightly, it sounded like a threat.

The sun was starting its descent at 5 o'clock. The last glare of its rays hit the minarette of the Grand Mosque as Eddie drove towards the old part of Hamra. By the time he was walking down the alleyways of the Souk, the late afternoon light had softened to a red glow in the sky making the clay buildings pink in the reflection. Underfoot, the sand was warm from the earlier heat, but now dirty with litter and discarded fruit stones. Here and there a trail of betle nut juice spat from red toothed Pakistanis, lay like thin veins of blood on the top of the sand. The spices, warm and fragrant, wafted their scent over all the buildings and the restaurants, whose doors were open to the street and emitted pungent odours.

Eddie, however had no time to look about him, his mind was totally on the meeting with Aziz, and getting the assurance he sought. When he arrived at the juice seller's shop it was closed. He swore under his breath "What now?" For a moment he thought he might have come to the wrong place, but stepping back against the wall and looking along the row, he could see that this was the only Juice seller in this alley. He tried the door. It opened easily and a small bell on sprung metal jangled. Aziz was sitting behind the counter out of immediate sight.

"I thought you were never coming." the small man said springing up and walking swiftly to the door. "come on, follow me."

The walk became a sprint as the sun finally went down and inky darkness spread through the Souk. There was no public lighting, only pools of light shining from the small stores and houses provided the two men with a safe passage through shadows and darkness. Narrowly missing his footing on a stone, Eddie called to Aziz in front of him "Hang on, I'm going to break my ankle at this rate."

"Sh!" the small man put his finger to his lips urgently "Quiet, we don't want everyone to know where we are going do we?" and he was off again, down a narrow alley, across a small cross roads, through the gold and silver Souks, down another stretch and through a warren of tiny paths. Shadows and black hollows were everywhere, turning a safe footing in daylight into a treacherous assault course at night. Eddie was fighting to keep up with his companion, if only for the fact that he had no idea where he was now. He had lost his way back at the gold Souk.

Finally he saw Aziz come to a complete stop. Inching forward, the Lebanese poked his head round the corner of a building, there was a small road to cross and lights were shining from round the corner. He turned "Come on." he called softly and ran swiftly across the road, Eddie followed instantly and they both arrived at a corrugated zinc door at the same time. Aziz undid the padlock, pushed the gate open and shut it as quietly as he could behind them both. He leaned back on the gate and breathed heavily.

"Were we followed or something?" Eddie asked anxiously

"Of course not," the other man said in astonishment "that is why I am so careful, then I am never followed."

Eddie looked round the yard in front of them and the

warehouse behind. There were stacks of pallets piled high with boxes everywhere, a fork lift tractor was parked in front of them and a pick up at the front of the Godown. Lights hitched up onto long poles were placed at strategic intervals along the wall surrounding the yard and the area was as bright as day.

Aziz motioned towards the godown and took out a bunch of keys to unfasten the padlock, then selecting another key he inserted it in the lock and the outer door opened to reveal another door precisely placed behind the first. Yet another key was used on this and they were inside the building.

"Very good security for out here." Eddie was impressed.

"It has to be, we aren't importing peanuts." Aziz said shortly.

In front of them the warehouse extended emptily for over three hundred metres. The lights were shaded casting illumination only on the area over which they hung. The silence was complete apart from a moth caught in a suicidal dance in the main light. Eddie gazed fixedly at the insect rising and falling back only to rise to the temptation again. For a moment he saw himself as the creature. Maybe he was a moth being drawn to blazing light, maybe he would also find that it would kill him. The man shuddered and then cast aside the fancy and walked over to the corner of the godown following his companion. There, already opened, was a container, and amidst a pile of shavings and straw he could see various items of bathroom equipment.

Eagerly he bent forward and examined the merchandise on the floor of the warehouse, behind them in the container were sealed boxes stacked to the roof.

"This is what you wanted me to see?" Eddie thrust his hands in his pockets and turned over a pile of straw with his foot.

"It's the container really, you must look at it." The Lebanese stepped inside the great steel box and took something off a pile of cardboard, "I have a torch to help you, come."

The torch beamed light over the interior of the container, between the stacked boxes a path had been cleared through to the wall. "To show you that the real consignment is safe from discovery, I want you to go in search of it yourself."

He swung the torch round to Eddie's face and he flinched and took it himself.

"Aw come on Aziz, I'll be here all night moving this stuff" Eddie protested. He swung the light across the stack of boxes, "I'll make it easy for you, give you an idea."

"Go on then."

Aziz stepped out of the container and carefully removed a hand basin out of the way. "Now listen!" he sat down on an unopened box and pointed inside the steel box. "First the consignment is packed in boxes completely covered with advertising, just as you would see in the UK. Famous brands of Whiskey, Gin, Rum and so on. All advertised on the exterior of the boxes. Second, you have no need to move a single box to find them." he stopped.

"Is that it?" Eddie asked and swung the torch again.

"That's it."

The salesman was uncertain. "Are you sure? You aren't having me on?"

"Not at all." the little man assured him, "the container is yours Mr Detective."

Eddie swung the torch around the interior of the steel box and pretty soon found that all the boxes on view were plain wooden crates or cardboard bound with strong nylon stranded belts. Not one on either side advertised anything more alarming than a serial number and a description of what was in them. Eddie reached the end of the path and gave up.

"Nothing here at all." he called to Aziz, sitting casually, one leg crossed over the other.

"Mm" he nodded his dark head "Keep looking." he instructed.

Within a moment Eddie had retraced his steps and stood over the Lebanese.

"Boxes with advertising on them? Like Black and White Whiskey and Gordons Gin?" he asked.

"Correct."

"Not there." the salesman said emphatically "Not among the boxes anyway."

"Quite!" said Aziz triumphantly.

The Englishman was becoming pink in the face and he could feel his impatience growing "Where then?" he asked, his voice rising.

"That is for you to find out- pretend you are a customs man."

"That's a stupid idea," Eddie said in disgust "I'm not trained to find things."

"Neither are Hamran customs men." Aziz said quietly "they only find something if they know where to look, or if they get a tip off. However if the goods were in a very obvious place, they would of course find them. They have to be hidden, go on pretend you are a Hamran customs man and go and find the hiding place.."

Eddie was beginning to feel foolish, but he put his mind to the task and started another inspection. Reaching the end wall once more, he touched the metal and then pressed forward, it did not give, it was not loose in any way. He examined the two seams between the steel panels, but there was no sign of a lever or handle and no obvious entry into the wall. However it did give him an idea, and charging out suddenly he bounded round the side of the container and examined the metal structure from the exterior. There was nothing to offer any clue. Eddie then went back and shone the torch onto the end wall and quickly did the same along the outside. There seemed to be no difference in length. He was beaten.

"Give up." he said walking back to Aziz and handing him the torch. "Thought I had it for a minute, but I was wrong."

"Good! I'm glad you failed, it will convince you of the security of the system. Come, I'll show you." The two men walked back inside the container again.

"You had the right idea, my friend, but you did not believe your eyesight." he said over his shoulder. "Look between these two seams." the small man took a knife and inserted the blade between the floor and the upright panel, he twisted and lifted and he was able to insert his fingers under the steel. He began to lift the panel which then slid up easily until the whole piece of metal had disappeared behind the ceiling panel which was now in front of it. Aziz ducked his head inside the cavity and fixed two heavy pins into position.

"Now it won't come down on your head." he emerged again and shone the torch inside the oblong cavity. "Look for yourself."

Eddie stood looking over the shoulder of his companion, his mouth open. From the floor to the ceiling, packed tightly in the narrow space were boxes of every kind of spirit he could think of. Every box was sealed and covered with advertising. There was no mistaking what any of the boxes contained.

"Phew!" the man let out a low whistle "who would have believed it?" he leaned forward and peered further "Is it packed with the same boxes the width of the container?" he asked.

"Of course, no good going to all this trouble to bring in only one or two boxes. In for a penny, better to be a pound." he said brightly.

"Why keep the bottles in the original boxes wouldn't it be safer to have unmarked ones?"

Aziz looked at him in horror "Never!" he said "they would never sell." The salesman raised an eyebrow, "think of what they can do with Sediki these days" the Lebanese went on "they can make it taste of anything, in fact I've had very good Sediki Gin, Whiskey and Rum. They are very clever, a bit of flavouring, a touch of colour and you can have anything you wish. No one is going to believe that what you sell him is the real thing unless the original labels are on the boxes and on the bottles."

The two men picked their way between the crates. "Would you believe it if someone tried to sell you a bottle without a label or a box of bottles without the proper advertising and unsealed as well?"

Eddie grinned ruefully " True, no one would."

"Correct. The little man said and began to pull the pins that were supporting the sliding steel panel.

"Just a minute." the Englishman touched his arm, "hang on, I looked to see whether the outside was larger than the inside, how deep does it go?"

"Oh I agree that you had the right idea, I told you, your eyes let you down. That is what we depend on, that no one would be able to tell by just looking. This section is only two boxes deep, twenty four bottles. When you compare the interior minus two boxes with the exterior in a container this size, there appears to be no difference. Only if you were to measure it with a tape and get the accurate measurements would you know that there must be a cavity inside." Aziz pulled the pins "we must close this now, we shall have to go soon, the watchman will be coming."

Eddie shone the torch and the Lebanese carefully pulled the steel panel down until it lodged back into position, flush with its partner over the top, and as close to the floor as it would go. he kicked some dust into the minute groove that was left and there were no signs that anything had been disturbed.

The Englishman was excited in spite of himself. he had urged himself to caution and up to that point he had been able to stand outside any decision, totally uninvolved. Seeing how the container worked was swaying him to the decision and he knew which way it was going to go.

"Come on," Aziz urged "Let's go quickly now, and no talking until we are away from here." and holding the door of the godown open until Eddie had slipped through, he cast a last eye on the container. he appeared to be satisfied and quickly inserted the two keys and finally the padlock. The outside gate seemed to be flimsy in comparison and swung open with a rattle, but Eddie reasoned it was not our of character for the area, most godwns had this type of gate.

Neither of them spoke until they had crossed the road and were walking quickly down into the Souk away from the glare of the godown lights.

"We will go to Ahmeds." Aziz called over his shoulder and started to move off down the alleyway more quickly. Eddie broke into an ungainly run as he realised that he would have to keep up, if only to find his way out of this labyrinth.

"Ahmed's?" Eddie wondered if he was about to meet someone else in this mysterious business deal.

"The juice seller." the dark man said, "hurry!"

They both hurried, and stumbled into pot holes and dents in the path. The sounds of the Souk had diminished with the closing of business for the night. The only places left open were the larger restaurants and most of their customers had gone home. The moon in its final quarter shed little light over the passageways, but increased the shadows that loomed on all sides of the two men as they sped through the Arab quarter. The lingering aroma of cooking would have been enough to indicate their destination, but there was no need, light still shined from the juice seller and they opened the door thankfully and collapsed onto the seats.

Eddie was aware of a Pakistani in a brown Shiva Kamis hurry forward and pull the shop blinds down over the glass panel in the door and then the shop window. The closed sign was put up and the man opened the door and stepped out closing it behind him.

"That's old Ahmed is it?" Eddie grinned as he caught his breath "God!" what I couldn't do to a gin." he puffed and panted and stretched out his legs. "just think of all that gin in that place and not a drop to drink." he shook his head "Criminal!"

16

AZIZ brought a spirit stove from behind the counter and a blue enamel cup with a pouring lip and a long handle.

"I can't give you gin, but coffee we both need." he placed two spoonfuls of finely ground coffee into the enamel pot and from a box in his pocket he produced two seeds the size of peanuts and placed them on top of the powder, he added sugar and then filled the pot with water.

"Light the stove." Aziz told Eddie who was taking little interest in the proceedings "The matches are just by your arm." As the liquid came to the boil, Aziz removed the pot from the fire, allowed the coffee to subside and then replaced it. He repeated the process three times and then poured the concoction into small coffee cups without handles.

"You have seen how it is done now." the Lebanese took a sip of the fragrant coffee. "the container I mean."

"Mm, I have to hand it to you old chum, it seems pretty well tied up to me" Eddie said frankly and hazarded a sip from his cup "what the hell is this stuff?" he asked grimacing.

"Arabic coffee, some call it Turkish." Aziz replied "it is the best way to make coffee, naturally."

"Oh naturally!" Eddie mimicked.

The little man grinned, his eyes crinkling "You'll acquire a taste for it, you'll see."

Eddie ignored the inference that the partnership was already decided.

"Tell me, why don't you import drugs?" he was curious " not that I'd want anything to do with it, but I would have thought the money was better."

The Lebanese smiled and shook his head. "Not so, in this place we get all we need from Pakistan already. Haven't you noticed the bad driving during Ramadan? Hashish has always been the alternative to alcohol here, no, booze is best. More people want alcohol than drugs, and better profit in any case."

"Just a thought." the other man murmured.

"I shall have to have your answer," Aziz looked at Eddie intently. "I did say I would need to know quickly."

The mention of the deadline brought Eddie's mind back to the last time he had seen the small man in Al Jalawi. "Yes, about that time you left me high and dry in the Phoenicia! What happened to you, I looked for you everywhere, you just vanished on me."

Aziz scratched at his curls " Sorry about that, but you know we had been sitting there too long, I really had to go before someone saw me."

"Someone did see you, and me too." Eddie leaned forward and looked the small man directly in the eye. "the Arab, remember?"

Aziz affected not to remember anything about the Arab. "You know, the one with the gold worry beads, I've been meaning to ask you about him, I've seen him before."

"Where?" his companion asked sharply.

"Oh" Eddie wrinkled his forehead in a effort to remember the precise situations. "outside the Grand Mosque. That was the first time, then outside my flat once, then in this shop the day I came here with Jenny. The last time in the hotel last week."

Aziz appeared to relax a little and then thought "Outside your flat?"

"Yes."

"Your flat or on the opposite pavement?" he persisted.

"Opposite."

"What was he doing?"

Eddie tried to remember, but all he could see in his mind were the penetrating eyes, the curved nose and the worry beads. "Just standing I think, and then he walked off somewhere."

"Somewhere" Aziz was pressing.

"Down the street somewhere."

"In which direction?"

"Aw, I don't know, towards town I think. What does it matter any way?"

The Lebanese exhaled as though he had been holding his breath. Eddie grinned at him.

"Don't worry he wasn't near your flat."

"What?"

"You didn't tell me you lived opposite me did you?"

Aziz smiled shamefacedly "I don't really live there, it's a sort of business address.

"A secret business address?"

"Well---"

"Not my place to pry old chum, just thought I'd let you know, but at least I can contact you there now."

Aziz looked alarmed "No Eddie, I don't think so, that is not a good place to contact me. It would be better to leave a message at David's." He placed his hand on the Englishman's arm "promise me you will not contact me there?"

"OK no problem," Eddie said smoothly "anyway what about that Arab, I'm not going to let you get away with it that easily."

"Mm?"

"There is something about that chap isn't there? He's always looking at me as though he wants to speak to me or tell me something, or just keep an eye on me."

Aziz eyes danced and his face crinkled with laughter "No need to worry, I think I know who he is----"

"You know darned well who he is." cut in the Englishman.

"No, I say I think I know who he is, but don't worry, I'll find out if he is after something, or what he is trying to do and let you know."

"How can you do that?"

The small man put an index finger alongside his nose and tapped it knowingly.

"All right, all right, them as asks no questions etc ete." Eddie said impatiently. He wished that dealing with the Lebanese was more straight forward, the man seemed to love mysteries.

"It's occurred to me," Eddie said loudly "that I could go off now and tell anyone what I know about this business and who is involved in it, and you would be in dead lumber."

"Yes?" Aziz drank until he reached the sludge at the bottom of his cup.

"You've taken a big risk, telling me and showing me so much." he grinned showing that he was not seriously considering it.

"I don't think so," Aziz was unconcerned, "who supplies you with your gin?"

"Some chap at the office."

"Who supplies you with your Sediki?"

Eddie paused " Some chap at the office."

"Where do you think this 'chap' at the office gets hold of such things?"

"I don't know, I just pay for it." Eddie thought "does it come from you?"

The dark haired man shook his head "I don't know, but I can tell you this, you would never be able to get hold of your supplies again." he played with his cup, tipping it and rolling the contents backwards and forwards. "terrible thought isn't it! No more parties, and the word would get around, no one would trust you."

Eddie glared at the man, his eyes bulging impatiently.

"It was only a thought." he said defensively.

"Never think it again, my friend, please I ask you, not even think it." the small man said comfortably.

Footsteps outside the small shop brought the two men back to the urgency of the decision. "I have to have your answer now." Aziz prompted Eddie.

The salesman knew the answer had been decided long ago "Yes, I'm in." he said.

"Oh good! Very good!" Aziz jumped up from his seat and extended his hand.

You will not regret this, my friend, you are going to be rich." he gabbled, his dark eyes dancing with delight.

Eddie shook his hand enthusiastically "I know, I'm certainly going to be rich, I can sell everything that comes in."

"That's exactly what we expected," he was assured "anyway," he looked around him and went to the door and peeped through the blinds "we shall have to go now. I'll get our friend back in."

Aziz switched off one of the lights by the door to give them some cover and ushered the salesman back out into the alley The Pakistani slipped back in and before they were a few yards down the Souk, the last light had been extinguished and they could hear feet pattering off in the opposite direction.

The car edged into the night traffic "What happens now?" Eddie asked.

"I'll contact you, do nothing at all until you hear directly from me"

The salesman nodded his head, they stopped to allow two women to cross the road and he turned to Aziz "How many people do you have working for you?"

The Lebanese nudged his arm to indicate that the road was clear and they moved off again.

"Quite a few, but do not worry, they are all loyal. If they were not my other deals would have fallen through, and they never have. I always use the same men. You will only know the ones that you need to know, the less you know, the less will slip out by mistake."

"I shan't let anything out." Eddie was offended by the inference.

"Quite!"

The Mercedes negotiated a diversion around some piles of masonry and then a Caterpillar Tractor that had been abandoned in the middle of the road.

"You can drop me in Ibrahim Street." Aziz pointed further down the road.

As he got out of the car, his companion had a thought. "Does David do the clearing and forwarding for the containers?"

Aziz answered shortly "Yes."

Eddie whistled softly, so he's involved as well!"

The Lebanese held the door open and sat back in his seat "Not really, he only does the paperwork, he will not know about the contents, so say nothing."

"Ok! Not a word."

Aziz once more got out of the car and poked his head inside "I shall contact you next week, wherever you are so don't worry. Good night Eddie, my friend."

"Good night Aziz, you old rogue!" Eddie said and laughed delightedly to himself, his spirits bubbling up like fizzy pop.

The Lebanese stood and waited on the pavement and watched while the Mercedes made its way up the street and rounded the corner. He then walked back the way they had come and hailed a taxi, followed the car back to the street where they both lived and entered Flat No 3.

17

SINCE the meeting with Aziz in Al Jalawi, Eddie had barely given Corinth a thought. True it had been on the tip of his tongue to ask Aziz about her, but his interest in the business had supplanted the thought.

Now he once again conjured her up in his mind and the bold longing started to work on him. It was strange how eyes affected him, he reflected. Whenever he thought of Corinth he first thought of her distinctive eyes, black and penetrating, and every time he thought of his Arab (he had now begun to think of him possessively) he remembered most of all the piercing eyes. He dismissed the thought of his Arab and concentrated solely on Corinth. It helped to pass the time on the long road, and more than helped to obstruct any thoughts that might crowd in about his wife.

Jenny was beginning to behave more and more oddly in Eddie's view, he had to admit to himself that her relationship with him was rather like that of Corinth and David. "Saints preserve me from emancipated women." he thought, forgetting neatly that he hoped to continue the pursuit of such a woman. Jenny seemed to spend most of her time away from the flat these days, and her husband thought he knew where she was spending her time. To tackle her on the subject was to turn every conversation into a fiasco. She admitted everything and turned it to her advantage, making Eddie appear to be the one at fault. he had no experience to deal with the situation, but he knew that if his suspicions were correct he would soon learn. Mind you, he thought, he would never believe that Jenny was unfaithful to him, not so much that his faith was in her integrity, rather that his pride would not allow him to admit that it was possible. He resolved to put the matter out of his mind, and let Jenny get on with it. After all, he reasoned with himself, he was going to be pretty busy from now on, and would have secrets to hide. Maybe it would be better nor to question her too much, it might invite close questioning of his activities in return.

His visits this week were to inland border towns. Here She-ite Muslims had built beautiful mosques, dainty in the extreme, a fretwork of white painted concrete, as delicate as lace. here also the influence of ancient Persia had left a legacy of irrigation that other Arab towns might envy. His first stop was at the home of a date farmer about two hundred miles from the coast. The sudden stepping into blessed shade under tall palms pressing closely together was an experience that Eddie simply could not describe on his return to Hamra. There was a smell of foliage, vegetation, and the impact on his senses was almost the same as the first mown grass at home after a cold winter. It was spring fever, a feeling of renewal, as though trees and grass had not died off in the world after all. He had no idea that he missed a garden and trees so much, the beauty of the scene he hardly appreciated, it was the impact on his senses that made him so aware. The sense of smell, the sense of sight, a deep velvety shade after the desert sun. A sense of hearing as the splatter of water sounded throughout the irrigation ditches, dropping from one height to another, and finally the sense of taste when a bowl of ice cold water was presented to him. It was deliciously sweet.

Eddie wished he could stay there for a long time, sitting beside the irrigation ditches they called a falaj; he watched the young children of the families who worked there, chase each other through the trees. The unmistakable sounds of drowsy bees made him think for a moment of England in summer and he looked wistfully into the water. The farmer offered his hospitality, presenting a wicker basket full of warm ripe dates. They burst onto the salesman's tongue separating easily from the stone. He had always found it difficult to believe that the Bedu were able to survive on Dates and water alone, now he could well understand it. It was the nearest Eddie had ever come to understanding and appreciating Arabia.

He finished his calls early that week and returned to Hamra on the Tuesday. he was anxious to buttonhole Reggie and get permission to go ahead with his plans.

The Chief was not encouraging when his best salesman indicated that he not only wanted to take on another product but also become a partner.

"Oh Eddie!" he said shaking his head "I hope you know what you're getting into." he pursed his lips.

Eddie was put on the defensive "Plenty of ex Pats are going in for this kind of thing." he said offering a packet of cigarettes.

Reggie took one and held it in his fingers for a moment while he shuffled through some papers. Finding the one he was looking for, he leaned forward and took a light.

"Here, take a look at this, top sales for I don't know how long." Reggie flicked the paper in front of him with an index finger. "how long are you going to keep that up if you take a second product?" he drew on his cigarette "there are only so many hours in the day, anyway there'll be a dickens of a lot of paper work to handle, and that'll take up more time. Aren't you in danger of biting off more than you can chew?"

Eddie puffed contentedly and crossed one leg over the other. "Don't think about that, it's all under control, just concentrate on the fact that I'm asking you as my employer whether I have your permission to go ahead or not."

"Yes Eddie, my boy, I understand all that, but remember I'm your friend as well. I don't want to see you getting into something that might spoil your career with the firm."

"You mean you don't want the sales figures to go down while I spend time on my own product." the salesman said grinning at his chief.

Reggie nodded "Yes, I must say that concerns me somewhat, after all, that's what you were brought out here to do, sell this company's products. They pay for your flat, schooling, medical expenses, air fares, all the rest of the perks you get at the end of the contract, it would hardly be natural of me not to be concerned about it, but I do speak as your friend as well you know."

"Right. I appreciate that, Reggie, but let's get down to some details first." Eddie stubbed out his cigarette and leaned forward in his seat. "What if I guarantee that the sales of engines won't go down--?"

"But that's---"

"Please Reg," Eddie cut in "hear me out first!" Say now the sales figures don't go down, would there be any objection to my going into my own business as well?"

"No—o" the chief responded carefully.

"Right, now then, say the figures after a time started to go down, in spite of all I try to do, then you would have a right to get pretty annoyed, yes?"

"Definitely!" Reggie said cupping his chin in his hands.

"So you need some kind of insurance. What if I change my contract so that I only get the fares, medical expenses, schooling etc. etc. if the sales stay on a level. If they don't I forfeit all those things including the 1% bonus at the end of the contract."

The Sales Manager was taken aback. "You must be pretty sure of yourself, Eddie, to want to enter into that kind of guarantee." The salesman leaned back in his chair and looked seriously at his chief.

"I am, very sure." he laughed and slapped some sand off his trousers "I tell you, bathroom equipment is selling like hot cakes, just as engines are." he added quickly, "either way I'm not going to be out of pocket, but if you don't have to pay for me here, you won't be out of pocket either."

Reggie narrowed his eyes and thought, it would be a pretty good deal, he would have hated to have lost his best salesman, and if he could ensure that the new venture would not cost the company anything, even better. If his sales figures did happen to drop drastically, then Eddie could always be sent home.

"You would have to stay on our visa." Reggie insisted.

"Quite all right old chap." Eddie responded easily.

"Not sure if it's legal, you getting tied up in your own company and staying on our visa you know." Reggie frowned trying to remember an instance where it had been managed before.

"What about McArthy and those Supermarkets/" Eddie prompted him.

"Of course! I knew there was a precedent, yes he got away with it didn't he?"

"I think things can be managed when you know the right people." Eddie was thinking of Aziz, he was sure to be able to sort that one out.

"Well, I shall have to think about it." The manager fiddled with his papers and placed a hand tenderly on his bald patch to shield it from the air conditioning.

"Need to look at your contract and sort something out." he lifted his head and shouted at the glass door. "Shafique!" then "Coffee!"

"Thanks Reggie, I'm very keen to get going, all I need is the go ahead from you."

"Working from home?" Reggie asked curiously.

"Yes, no office or anything like that, just me and the order book, you know, that kind of thing." Eddie smiled.

"Where's the godown?" the chief was interested.

"Er- down the Souk somewhere, don't ask me where. God! It's like a warren." Eddie eased himself out of the question.

Shafique in dark blue, his baggy trousers and long shirt flapping in the breeze from the air conditioner, brought in a tray. He laid it on the desk and turned to Eddie.

"Good morning Mr Miller." he said politely and he looked directly at the salesman.

"Do I owe him money or something?" he asked cocking a thumb over his shoulder in the clerk's direction.

Reggie laughed "I don't think so, you haven't ordered any more hooch have you?"

"No, none at all." Eddie said thoughtfully "I've never seen the old chap look so pleasant, he always seems to have a grudge against the world."

Reggie reached for his cup and took a sip "Anyway to get back to what we were talking about. If I go along with this, there is still the matter of Hamra."

"Meaning?"

"I've known quite a few people out here go into business, it isn't always plain sailing."

"Meaning?" Eddie repeated offering his cigarettes once more, Reggie shook his head.

"Arabs have a rotten way of doing business sometimes, especially with people like us."

"You mean true blue Brits?" he gave a mock salute.

"No, just Ex Pats in general. They set up in business, let the poor Ex Pat do all the work. It takes off everybody is happy, and then Bang! One morning, it's all over, the Arab has taken over and the man who has made it all work for him is out on his ear." he sipped again " seen it happen more than once." Reggie replaced his cup on the tray.

"I don't think that will happen to me," Eddie said confidentially.

"They all would say that wouldn't they?" Reggie remarked reasonably.

"What about McArthy?"

"He was lucky, he had the right partner."

Eddie was unaware of the significance.

"There are all sorts of Arabs out here Ed, you know that, but the higher you go usually the better you get. McArthy went into business with one of the Princes's men."

"Oh."

"Bit of influence goes a long way, but the partner was already very wealthy and tied up in all sorts of other businesses, mostly oil I think, and so he had no designs on the supermarkets and left McArthy to get on with it." The chief got up and redirected the flow from the air conditioner "My bald spot gets cold." he explained and went on "if someone gets involved with a relatively poor Arab, and there are some," he said quickly seeing the look of disbelief on Eddie's face. "poor Arabs are those with only a few thousand sterling to invest, the rich ones have millions." Reggie explained "yes, get hitched up to a poor one and you have a problem, who's your partner?" he asked suddenly.

For a moment Eddie was trapped. Reggie had lived in Hamra for nearly ten years, he knew all the top people by name. If Eddie was to make up a name, it would only make his chief believe that his partner was one of the poorer Arabs, because he hadn't heard of him.

"Um"--- Eddie began cautiously "well"---

"Oh all right! I get the message." Reggie rescued him "I know these bods don't like it to get around until they have a big success. In any case it isn't any of my business really, just curious." Eddie breathed out silently in relief. "just don't want to see you get in a hole over this." his chief assured him.

Eddie smiled his gratitude "Damned good of you Reggie, old chum." his humour was restored "much appreciate the advice."

The salesman took a handkerchief and wiped the back of his neck. Now that the worst part of the interview was over he realised that he was sweating profusely.

"Er—about your decision, Reg, need to know as soon as poss." Eddie pressed.

His boss smiled at the man sitting opposite him. "It's almost a foregone conclusion, I can't really stop you as long as you don't hurt this company, but give me a night to sleep on it and work something out with the contract. Come in tomorrow with the rest of the team and I'll give you a definite answer on how we can sort it all out."

Eddie sprang to his feet and gripped the Sales Manager's hand pumping it enthusiastically. "God! Reggie, you don't know how good you've made me feel, this is great, what is it?" he asked his voice rising in pitch.

"Great." Reggie answered, responding in a quieter manner, he stood up "I don't suppose you'll get much time for partying anymore?"

The salesman's face fell "No, I don't suppose I will, but I shall darn well try." he added brightening up again. "whose place this week?"

"Don't you know? the chief asked him puzzled.

"Should I?" Eddie had his hand on the door knob.

"That friend of yours from the embassy, David something or other, sent printed invitations round to all the reps. it's at his place this week, didn't you get one?"

Eddie was alarmed, a party at David's place, another chance to meet Corinth and he had no invitation, what was going on now? "He's not from the embassy, he's in clearing and forwarding." Eddie said absently.

"Well, you know who I mean." Reggie was not interested. He cocked his head on one side seeing Eddie's face so glum. "Have you looked in your post?"

The salesman recovered himself and cleared his throat, "Er, no, God! I'd forgotten about the post, I'll go and have a look."

"Right you are, see you tomorrow."

"Great!" Eddie opened the door "and thanks Reggie old chap," he said closing the door behind him.

In the reception hall Shafique came forward with a bundle of mail.

"For you Mr Miller." he smiled and gave a small bow.

Eddie looked at the old man wondering what he has done to deserve such attention from the Pakistani. "This is the one you must open now." the man urged handing him a large white envelope.

The salesman tore open the envelope and found the invitation to David's party inside. It stated simply that Mr David Awdle-Brown requests the pleasure of Mr and Mrs Edward Miller to a reception in his house on Thursday at 8.pm. R.S.V.P.

Eddie held out his hand for the rest of the mail but the old man shook his head.

"R.S.V,P." he said.

"Yes I know." Eddie said impatiently "I'll see to it."

"There is paper and envelope here, I shall deliver for you." Shafique urged again. For a moment Eddie stared into the eyes that were staring into his. Making up his mind, he threw his briefcase on the desk and extracted a pen from his pocket. With a flourish he wrote an acceptance for Jenny and himself, addressed the envelope and sealed it.

"Thank you." Shafique said picking up the envelope and handing him the pile of letters in his other hand.

"Thank you." Eddie said bending his head in an excess of courtesy and grabbing his case he swung round and ran down the steps of the building to his car.

18

IF EDWARD Miller's confidence had suffered a slight setback during the ups and downs of the two previous weeks, it was fully restored now. The man's ebullience returned in full strength and he looked on everyone he met as his bosom pal. Whistling tunelessly he bounded up the stairs to his flat and then stopped. Jenny was the only uncertain element in his life at the moment. These days it was becoming a habit to pause before he entered his home, he was never sure whether Jenny would be there or not. If she was, he was never confident about her attitude towards him.

Uncharacteristically he would open the door cautiously, almost as though he needed to prepare himself for his entry not knowing what he might find. He breathed freely when he found his wife pottering about in the kitchen. He was comforted to find that she was behaving normally, preparing a meal.

"Hello gorgeous!" Eddie folded her in his arms and kissed the back of her neck, her lack of response was encouraging, a normal response to his bear hugs. "Oh it's a great day Jenny!" he turned her round to face him. "you're looking good!" he made a clumsy attempt at a compliment, suddenly unsure of himself.

"Drink?" her voice was chilly and he let his arms fall to his side.

"Yes, er, fine" he walked into the lounge and looked back at her curiously as she wiped her hands. "had a good day?" he asked trying to gauge her mood.

Jenny nodded and reached into the cavity of the air conditioning panel and groped for a bottle. "Last one." she said drawing the panel back.

"Soon be plenty more." Eddie smiled happily to himself. Jenny looked at him sharply "by the way," he said accepting a glass "guess where the party is tomorrow."

"Where?"

"David's." Eddie set his glass down and extracted the envelope from his briefcase. "Look, I didn't know he had a double barrelled name."

Jenny took the card from him and read the invitation. "It doesn't surprise me with that accent. That sort always have to prove where they come from" she sounded cynical.

"Hell, Jenny, you're beginning to sound like a brain doctor!"

She laughed apologetically. "I suppose that's Bill again, he does it all the time."

Eddie stiffened and swallowed a large gulp of his drink "Bill?"

"Yes, he used to study psychology and he tries it on everybody. He's always trying to get to the bottom of Bobby, it works too. Oh that reminds me about Bobby." she sat down on the edge of the easy chair and rubbed at a stain with her apron.

"Never mind about Bobby." Eddie said irritably "or Bill Jolly either, I just don't want to know. What I *want* to know is what do you think of David and his party."

Jenny stood up and for a moment Eddie thought she was going to stamp her foot.

"Oh for goodness sake what am I supposed to think? It's another dreary party with dreary people all talking about the same thing week after week don't you ever get fed up with it?"

"Jenny. Jenny!" he held up the palm of his hand and lowered it again like a conductor "please just think, Abdul Aziz Street, the best place in Hamra, the most luxurious villa you could think of and among the best people, it's so good for business I could meet a lot of people there."

Jenny walked towards the kitchen "Are the rest of the reps going?" she asked

"Yes, I think so." Eddie watched her through the hatch. Her face appeared at the aperture, her silky hair falling forward.

"Then they'll have the same contacts won't they." she said brightly and disappeared from view, reappearing at the door with a spoon in her hand. "be honest with yourself Eddie," she said pointing the spoon at him "you're going to the party because it enhances your ego to be seen in that place, you also feel popular and like drinking. Right?"

Eddie could hardly disagree with her.

"So?"

"Be honest with yourself, don't make excuses, just say you are going to enjoy yourself."

"Bill Jolly again?"

"What?"

"All those fancy words and explanations."

"If you must know, yes, he makes me think seriously about what we get up to out here. I can now actually stand outside myself and analyse what goes on, that's all." Jenny said casually.

"Oh terrific! A bloody Einstein in the family." Eddie exploded.

"No, just a thinking female for the first time since I was an idealistic adolescent."

"A what?" Eddie began to think for the first time that he was actually losing his wife. She was talking and acting in a way that was totally foreign to him, would he ever be comfortable with her again? He bit his lip. Where was the old Jenny, the pipe and slippers little woman who danced attendance on him and hung on his every word? He would never be able to understand that the real Jenny had been hidden behind the one he had described all along. Without him realising it, he had never really known his wife at all. Of a sudden he felt wretched and his confidence fizzled out like a slowly deflating balloon.

"All right, all right clever breeches, that's enough for today thank you very much, anyway you know about the invitation."

"I shan't be going." Jenny sang out from the kitchen.

"Hells Bloody Bells!" Eddie stood up and slammed his glass on the sideboard. "what the devil is the matter with you now?" he walked deliberately into the kitchen, his step heavy. "You pompous bitch!" he waggled a finger at her, "I don't know what you are playing at, but it had better stop right now. Bill Jolly has a bloody lot to answer for, and if you don't stop it Jenny I'll- I'll-"

"You'll hit him- hit me- hit Bobby?" Jenny stood in front of him taunting, her arms folded, the light of battle in her eyes. Eddie faltered, Jenny had never stood up to him when he had put his foot down previously.

"What the hell's the matter with you?" Eddie yelled, throwing his arm out to her desperately. Everything was going so well, he had been so happy, although he was unable to explain how, he was going to be rich and make her rich as well, and here she was baulking him and making him feel miserable.

He had no idea how to deal with her, he was not a man who beat women, his threats over the years had never amounted to anything. When his temper and voice had risen it was enough to intimidate both his wife and son, especially when his eyes started to bulge and his fists clenched. Instinctively he knew that he would never be able to use those threats again, his bluff had been called.

"OK, Jenny, there's only one way to deal with this." his voice was subdued and flat, he felt drained of a sudden "I shall have to send you and Bobby home."

His wife unfolded her arms and clutched the draining board "You wouldn't" she said in a whisper, and then in stronger tones "Bobby, yes, that's what I wanted to talk to you about, but not me, you wouldn't send me home would you?"

Eddie was sure of the upper hand now, "If this business with Bill Jolly doesn't stop, I'll send you home."

"Reggie wouldn't let you."

"Reggie wouldn't have a say in it." he countered.

"How would you manage without me?"

Eddie laughed shortly and slapped at his forehead "Good grief, Jenny, how do you think I manage now? I'm away for most of the week, don't worry about that I'd manage, get a house boy or something." There was a pause, each of them thinking bleakly about such an appalling idea. Jenny looked her husband in the eye and said steadily "If only we had been able to talk to each other."

"Oh talk!" Eddie said disgustedly.

"Yes, talk, Eddie, but most of all if you could only have listened to me."

"I always listen to you."

"No you don't, you hear me but you don't listen."

"Don't start that analysing nonsense again, I tell you I've had enough of it."

"All right, just a minute let me turn this off." she reached behind her and switched off the electric stove moving a saucepan to another ring. "come on, I'll pour both of us a drink and we'll sit down."

The man reluctantly followed her into the lounge and accepted another drink. He felt like a schoolboy about to be lectured by his mother.

"I'm sorry you're upset." she began as they sat down.

"Of course I'm upset," Eddie's voice was impatient, his manner threatening to become arrogant again.

"Yes, well I'm saying sorry but----" she held a small hand up as she saw her husband attempt to speak "but I must say this, I've lived with you like a mouse." Eddie's eyebrows shot up and he grinned. "Yes Eddie, a mouse. I've been a good wife to you and you know it." He nodded noting at once her fine silky hair, her beautiful eyes, her soft neck, he was weakening as he felt desire overcome him. Jenny, quick to see the signs hurried on. It was only when I met Bill that I started to realise that I had been living a lie."

"Great!" Eddie shifted his position to the edge of the cushions, "that's great, he tells you that you've been living a lie. Well, I've heard of some lines thrown to married women in my time, but that's a real beaut, yeah, a real beauty!" he spluttered into his glass.

"There you go again," Jenny said in despair "you simply will not listen."

"What do you expect from me, Jenny? That I should take all this lying down?"

"Just listen!" she shouted banging her glass down on the coffee table. It was enough to silence him for a moment, she continued." Bill didn't tell me that I was living a lie, he merely introduced me to some new hobbies." her voice faltered "just new hobbies, little things to help pass the time. Painting, drawing, conversation." her voice was suddenly miserable. "nothing that interested you, nothing that interested anyone except perhaps Bobby. "Jenny looked into her husband's face and was surprised to see him listening intently, "gradually I found that I was becoming a person in my own right."

"It didn't take long did it?" Eddie said caustically, "he's only been here about a month."

"Perhaps he came at the right time, just when I needed someone to help me."

Eddie looked up at the ceiling, he understood very little of what his wife was saying, all he could see were Bill Jolly's intentions towards Jenny.

"I saw the way I lived with you," Jenny continued "let you walk all over me."

The man looked at her sharply and opened his mouth to protest but she went on.

"Good little wife doing her duty, spending all her days merely waiting to be a servant to her husband, but what about duty to myself?" she asked and her husband looked blank. "Everyone has a duty to themselves and that's what I learned by broadening my horizons, reading books, making conversation with an educated person. There is a duty to oneself." she repeated.

"Where does that leave me then? Eddie asked petulantly.

"You fulfill your duty to yourself, Eddie, all men do I simply need to do my duty to you and to myself."

Eddie scratched at his head and wished he hadn't started listening to this rubbish.

"I do my duty to you." he was puzzled.

"Of course you do, as well as to yourself. You work for me, provide me with a home, clothes, feed us and all the things we need. Yes, that's what I mean, I've been paying my duty to you and you have led a balanced life by paying your duty to both of us, yourself and me. Now I propose to balance my life and see to myself as well." She stopped and looked at her husband expectantly to see if her explanation had been understood. She was disappointed, Eddie still looked blank. In spite of himself though, he had seen glimmerings of understanding in what she had said. He reminded himself of the fact that he would soon have much to be kept secret from her. He thought it politic to allow her to win a little ground after all.

"Hobbies, chats and conversations?"

"Yes, company really, he's lonely as well." Jenny answered eagerly.

Eddie ignored the thought, all men were lonely in Hamra. He came to a decision.

"If you promise not to analyse me using those long words, and provide the sort of home I'm used to-damn it all Jenny." he broke off "I do like some comfort when I come home, those roads can be hell. Just go on as you used to, and if you have to visit that awful wet week of a man, well, all right, just keep him away from me that's all." he grinned ruefully " the emancipated little woman eh?" he looked at her and she blushed. Eddie leaned over and kissed her on the cheek, the tenderness surprised her.

"About Bobby!" she said striking while the iron was hot. Eddie withdrew as though sting.

"Bobby" he said flatly.

"I think he ought to go home."

"Where to?"

"My mother's." Jenny said. "the life is no good for him out here, there's no opportunity for him to develop."

"Georgie manages all right." Eddie said not liking the idea of losing his whipping boy.

"Yes, but Georgie is what you would call a real boy, isn't he?" she said slyly "Bobby is artistic, there's no way he can develop those talents out here."

"Jolly again?"

"Not really," she sighed "I've looked for some kind of talent in Bobby since he was a baby, and only now since we've been painting can I see something in him." she could see her husband was thinking. "it's not good for a boy of his age to be shut up in his room all day long."

"I've always said that, now haven't I said that before?" Eddie appealed to Jenny.

"Yes, and you're right." she unconsciously flattered his ego.

Eddie thought for a moment "S'right really, I suppose you've got the right idea, all right we'll send him home." he thought again, "does he want to go?"

"I think he will," she answered, I haven't talked to him about it, but I think he'll jump at the chance, he gets on well with mother." Eddie was wise enough to keep what he thought about Jenny's mother to himself.

He sprang up, his spirits returning, "all right now, he said "coming to the party?"

"Oh that dreadful party!" Jenny said grinning, "all right, since you asked so nicely, I'll come."

He drew her into his arms and lifted her off the floor "Come on, time for my oats." he said coarsely.

"And that's another thing." she said as the bedroom door closed behind them.

19

ON THE Thursday morning, Edward Miller was given permission to enter into a partnership and start his own business. He was deliriously happy at the news, promising great efforts and even bigger figures in his gratitude. He assured the chief that he would never regret his decision, and was already drawing up a list of prospective customers in his mind. It was agreed that no one would be told until Eddie had signed his partnership agreement.

Jenny accepted her husband's high spirits as relief after their brief argument and reconcilliation. She smiled knowingly as once again she fell into the roll Eddie demanded of her, reserving for herself the luxury of knowing that she had made her stance, and that if she ever needed to do it a second time it would not be so difficult. She had gained a freedom, and the knowledge was enough for the moment, she had no need to prove it.

The party was a double celebration and in spite of herself she was looking forward to it. Jenny had never been in Abdul Aziz Street except for a short drive to look at the villas when they first came to Hamra. The Palace at the end of the lovely avenue of trees, was hidden behind high walls and forbidding gates, A glimpse of the golden Dome from behind tall palms was all that could be seen from the street.

Martha had been delighted by the invitation and bustled in and out of Jenny's flat all day. There had been long consultations about what to wear and what shade of lipstick went with what, and in the afternoon when most people were taking a nap, the two women went to have their hair done at the hotel.

As Martha was settling herself into the back of the Mercedes that night, she was bursting with comments about the young hairdresser, Elaine.

"Did you see her black eye?" she said to Jenny "it's those Palace parties you know."

"What is?" Eddie looked back at the colourful woman.

"Elaine, our hairdresser goes to the Palace, dreadful parties up there all sex and booze!"

"Ooh! I want to go, I want to go!" Eddie giggled at Don.

"Don't be silly, Eddie, it's serious."

"I'm sure it is Martha, old honey bun," he grabbed at his friend " Hurry up, we'll never get there and I've got a thirst."

"Eddie!" Martha slapped him on the shoulder "she's English."

"So?" The doors closed and Eddie drew away from the pavement

"Well, it's terrible."

"If it's terrible she won't go again will she?" Don said reasonably.

"I don't think it works like that, she has to go or she'll get chucked out of Hamra."

"Good old Martha, ever the little stirrer." Eddie nudged his friend.

Don said over his shoulder, "Give it a rest, Martha."

"She's right though," Jenny said nodding her head.

"Not you as well." Don was surprised.

"It's a well known fact that the Princes are perverted and import all sorts of girls just to have wild parties. Then they won't give them exit visas to go home and they're stuck." she was angry at male unconcern.

Eddie whispered loudly to Don "Don't get her going, she's learned some long words in the last few weeks, it's awful."

"I thought you said that they get chucked out of Hamra," Don said to his wife.

"Yes."

"Well, she can't get chucked out if she can't get an exit visa can she?"

Eddie slapped his friend on the knee, "Well said Don, old bunion, lot of nonsense, women talk."

The two women gave up and looked out of the window as the car swung into Abdul Aziz Street. Don turned to his wife,

"Now that's enough Martha, no mention of black eyes and Princes tonight, just behave yourself." and he struggled out of his seat and opened the door for the women. Martha pulled her tongue out at him and swept magnificently to the gate of the villa.

It was all the same as before, Eddie thought, the perfume of the flowers; the lights subdued and hidden but spilling out from cracks and small windows highlighting areas of vegetation and low branches of palms surrounding the garden. The oak door with it's panels, David welcoming and making them all feel at home straight away. His heart had started to beat faster as his eyes searched the hall and he stood on tip toes to see over the many guests that were moving slowly into the main lounge. There was no sign of Corinth, but that did not mean that she was not going to be there.

Drinks were produced and in the crush groups of guests were pressed close together, still there was no sign of Corinth, Eddie wondered if Aziz was here, it occurred to him that he had never seen David without either Aziz or Corinth being with him.

David, his tall thin figure spotted easily from the other side of the room, was energetically encouraging guests to return to the hall so that the suffocating press of people would spread out. Gradually groups went to sit down on the benches, some perched on the Kuwaiti chest and more stood around until they were breathing much easier.

The conversation was fluid, most of the guests were in high spirits and the protests and laughter over the lack of room had produced a relaxing effect and more cause for chatter. Eddie could not keep his thoughts or his eyes on the group he was with, they remarked on it.

"You're very quiet tonight," Reggie said sipping eagerly at his Rum. "thought you'd be cock a hoop and doing hand stands," he said grinning.

"Yes," Eddie answered vaguely "I am." and his gaze was drawn to the door behind the bar. If Corinth was anywhere she would be behind that door somewhere. The question was, how was he going to get to her?

"Did you notice his name on the invitation?" Martha was saying to Jenny.

"Yes, chronic isn't it?"

"Never heard of that name before." Reggie's wife, Ann joined in.

"Probably made it up. "Martha said giggling, "I don't know though," she stopped and thought "all those double barrelled names are a bit peculiar aren't they, you know the kind of thing, Fitz something or other."

"That's easy," said Don, his interest aroused "That means born on the wrong side of the blanket to Royalty."

"Go on!" Martha looked at her husband with respect "fancy you knowing that." she said looking around at the others to invite their admiration.

"Hidden depths, Martha." Reggie laughed.

David had struggled across to the group, and flicking a stray wisp of hair out of his eyes, greeted them.

"Quite a squash isn't it?" he said in his prissy way "Everybody got everything they want?" he enquired solicitously. "Plenty of drinks, just take what you want if you get thirsty before the boys gets to you." he instructed.

"Eddie!" he took the man by the arm "a word in your shell like," he said fatuously and drew him aside. "someone to see you in a short while, I'll let you know when, just go through the door behind the bar into the library, I think you know where it is." Eddie pulled away sharply and looked him in the face.

"All right." he said He was getting desperate to see Corinth again, but having David make the arrangements gave him a very uncomfortable feeling, there was something unhealthy about it.

"Here David!" Martha was calling him back to the small group, "I'm curious." she said.

"She's very curious," Don said jokingly "all the time."

"Oh shut up you!" Martha laughed at her husband. "No, seriously David, I want to ask about your name."

David smiled politely and took a glass from a passing tray "What's the question, dear lady?" he asked bowing in her direction.

"Awdle-Brown- where does that come from?" she looked at Don "my husband says that Fitz something or other means something to do with royalty, what does Awdle mean?"

"Ah!" David smiled posing elegantly with his glass. "I'm certainly not anything to do with royalty, that's for sure." he let out a short laugh and went on seriously "Awdle is a strange name I agree and for the life of me I don't know why it was attached to our name. It has something to do with a Welsh poem you know."

"Welsh?"

"Mm—seems someone way back in our family fancied themselves as a bard or something. I keep meaning to look it up somewhere, but I never seem to have the time." he bowed slightly to Martha and then to the other ladies "Now you see, when you think of me at all, which I hope will be often, you will think of me as a Welsh poem." and smiling gracefully he withdrew and strolled across to talk to other guests.

"Wow!" Ann said feelingly "it oozes out of him doesn't it?"

"What does?" Martha asked giggling.

"Charm- oh boy! Does he have charm." Ann looked at Reggie who responded by saying to Eddie "That look means, 'why don't you have any?'"

"I know just what you mean," Don said sympathetically and then in an undertone "something not quite a hundred pence to the pound there if you ask me."

"Mm" Reggie said into his drink.

Eddie was impatient, he kept his eyes on David as the man made his way round the room, and by going to the bar for another drink he managed to detach himself from the group he had been with. He managed to stay separate from them by working his way around the edge of the room pretending to look at the pictures and indicating that he was fully immersed in his thoughts.

One of the house boys entered from the door behind the bar and went in search of David. Eddie caught the tall man's eye and placed his drink on the bar. He took a handkerchief from his pocket and drew it across his forehead, the room had become increasingly stuffy, and he walked through the door to the passage beyond.

Once again the only light burning was that outside the library and once again his nerves tried to get the better of him. There was so much to say to Corinth, there were so many questions to ask, arrangements to make. Suddenly it was as important to see her as it had been in Al Jalawi. He turned the door handle, the room was brightly lit, the curtains, velvet and heavy, closely drawn. The books that lined the walls glowed in various hues with golden decoration. Eddie noticed all these things as his eyes swept across the room to the imitation fireplace and the pink rug. This time Corinth was not there. Sitting in the easy chair by the coffee table was Aziz!

Aziz was sitting with his legs crossed, in the very chair that Corinth had draped herself across the last time Eddie had visited the room. He held up a hand as the salesman entered and waved briefly.

"Hi!" he said smiling.

"What are you doing here?" Eddie said indignantly, bitterly disappointed.

Aziz looked surprised. "I come here often," he said "David knew I wanted to speak to you, so he lent me this room."

"Yes, well- I didn't expect to see you in here." The Englishman was discomfited by the thought that Aziz could not be expected to know anything about his hoped for meeting.

"How did it go?" the man asked "with your company?"

Eddie brightened and sat down opposite the Lebanese. "Great! Absolutely fine, no problem at all, I'm in."

"Very good, very good." The Lebanese was delighted and laughed out aloud. "We shall do wonderful things, we shall make plenty of money, my friend."

"You can say that again." he looked around for a drink.

"Over there by the decanter." Aziz pointed to a side table. The salesman poured himself a drink and sniffed at it. He looked up at his companion appreciatively

"Gin." he said.

"The real stuff always."

"That reminds me," Eddie's thoughts were travelling along practical lines. "What happens now? I want to get this thing tied up so I can get going."

"That's what I came for tonight, you can see I'm not dressed for a party."

Eddie thought he looked smart enough for anything and nearly said so, but his companion was continuing. "the next step is to sign the agreement, we shall have to get you to a solicitor."

"Solicitor? I didn't think there were any out here."

"Notary then, a legal man who witnesses agreements and papers and things that have to be legal."

"All right, where?"

Aziz took from his pocket a notebook and pen "I'll write it down, but it will have to be in Arabic. Give it to a taxi driver, don't go in your own car, you might be followed."

Eddie was alarmed. "Is it likely?"

"No, not at all." the Lebanese said lightly, "but the moment we make ourselves suspicious enough to get followed, then we are already in trouble, you understand?"

Eddie was not quite sure, but he nodded.

"Take a taxi, just pretend you would be followed in your own car. I can't tell you strongly enough, you must behave at all times as though you think someone is following you, then you can be pretty sure that no one will."

The dark haired man wrote quickly from right to left in Arabic script and tore the page out of the book.

"There, don't lose it, be there Monday at 3 pm."

Eddie was uncertain "I don't know if I can be back in Hamra by then."

"Yes you will." Aziz grinned.

"How do you know?" The fact that Aziz always seemed to know more about the salesman's affairs than Eddie himself made him angry.

"Because you will make it happen, you will arrange to be there."

"Oh all right, I suppose I can arrange it."

"Of course." Aziz said and Eddie for a moment felt like hitting the man.

"What happens after that?"

"I will contact you again."

'Really' Eddie thought, 'it's like cops and robbers,'

Aloud he said "Is the Arab happy about the arrangements?"

Aziz was taken aback for a moment, but he answered easily enough.

"Ah yes, he is perfectly content," and shook his curls, passing a hand over his forehead. "I must go home to sleep I'm tired."

Eddie held the glass to his chest and looked around the room.

"Expected to see Corinth this evening." he said casually, hoping to draw the Lebanese out.

"Why?" it was a curious question in view of the party.

"Well," said Eddie scathingly "when I have a party in my flat I expect my wife to be there."

"Corinth isn't"--- Aziz gulped nervously "I mean Corinth never does what she is supposed to do, she just does what she wants to."

"Is she home?" the salesman asked again, not noticing Aziz's hesitation.

"Yes, she has been in her room this evening, but I suppose she may come down later. She will please herself." he stood up "I am not going to the party, however, I am going to sleep. So good night to you Eddie, I'll see you after Monday."

"Right you are old chap" Eddie stood and placed his glass on the table. "thanks for the info." he said letting himself out of the door. "Cheers!"

It was becoming obvious that Martha was drunk, her face was red, her eyes watery and her stance was becoming shaky. Jenny constantly intercepted her drinks and made the house boys add larger quantities of mixers to them, but her friend steadily advanced into inebriation.

Her laugh became louder and she was giggling too much. Don hardly seemed to notice, but Reggie and Ann looked on with ill concealed alarm. It was par for the course when Martha went to a party, but this time they were on alien territory and none of them were happy about it.

"I think you've had enough." Jenny whispered into her ear.

"What?" Martha almost shouted back at her, "yes love, I know, I always do have more than enough." she giggled loudly.

Jenny pressed her arm and said again quietly "Make that one last, Martha, you're making an idiot of yourself, there are too many strangers here for this."

Martha frowned in an exaggerated way and drew back an inch or two in order to bring her friend's face into focus.

"You're just fed up 'cos Bill isn't here." she said deliberately weighing every word.

"Don't be silly!" Jenny said, looking up at the group and catching Eddie's eye.

"Who're you calling silly?" Martha was becoming belligerent, "everyone knows he's not here tonight because Eddie is—and you wish—you wish he was." She accompanied the last words of her sentence with a pointed finger aimed at Jenny's shoulder. She had no time to smother Martha's words, or try to laugh them off, Eddie was already grabbing the woman by the arm. Martha looked up at him in a vaguely surprised manner as he brought the full force of his large eyes down into hers.

"Listen you half baked busybody!" he spat through his teeth glaring down at her "pack that kind of talk up now, or I'll throw you through that window over there." he swung her around to face the great bay window at the end of the room. Martha gazed at it uncomprehending for a moment and then back at her captor.

"Steady on old chap," Don laid a hand on Eddie's arm, he shrugged it off angrily and Reggie gave him a warning glance not to try again.

"Yeah!" Martha shook her head stupidly "Shteady on!" Reggie tried to cut in between them and said heartily

"Poor old Martha, had one over the eight, you'll have to excuse her Eddie, she doesn't know what she's saying." he laughed unconvincingly while Ann looked round the room to see if their argument had been heard over the top of the noise in the room.

Eddie released the middle aged woman with a push and a pointed his finger at her. "No more, Martha, remember, or I'll give you a good hiding." His face was scarlet and his eyes were bulging, he longed to punch his fist into her silly face and release the tension that had sprung up in him like coiled wire.

From behind him came a voice as cool as iced water "Good evening Edward." He whirled round, his mouth open. his expression ridiculous. Corinth was standing before him in a perfect pose. She was wearing a pale blue gown, a white band around her hair, her eyes were as deep and black as he remembered, her face white and composed. To Eddie she looked like an ice queen.

After a moment's hesitation that made him look like a stunned ox, he recovered sufficiently to greet her and introduce her to the group. Jenny watched her husband fall over his words and produce nervous conversation, generally behaving in a way which he himself would have recognised as ludicrous and she wondered. She looked at the girl as she answered and conversed in general terms, her face cold, expressionless and passive and Jenny shivered. There was something about her that was just unwomanlike. She set out neither to entice or to reject. She was just there, sitting comfortably between positive and negative, and yet she was sending Eddie into a flat spin.

To Jenny, there appeared to be very little about Corinth that was desirable to a man. her figure was so slim as to be more like a boy's. Her features were certainly not pretty, her nose was too big, her eyes too small, and yet Jenny had to admit that there was something quite fascinating about her. Maybe the eyes, she thought, and at that moment Martha lurched into her elbow and she was reminded of her friend. With a murmur of excuse, she steered Martha to a settee by the window and propped her up against the cushions, after waiting a moment she was glad to see her friend falling asleep. She left her and went to tell Don, who gave her a grin and renewed his attacks on the whiskey, he would not have to go home so soon now.

While Reggie was chatting to Corinth, Eddie was racking his brains for a way to get her on her own. he thought he saw an opportunity when she excused herself in order to go and talk to the other guests but it was not to be. He found it impossible to find an excuse to leave the group he was with, and doubly impossible to find a plausible reason that would dovetail with it in order to get Corinth on her own for a private word. Reggie was a man who could sum up events very accurately even if Don was too far gone with Whiskey. Then there were the women, Jenny would ask why he wanted to see Corinth in private and Ann would think the worst..

Inside him his muscles contracted increasingly with apprehension until he found he had cramp in his leg. he kept reminding himself that this might be the only chance he had to speak to the girl and the fact was driving him mad.

Eddie's eyes followed Corinth around from group to group and he became so jealous as he watched her being flattered and feted by other men, that he could barely suppress the urge to go and grab her by the arm.

"Time to go." Jenny said in his ear "Martha and Don are ready."

"To hell with"--- he began looking around and caught Reggie's eye, "Oh all right." It was inevitable, there was no way to avoid it, they would have to leave without Eddie having achieved what he had set out to, a meeting with Corinth to arrange a place where they could be alone together at last.

After David had seen them to the door and bade them goodnight, Corinth opened the door again. Jenny and the others were already down the path by the gate, Eddie had lingered hoping until the last for a glimpse of the dark haired girl.

"Oh Edward!" she said, her voice soft and in his ears enticing, he turned back his face wreathed in smiles. She looked behind her, David had gone. "Eddie, I'm so sorry about the hotel, you know." she whispered so that he had to bend forward to hear her.

"Yes, yes, I know, never mind, when?"---

"Ssh!" she placed a finger to her lips and looked over his shoulder at Jenny waiting at the gate facing them. "I'll get a message to you," she went on "don't worry, it will be all right." Eddie was about to touch her hand, but she had withdrawn and was closing the door. His 'goodnight!' echoed back from the oak panels.

So after all he had managed to get a word with Corinth on her own, the evening was not the disaster it had seemed. There was no arrangement, but there was enough hope in that whispered conversation for Eddie to build castles on. He was relaxed and thoroughly at peace with the world as he drove his friends home. He had forgotten immediately about Martha and would have ignored her behaviour in any case had he not been so wound up. Now he laughingly helped Don to manoeuvre his wife up the stairs, slapped him on the back and bounced up the remaining flight to Jenny waiting at the door.

She had watched him curiously ever since Corinth had appeared on the scene, and still she could not understand what it was that made her normally confident husband become like jelly in the girl's presence. She made up her mind not to comment on what she had seen, but decided to keep it in reserve until she wanted to assert her independence again. It might stand her in good stead.

20

BY MONDAY, Edward Miller top salesman, had managed to arrange his calls so that he was back in Hamra. Jenny had been pleased to see him, for she had started arrangements that would send Bobby back home and she needed to discuss them with him. Eddie however, was fidgety and insisted on leaving all the decisions to his wife. He excused himself by inventing a sale that was going wrong and that he needed a great deal of concentration to sort it out. In his mind he knew the time had come to tell Jenny of his business venture, soon everyone would know, Jenny had to know first.

It was a question of how much he left out, rather than how much he told her. He could see some sticky questions ahead. He resolved to sign the agreement and then come straight home and tell her what he had done, that way nothing could influence him, no nervous doubts and worries, it would be too late. Not that she had ever interfered with his work, but this was rather different. He left her having an afternoon sleep and crept out as quietly as he could.

He had forgotten that it would be difficult to get a taxi at that time of the afternoon, most businesses were closed until 4 o'clock and a large part of the population of Hamra were sleeping. Eddie walked in the violently hot sun between the tall buildings, endeavouring to keep in the shade on one side or the other until he came to a small square.

There where a garden had been planned and only partly executed he saw a taxi parked. The vehicle was standing under the only palm tree yet planted and as he picked his way throught the spilled cement and broken concrete blocks, he stumbled over a pile of sawdust. It was there to be placed between the grass seed that would eventually be planted, swelling with water when sprayed and thus holding the fragile growth of the alien vegetation until it was established. Now it was an attraction for goats who tossed their heads at the flies buzzing around their long ears and showing evidence of wood dust around their mouths.

Eddie banged on the roof of the taxi, waking the driver who was sleeping in the back seat. "Working?" he leaned in at the window.

The driver sat up quickly and jumped out of the door and into the front seat. Turning the key, he indicated that his passenger get in. Eddie handed him the paper that Aziz had given him.

"You speak Inglese?" he asked the driver.

"No Inglese." the man responded waggling his head. He read the Arabic script and waved it above his head. "Ok, ok." he said and manoeuvred his vehicle out of the square.

The taxi was taking Eddie to a part of Hamra that was unknown to him. He had assumed that he would be taken to the Souk, but the taxi turned north and drove down almost empty streets through the centre of the city. Gradually the large plate glass windows were replaced by smaller ones, and the newly built houses, by older Arab type dwellings. Finally the car turned into a street where the inhabitants seemed unaffected by the habits of the rest of Hamra, no one appeared to be sleeping here. Carts filled with vegetables and fruits lined the broad road. Arab women completely covered in Abbaya and veils chattered like monkeys, turning over the produce, squeezing it, and throwing it back contemptuously. Eddie got out of the vehicle a little uncertainly and turned to the driver, wishing he spoke English. He seemed to understand what was wanted however, and pointed to a doorway in a baked clay house.

"There?" Eddie asked surprised.

The man nodded "Two Dinah." he held out his hand and Eddie paid him. The driver swiftly let in the clutch and moved away up the street and round the corner. The Englishman was left standing on a piece of road that had at one time been a pavement. He was surrounded by goats turning rubbish over outside a small solid house, the windows shuttered and the door closed The building looked as though it had no occupants and had been that way for some time, but then, most Arab houses looked like that. Eddie picked his way between the goats, who took little notice of him, and approached the door. He rapped with his knuckles producing a sound that alarmed him, it was like knocking on a large empty box, the echoes rebounding from the walls.

At first there was no response. The afternoon sun beat down, the chatter of the women and the gruff male voices floated over the thunderous sound of the heat in his ears. Slightly worried by now he knocked again, louder this time. In response there was a rustling behind the door and he looked expectantly into the peeling green paint and the splintering wood. He was aware of someone looking at him, and the feeling grew then he noticed a spy hole in the door on a level with his eyes.

Someone was making sure who the visitor was. Angrily now he raised his fist to rap again on the door, but it just as suddenly opened in front of him. The Englishman could hardly discern who was standing in the doorway, the sun was too bright, the house too dark, there appeared to be no light coming from the interior at all.

"Come!" a voice said peremptorily and Eddie did as he was told, nervously looking into the darkness.

"Wait!" the voice said again, and the door was closed behind him. They were both left in complete darkness. The guide switched on a torch and Eddie found himself in a corridor. The passage was barely wide enough for his broad shoulders and they touched the sides as his companion urged him to walk on. There was a door to the left of him and the voice behind said "Please to go in."

Eddie was beginning to feel angry again, all the mystery seemed unnecessary, surely other people signed agreements without all this hassle. He turned the handle on the door however, and walked into a room that was only marginally better lit than the corridor. From a door in the corner, a small patch of daylight threw a weak pool of light onto a dirty floor. From between the wooden shutters tiny cracks of light pin pointed grease marks and patches on the wall nearest to them.

Eddie swung round on the guide, but the torch had gone, the door evidently closed behind him. He was about to move back towards it when from the centre of the room there was a click and light beamed out from a naked bulb. Underneath it was a desk, very old, obviously rickety. Behind the desk, a chair and again in front of it another chair, he looked around startled, the rest of the room that was hidden in shadow was empty. Only the walls, dark and dirty with grease and streaks of paint bore evidence of previous occupation. Eddie was wondering what to do next when the door in the corner opened and a man came in carrying a pile of papers.

"What the hell's going on?" Eddie erupted in relief.

The man came towards the desk and laid his papers on the top.

"Oh my dear me!" he said rubbing his hands together, "please do not be angry Mr Miller, precautions have to be taken you know." The Notary was Indian, dressed immaculately in a dark suit and tie, his shirt violently white against the dirt and shadows of the room. "Now then." he said and took a pair of spectacles from his pocket. Placing them on his nose he looked at his client more closely, smiling obsequiously into his face, he appeared to be satisfied with what he saw for he held out his hand.

"Good afternoon Mr Miller." Eddie reluctantly took the brown hand wondering at the smoothness of it. "Please sit down, sit down." the Indian urged, taking the seat behind the desk himself.

The man rested his chin on his elegant hands and looked again at his client, he appeared to be weighing his words.

"Mr Miller, I wish you to tell me why you have come here to-day---to-day." he repeated comfortably over the desk.

Eddie sat up startled, "What do you mean?" he asked angrily "You know why I'm here."

"Do I?" the man said, his eyes flickering as he recognised the impatience in the other

"Of course you do, you—you"—he let out a breath of exasperation. All the mystery, all the secrecy and now this.

"Aziz told me to come didn't he?"

"Dear me, dear me Mr Miller we must not mention names, I do not know that name, in fact I have never heard it before, so it means nothing to me, nothing." he was still smiling, but the expression was wavering as he apprehensively gauged Eddie's temper. "Please," he went on holding up his hand, let us start at the very beginning and then we can order this interview correctly.

"Mm?" The Englishman was beginning to feel completely confused, for a minute he began to think he had come to the wrong place, but then the man was calling him by his name, 'he expected me,' he thought.

"My name is Mohun Nair, I am a lawyer, oh yes, first class." Eddie looked at him in amazement, wondering what course the man was taking now. The Indian paused and flicked his wristwatch backwards and forwards on his lean wrist, the gold bracelet glinting in the light from the bare bulb. He watched it for a moment and the looked up. "Your name is Edward Miller, a salesman in this country, correct?"

"You know it is." Eddie snorted, crossing one leg over the other. Sweat was beginning to pour down the back of his neck. The room was close and shaded from the sun, but it was stuffy and the smell of the dust was suffocating, he took his handkerchief and wiped at the base of his hair. The Indian was looking at him, his head cocked on one side, he took off his glasses and tapped them gently over the papers on his desk.

"Yes, all right." Eddie responded.

"Good." Mohun Nair declared as though everything was going well. He replaced the glasses on his nose and picked up a paper.

"Please now to tell me what you are here for." The Englishman felt that the Indian was running circles round him for his own pleasure, he had no idea what was in the lawyer's mind and began to dislike him intensely.

"You know darned well, I've come to sign some papers." "Ah! What kind of papers?"

"This is ridiculous!" Eddie said springing up from his chair and thrusting his hands into his pockets, "is it such a secret?"

"It might be." the man said enigmatically "please sit down Mr Miller, sit down."

There was only one way to play the game with Mohun Nair, Eddie decided and that was his way. If he was to get the matter over and done with, he would have to answer his stupid questions and commit himself. He must know why I'm here, he probably has the papers there on his desk, why is he asking me these questions then? Eddie was beginning to feel uncertain of the situation, as though he were being trapped into making an incriminating statement.

"I've come to sign partnership papers as well you know." he said finally "I'm going into business to sell lavatory paper." he added sarcastically.

The dark man sat up and threw his spectacles onto the desk.

"Lavatory paper?" he said, his voice almost an octave higher, his eyes staring.

"Just a joke, old chap, just a joke." Eddie grinned at him happy to have discomfited the lawyer "bathroom equipment then."

The Indian lawyer sank back into his chair and replaced his glasses on his nose. Eddie began to wonder if he could see through them, he was so keen to discard them.

"You have a little joke with me." the Indian said and attempted a short laugh.

"Yeah!"

"Of course I know about this business, I have the papers here, but-----"and he waggled his finger at the salesman "I have to be very careful, you might have been an impostor."

"Hardly likely, old chap." Eddie said sitting down again and crossing one leg over the other.

"That is not true Mr Miller, in this country very many crazy things happen, we have all to be very careful." the man was offended. "now we shall have tea." the Indian declared and before Eddie could say a word, he had clapped his hands and a Pakistani entered with a tray.

"I have to apologise to you Mr Miller, it is difficult to be hospitable in such a place, this is not my normal office you understand."

The fact that the signing of the agreement was taking place in an unofficial office was entirely in keeping with the whole deal, 'another mystery, another secret' thought Eddie. Tea was poured and a cup and saucer placed before each of them.

Eddie examined the cup as best he could under the poor light, it looked clean but he was suspicious.

"It is quite clean." the Indian said reading his thoughts, "I've been a practicing Hindu all my life, and although there are some things I do not adhere to, cleanliness has to be one of the most important." and he took a sip of the hot liquid.

Somewhat reassured, the Englishman did the same trying not to grimace. It was very hot and very sweet.

"Not to your liking?" the lawyer asked.

"It's all right." Eddie answered churlishly, anyone would think they were at a tea party, he thought.

Pushing aside the cup and saucer, Mohun Nair picked up two pieces of paper stapled together

"This is the agreement you must sign, please read it."

"Don't bother," the salesman said reaching out for the papers

"I'll just sign it."

The Indian drew back the agreement "No, Mr Miller, that is not the correct way to do this business, you must read it first."

Eddie blew out his cheeks and looked exasperated, "All right if I must." he said and reached out again and took the pieces of foolscap. The pages were divided down the middle. On one side the script was in Arabic and on the other in English. At the bottom of the second page were spaces for signatures.

The Englishman settled back into his chair and started to read the agreement. Mohun Nair, his glasses once more in place picked up another sheet of paper and started to read, extending his hand from time to time for his tea cup. The sounds from outside the building were muffled in the dark solid house, and the silence within was heavy on the ear drums. neither seemed to notice however and when he had finished, Eddie laid down the papers on the desk."

"OK!" he said.

Mohun Nair placed the paper he had been reading back on the pile and his spectacles on top. He took a pen from inside his pocket and for a moment held it in the light to capture the glint of the gold case, he appeared to be fascinated by it.

"You must ask questions!" he said narrowing his eyes at the pen.

"What questions?" Eddie was baffled.

"Anything you wish to ask, before you sign." the lawyer held the pen close to his chest and leaned forward in his chair eager to listen.

"There's only one question I have to ask." Eddie said without much hope of having it answered.

"And that is"---? encouraged the man,

"Who the partner is, his name isn't on the agreement." Eddie tapped the papers.

"Ah!"

"Yes, Ah!" Eddie grinned.

"That is something I cannot tell you." the lawyer was plainly put out. He replaced his spectacles and shuffled in his chair, easing one leg over the other.

"Why not?" Eddie pursued, knowing very well but enjoying tantalising the official.

"Well, you see Mr Miller," and here he leaned forward again confidentially "I don't know myself who he is."

"Really?" now Eddie was surprised, he had really thought that the lawyer would know, in fact he had assumed that he, Edward Miller was the only person not to know.

"Yes, I'm afraid, really!" Mohun Nair threw up his wrist into the light and flicked his watch from side to side, the bone sticking out on his thin wrist "this is an affair I have to settle with my conscience," he went on "very difficult."

The Englishman was tempted to ask how much in pounds Sterling it had been difficult, but resisted the temptation. Instead he nodded his head sagely.

"Yes, I see very difficult for you." he said earnestly.

"Now to sign." the lawyer jumped from his seat and flourished his gold pen. He presented the exact line for the signature and held the paper steady.

For a moment Eddie hesitated and looking into the Indian's eyes he almost asked 'Am I doing the right thing?' then thought better of it. The decision had been made the week before, now all he had to do was confirm it. With characteristic energy, he scrawled his signature over the bottom of the agreement papers.

In less than a moment he was being ushered out of the dark hall, a torch lit his way to the door, switched off while it was unbolted. With great surprise he saw a taxi waiting outside for him and although he was dying to ask how it got there, he was unable to question the driver for once again he could speak no English.

Now Edward Miller was a partner in a business in Hamra, and the next difficult part was to explain it to his wife. His mind still dwelling on the afternoon's bizarre proceedings, he bounded two steps at a time up to his flat.

21

DURING the course of the next few weeks, Jenny became more and more involved in her new activities. She had accepted the news of Eddie's business venture with very little comment and happily contented herself with her own affairs. Eddie signed his new contract with the company and his friends congratulated him on the new enterprise. A large packet came for him in the mail in which pamphlets and brochures proclaimed the glories of cisterns, bath taps and other paraphernalia, along with an order book came a note unsigned. It said 'Get started, sell a lot.' He needed no second telling and threw himself into the new business.

He visited all his old contacts and formed new ones, The bathroom sales interoperating with the engines, so that the sales of both soared. Each Thursday he attended sales conferences with his friends where he proved that he was still top salesman in the company, and at the end of the meeting Reggie would point him in the direction of the toilets, where hidden in a cupboard, a package containing two bottles of gin would be wrapped in a towel.

At first he protested that he had forgotten to order them, so they did not belong to him, but Shafique soon gave him the hint that they had been ordered on his behalf, and guessing that they were the free perks from Aziz, he collected them each week cheerfully and gave up ordering Sediki until it was his turn for a party.

Most weeks he was away from Hamra until Thursday conferences, he rarely saw the inside of his flat until Thursday afternoon and slept most of Friday to make up for his lost energy during the week. He knew the commission was piling up, he was getting his gin and he was completely happy. The only thing he grumbled to himself about was the fact that although he was in touch with the Lebanese by sending in his orders, he had seen nothing of the man since David's party. He had no real reason to need to see Aziz, but he would have liked to chat to someone about how the business was going. Aziz was the only person who could tell hin the exact success of the operation.

Bobby had gone back to England, and indeed he was hardly missed by either parent, but before he went, Eddie asked him to point out which flat belonged to Aziz. During the last weekend, he had spent some time in his son's empty room staring down into the flat, but there had been nothing, not even a light. It was an exasperating feeling not being able to contact the most important person in his business venture. Then of course, his thoughts would turn to Corinth. Even though his life was now totally full and spare hours hard to come by, he did find that the evenings away from Hamra sometimes dragged and it was then that his thoughts would turn to the dark haired girl. He longed to be able to touch her and spend his nights with her. He had never received the message she had promised and wondered now if he ever would.

After over a month of silence, Eddie was handed a note from Aziz. Shafique presented it to him one Thursday morning as he rushed in for his meeting. he looked at the elderly Pakistani, wondering if he was in the pay of his Lebanese friend, he always seemed to be doing errands for him and taking messages.

The note said "At my flat 2-30." It was unsigned, but it could not have been from anyone else.

Eddie was in a hurry to get the conference over that morning and excused himself early, declining a party invitation to Reggie's villa down the road on the excuse of pressure of business. That brought a derisory cry from the company reps who openly laughed at him.

"Never did I think to see the day, Ed, when you'd refuse a party."

"Yes, it comes to something doesn't it, when old Eddie is opting out of a shindig?" they bent their heads together laughing.

Eddie waved to them cheerily, and laughing shut the door on them all, hurrying down to his Mercedes.

It was almost time for Salah and Arabs and Pakistanis were already entering the mosque on the other side of the street, the road was full of scurrying feet, carts carrying carpets, vegetables and tin pots were hastily being covered over so that their owners would not be accused of taking money during the sacred twenty minutes it would take to complete the rite. Eddie, sitting in the car, waiting while the condensation cleared from his sunglasses, fastened the windows tighter as the Mezerin began the call to prayer. The totally unmusical voice was echoed after a moment from half a dozen other minaret's around the centre of the capital, producing a raucous din amplified to an amazing degree by the loud speakers on the towers.

The Englishman edged the car between the mass of bodies making their way across the road and was startled to see once again his Arab. He was standing at the entrance to the mosque with another tall man leaning on a stick. Their camel coats wafted in the warm breeze and they were in deep conversation with each other, the one with the hooked nose playing languidly with his gold beads. Eddie breathed a sigh of relief, at least this time he had to admit that the man was looking anywhere except at him. He shrugged to himself, maybe it was a coincidence after all.

Aziz opened his door as soon as he saw the salesman approaching

"Hi!" he said and shook hands briskly and invited him in.

"I didn't think I was ever going to see you again, old chum." The Englishman said looking around the sparsely furnished room. "I've been on the look out for you every time I came home, but there was no light over here."

"Not here for some time," Aziz explained "but how about you? You've been doing good?" he was smiling, his brown eyes dancing with merriment.

"You can say that again, I've loads of contacts lined up. I can sell all you bring in." Eddie was pleased to be able to talk about the business with Aziz at last.

"Good,good!" the little man seemed abstracted "Yes, good." he said again. he sprang up "Beer?" he offered opening a small fridge.

"Beer?" Eddie was surprised "bringing that in now as well?"

"No, David gave me some cans" he said straightening up and produced two glasses.

"Where did he get beer from? Made it himself?"
Aziz laughed "No, real stuff."
"People downstairs from me started to make beer, it's useless, you can't hide what you're doing, it smells so much, in the end they had a fit of nerves and poured it all down the sink. Just think, a whole dustbin full, the place stank for days and the population of cockroaches increased overnight. If they try it again we intend to turn them over to the police ourselves!"
Aziz, who had started to laugh at the beginning of the story now looked up at him sharply "You would do that?" he asked incredulously.
Eddie sighed deeply "No, old chap, just a joke, God! It's only a joke."
Aziz was comforted "British humour." he said handing his companion a glass of foaming lager.
"I didn't think it was," Eddie said puzzled "just the way I say things sometimes."
"British Humour." Aziz said again "difficult to understand at times."
"Sorry!" The Salesman was put out "I had no idea." he said and buried his nose in his drink. "God!" That's great!" he said "I haven't had a lager for over a year." he crossed one leg over the other and placed an arm along the top of the chair. "So then, what's new?"
"Message for you." Aziz sat down elegantly and pulled his jacket straight.
"Oh?" Corinth at last, he thought.
"This time it's for you alone, you're invited to a party tonight."
Eddie opened his mouth and shut it again.
"Where?"
"At the palace in Abdul Aziz Street."
"The palace?" Eddie echoed "in Abdul Aziz Street? You don't mean the villa?"
"No, the palace, and you can only go by yourself, men only."
Eddie pursed his mouth and scratched at his red curls, "Ooh- I don't like the idea of that." he said shaking his head.
"Why? it's supposed to be an honour."
"A bit too near the fire for me, old chum." he replied placing his glass on the table and reaching into his pocket for a packet of cigarettes.

"Fire?" Aziz looked puzzled.

"Just an expression- no not humour- a bit near danger if you like. I've heard of some terrible things about that place."

Aziz laughed and his curls shook "They're probably correct as well."

"Have you ever been there?" Eddie asked.

"I'm not important enough." the Lebanese answered evading the question.

"What's important about me then?" How did I get an invitation?" he paused "how come you are giving me the message, shouldn't there be a card or something?"

"Eddie, Eddie," Aziz held up his hand, "you have to understand Hamra to understand these parties. Nothing is written down, it's always by word of mouth. It isn't official, very casual in fact. The Princes decide who they want to meet and send messages through, sometimes, several people, until it gets to the right one. That way they can't be implicated in what happens."

Eddie was frankly puzzled "What do you mean 'what happens'?

Aziz was vague "Whatever happens at the parties, you know, girls and sex and things like that." Eddie was thoroughly alarmed.

"Where on earth did they get the idea that I would be interested in that sort of thing?" he asked "I don't need girls, I've got plenty going for me without that sort of thing." he said almost huffily.

"Don't worry, you don't have to take part if you don't want to. Just greet them and if you don't like what is there, you just go home. No one will mind."

The Englishman was silent wondering what on earth he was getting into and not liking the idea one bit. However much he enjoyed his parties, they had never been an excuse for chatting up the girls and taking them into a bedroom as some of his friends tried to do. He enjoyed the social chat, the drinks, the food, the general feeling of well being they produced.

"The food is excellent." Aziz said reading his thoughts. "The alcohol all from genuine sources, imported of course." he smiled slyly.

"Ah!- We supply the booze up there, right?"

"Right, the Lebanese nodded his head "but that isn't the reason why they've asked you. They have no idea that you are involved, just as I said, no one except the partner and us know you have anything to do with the booze."

"Why then?"

Aziz shrugged "The fact that you are selling a lot of goods in Hamra is good enough reason. Someone might have mentioned you and they are curious. They do like to know what's going on in their country, especially when it concerns Ex Pats."

Eddie could accept that answer, then he thought.

"Do I tell Jenny?"

"If you like, it isn't a secret." Aziz said.

"Thank God for that." Eddie sighed dramatically, "it must be the only thing that isn't secret since I met you."

The Lebanese looked slightly hurt and the salesman laughed at him. "You have to admit old chum, it's like getting tied up with spies going into business with you."

Aziz clapped his lips together and showed his displeasure.

"Now what have I said?" Eddie said childishly.

"You make fun of me." Aziz said, pouring another lager into his companion's glass.

"No!" Eddie tapped the small man's arm "just teasing." he said "anyway, go on."

"What?"

"What time do I have to go, and what happens if I don't go?"

It was Aziz's turn to look alarmed. "You have to go." he said "no one turns down an invitation like that."

"Pity!" Eddie said, wishing that someone had started the fashion before this.

"You must be there at nine o'clock. Take your own car."

"You can't come as well I suppose?" the salesman asked wistfully.

"Sorry, not possible."

Eddie breathed out heavily, "Oh well, nothing for it I suppose. Anything else you have to tell me?"

"No, nothing, just carry on selling. Oh yes! The first container is coming next week, probably be through clearance on Monday.

"Super!" the salesman's eyes sparkled "Good to see the product go out to the customer then sales will go up, everyone will want some if his neighbour has bought a new bathroom for himself."

Aziz lit a cigarette and looked at his watch.

"Have to go soon, I have an appointment."

"OK, by the way, how about that Mohun Nair?" his companion frowned, "you know the Indian lawyer, the agreement."

"I don't know him." Aziz said.

"Do you mean to say you didn't set up that meeting at the other end of town?"

"Yes, I knew the address, but the partner set up the meeting. He used the notary he could trust, I never met him, I don't think I know him."

"You missed nothing," Eddie laughed "I don't think he was quite sane."

"As long as you signed, that was the important thing." he stubbed his cigarette out and got up from the chair.

"Now don't forget, nine o'clock at the latest tonight, be very good and let nothing out.!" Aziz warned.

"Right! When do I see you again? No don't tell me, you'll contact me, yeah?"

"Correct." the Lebanese shook Eddie's hand "all the luck, Eddie, take care."

On his way to Abdul Aziz Street that night, Eddie noticed that the windows of Flat No 3 were dark and the curtains undrawn.

"Gone again!" he breathed to himself.

22

THE sky was black when Eddie drove down Abdul Aziz Street and through the avenue of trees. There was no moon and the stars were hidden behind dense cloud. A rustling of leaves suggested thoughts of rain, but it was unlikely, it rarely rained at all in Hamra, and before it did there was usually weeks of heavy banking cloud enclosing the heat in the capital like a blanket.

Armed guards, the personal guards of the Princes, stood smartly to attention at the Palace gates as the salesman was waved through. In the blaze of light within the courtyard Eddie could see a building of fairy tale fantasy. An oblong building sitting prettily behind immense fountains throwing water into the air up to the height of the flat roof. The windows, designed to open onto the courtyard, were all of brightly coloured glass, in a pattern of red and yellows that glowed and twinkled in the light from within. At the centre of the Palace an enormous bay like structure bulged out at the top of broad steps and then over the top a golden dome, heavy and bulbous. The five great windows in the bay were of plain glass enabling all in the courtyard to see the massive chandeliers in the room beyond. It was magnificent, but the finishing touch was the fretwork of glistening white cement, almost a filigree that covered the whole of the exterior walls. It was a Palace of icing sugar.

Eddie parked the Mercedes and found a man at his elbow. He was guided past the fountains and to a door at the side of the building which opened as soon as he reached it. Stepping inside, he was immediately confronted with a solid wall of bodies, men of all shades of colour wearing all types of national dress were standing about the entrance hall chatting. Not for the first time, he cursed his height, a good many visitors were tall and were blocking his view. He managed to see across to the end of the room where a clock started to chime. It was nine o'clock. A door by the side of it, that opened from floor to ceiling was thrust open and an Arab with a camel stick stood in the entrance.

"Gentlemen, please come in." the man said inclining his head to the company.

For a moment Eddie lost sight of him as the crowd attempted to get into some kind of queue in order to file through the door, and then when he came nearer to him he stopped in mid stride. The Arab standing at the door was his Arab, the one with the eyes and golden worry beads, the one that had been following him about all over Hamra.

Eddie felt a push from behind and involuntarily walked towards the door. He could not take his eyes off the man. His piercing eyes, his hooked nose, the immense pride of bearing, he noted it all as the Arab bowed his head to every guest when they walked through the door.

"Good Evening!" he said directly to Eddie as he hesitated on the threshold of the next room, and the Englishman cleared his throat and returned the greeting in a louder voice than he intended. A small smile flickered over the Arab's face as he bowed to the next in line and Eddie was through into the adjoining room.

He thought he must now be in a ballroom, it measured the whole length of the building and the width of the central structure. Four of the largest chandeliers that Eddie had ever seen hung down over a pale onyx floor covered in places with deep piled Persian carpets. Down each side of the room were booths the size of small caravans. Oblong boxes decorated in red velvet and gold trim, having wooden windows overlooking the main concourse and a close fitting oak panelled door. He would have dearly liked to ask someone what the boxes were for, but his eyes were almost immediately drawn to the end of the hall towards which the large queue was moving. On a dais covered with a bright red Persian carpet were three carved chairs, and in each chair sitting bolt upright was an Arab.

The princes wore white Dish dashes with gold trimmed collars. Over their guttras instead of the black camel rope, they wore a square crown made up of three strands of large gold beads. The three men looked remarkably alike even to the shape of their heads. They might have been triplets.

Eddie felt intimidated, he had no idea what was expected of him and he watched the other guests closely and copied them. He noticed that when each man approached the dais, they bowed and announced their names and business. He gave a nervous giggle to himself 'Edward Miller Bathroom Cabinets.' he said to himself, it sounded ridiculous.

As the long line of guests moved forward and were acknowledged, they dispersed to the side of the room. It was diminishing rapidly and as he moved closer Eddie was aware of someone at his elbow. A glance told him that his Arab was walking bedside him. He looked straight in front unable to think of what to say or do. A slight pressure on his arm stopped him, the Arab was speaking to him.

"We have met before Mr Miller." he said conversationally.

"Yes, I think we have." Eddie said as casually as he could. The guests in the queue overtook him.

"Don't worry, there is plenty of time, the Majlis will continue for about thirty minutes." the man held out his hand, "my name is Ahmed bin Hauz he said and briefly touched the Englishman's hand. "I understand you have just started in business Mr Miller."

"Er- yes, that's right, just started." Eddie had lost his charm, it had completely deserted him.   "Doing well I hope? The Princes like all business men to do well in our country."

Eddie cleared his throat and coughed discreetly "Yes, very well thank you." he managed to say. The very ordinary way in which the Arab was conversing was making Eddie feel breathless. It was hard to imagine that after the fears he had concerning the man, that he would be talking to him across such a small space.

"You may go forward now, Mr Miller." Ahmed was saying "just say your name and state your business and that will be all that is required. Afterwards you may take a seat over there." he pointed to the wall with the overstuffed settees where the guests were now sitting in a long line.

The Englishman managed to thank the man as he turned sedately and retraced his steps to the entrance hall. He was too confused to ask himself at that moment why the Arab had singled him out, he had not addressed any one else in the queue. It was almost his turn to bow to the dais.

Eddie took a step forward and bowed to the three figures on the dais, he was too nervous to notice anything but their immobility. It was almost as though they were made of stone.

Their eyes seemed to be the only feature that was capable of movement, three pairs of brown eyes flickered over him and flickered away again.

"Edward Miller, Importer of Bathroom Equipment." he stated quietly and instantly resented feeling intimidated by the three men. The Princes inclined their heads for a moment and resumed their erect position. Eddie turned in as sedate a fashion as he could manage and walked over to the couches along the wall. The Salesman stared at the men in their wooden thrones and watched the elegant inclination of their heads as each guest bowed before them. Their expressions did not change, their faces were empty, only their eyes would dart around on occasions, alighting on some guest or other, only to revert back to the glassy stare.

A sudden movement to the right of the Princes caught Eddie's eye.

"Ye gods!" he caught his breath.

Perched on a rail supported by ornately golden legs were two falcons, their eyes hooded with a leather cap, a small bunch of feathers on the top. Jesses were attached to their feet and to the end of the golden rail. He had stood barely a yard away from them and had not noticed they were there. A young Arab, handsome in sparkling white robes stood by them and when they became restless, stroked their feathers. Obviously Keeper of the Hawks. Eddie thought. he looked around the massive hall, from the chandeliers to the red velvet boxes, the three Princes with their beaded crowns and to the falcons restlessly standing on one leg and then the other. He watched the many nationalities in their colourful robes, the Sudanese tall and stately, the Nigerians tall and very black, Orientals with turbans, Ghanaians in Kente cloth, people from all nations, the blackest of faces and the whitest of skins. The people, the colours, the robes, the great hall was a mediaeval picture, only the guests wearing trousers and shirts could be called truly twentieth century.

The last guest had made his obeisance to the Princes and Ahmed bin Hauz appeared from the back of the hall, walking proudly his head held high and his camel stick touching the floor at each step. he walked up the carpet covered steps of the dais and bent down to speak to the Princes. He then straightened up and took a step to the side of them. In a clear voice and superbly educated accents he began:-

"The Princes, Abdullah Al Mukadan, Hassan bin Fitaihi Mukadan and Yusef Rashid Al Mukadan all thank you for your greetings.

There have been no requests for an immediate audience with their Royal Highnesses, therefore all other requests will be answered by their Royal Highnesses secretary tomorrow. Thank you once again, gentlemen, the Majlis is at an end."

As though a gong had sounded, the princes stood and all the guests got to their feet. The three men walked slowly down the steps keeping shoulder to shoulder and the young Arab, carrying the falcons on his wrists fell in behind them. The small procession turned and walked through an ornate doorway and out of sight. Ahmed, the master of ceremonies directed the guests to follow him to the entrance hall where some visitors went out of the side door and back to their cars, while others slipped through another door and into another part of the Palace.

Eddie lingered at the back of the crowd filing into the entrance hall. In spite of himself he was savouring the experience of being in the same room as royalty. It had been an impressive ceremony, a display of quiet authority and courtliness in beautiful surroundings. He thought for a moment of all the rumours that surrounded this Palace and smiled to himself. It was amazing what people made up, he thought. Looking back to the immobile features of the three men he had bowed to, the stateliness of their bearing, it was impossible to believe that there were grounds for any of the stories that were spread around Hamra. He had seen their dignity, felt the awe in which the guests approached the dais, it was barely possible to think of them other than in the light of stern Muslim rulers. Where had the rumours come from? People were always jealous, he knew well, perhaps that was it.

He was almost at the door when he thought of Aziz, even he had assumed the rumours to be true. he would soon be told the truth when he saw him next, Eddie thought.

The queue of men came to a stop as Ahmed said a few words to one of them. It gave Eddie a perfect view of the man. It must have been the first time that the Englishman could stare at Ahmed rather than the other way round. Eddie could not say anything but that Ahmed has been gracious. Every time he had seen the man he had been courteous and polite. However there was still something about the man that sent the hair up on the back of his neck. Those eyes, the coal black intensity when he turned them on you, Eddie thought, as though he could see your secret thoughts. he shuddered and the line of guests moved forward again.

"Mr Miller!" Ahmed smiled at him, "please go through that door over there and have some supper, you have been invited to stay."

"Thank you." the Englishman said and walked in his ungainly way across the hall and through the door.

23

THE room in which supper had been laid was small, an ante chamber. The buffet supper had been spread out on tables against the wall, but apart from one or two servants standing about, there was no one but Eddie in there. There appeared to be only one other door at the end of the room and it was heavily draped in red velvet curtains. Ornate gold leafed friezes decorated silky wood panelling around the walls, it was an extremely attractive room.

"Where did everyone go?" Eddie asked a servant.

A man in a dish dash but no headdress said " They have already eaten and have gone through, you must eat and wait here."

"Right then," Eddie, keen as ever to satisfy his appetite looked at the table which seemed little different from the hotel buffet on a Friday, save that in the middle of the many dishes sat an enormous swan made out of spun sugar. The sculpture was magnificent and he admired it before taking a plate and spooning onto it portions of everything that looked interesting.

"You would like a drink?" the servant came towards him carrying a goblet of silver.

"Yes, great!" he said eagerly.

"Whiskey, gin, rum?"

"Gin and tonic." Eddie said, his face breaking into a smile 'Good old bathroom equipment' he said to himself.

The Arab responded to the smile with a look which took the salesman aback.

The eyes flashed, the smile was beatific, but it was definitely sensuous. The smile froze on Eddie's lips and he looked around to the door in the hope that someone else might join him, but it remained firmly closed.

The Englishman took his plate to a small table by the door, his goblet had been filled with a very strong gin to tonic and he took his first drink keeping an eye on the servant, he soon forgot about the young man however in the enjoyment of his supper, everything was good, the food, the drink, the décor. He was though, beginning to feel a little uncomfortable sitting on his own in that room. From the other side of the door, the noise of guests leaving and car doors banging were becoming less and less until it had almost stopped. Eddie wondered what he was supposed to do when he had finished eating.

Then the door opened and an elderly man leaning on a stick entered the room, spotting Eddie straight away. He was about to speak, but before he did he looked across at the servants, the buffet table and the other door hidden behind the curtains. Appearing to decide that all was in order he addressed the salesman.

"Good evening Mr Miller!" he approached the table leaning heavily on his stick. The man was indeed old, his beard grey and eyebrows almost white. His eyes, though, were brown and sparkling, alive in his face and essentially kind.
Eddie stood up politely "Good evening!" he answered "are you going to join me?"

"Yes." the man looked across to a servant "a little fish I think." he said in excellent English. The young Arab scuttled across to serve the old man and looked at him and asked "A drink?" the expression on his face was cheeky.

"Of course not," the elderly man rapped out "water only."

Eddie was instantly ill at ease, he was sitting there with a strong smell of gin on his breath, he felt that it was impolite. He was not used to drinking in the company of Arabs and began to wish that the man had sat somewhere else.

"I hope you don't mind, the boy gave me this----" Eddie began, holding up the goblet.

The old man thumped his stick on the floor as he levered himself down into a seat opposite the Englishman.

"You are a Christian?" he asked and Eddie felt guilty.

"Well, er, yes, I suppose I am." he said, his mind instantly full of Christmas trees and three wise men.

"Then you can drink, you offend no one but yourself." the man said smiling kindly. "in this Palace, the Princes have decreed that alcohol should be available to anyone. It is the conscience that has to be satisfied."

Eddie had no idea what the elderly Arab was talking about, but he felt that he had been put at ease and was grateful. The two men ate in companionable silence and were undisturbed.

The servants gradually left the room until only the Arab youth remained. He whisked the plates away, refilled their goblets and brought them a dish of ice cream smothered in chocolate sauces, marshamallow and nuts. The old man rubbed his hands smiling "I like my pudding." he said and picked up a spoon.

Eddie thought he sounded remarkably like his grandfather and warmed to him.

"You wonder about my English?" the old man said, raising his eyes for a moment to his companion, he had not missed the fleeting expression on Eddie's face when he had said 'pudding'. "Mm I suppose so, yes." the Englishman was avidly spooning ice cream into his mouth.

The old man delicately wiped his beard with the linen napkin and laid it beside his plate. "I was educated in England." he said "spent most of my youth there."

Eddie tried to look interested, most well to do Arabs had been educated in England, it was nothing unusual, he thought.

When the old man had finished his ice cream he laid down his spoon and began to chuckle. "I had forgotten," he said " you do not know my name." smiling genially he went on " I must introduce myself to you, you will appreciate my name."

The man held out his hand to Eddie who took it warmly.

"My name is Sediki, Sediki Al Kadar." he announced with relish.

Eddie's eyebrows shot up and he grinned broadly,

"Sediki?"

"Yes, it is a name you know very well I am sure." the old man smiled back at him.

"But, it's the name of a drink." Eddie protested.

"It is now, but it has always been the name of a man. It means my friend."

"My friend!" Eddie repeated shaking his head.

"Yes, I suppose to the lonely men out here, the drink must be their friend, although I cannot see that it is a good friend to them." the grey haired man chuckled.

Eddie looked at Sediki in wonder, he liked him enormously.

"Coffee!" the old man called to the servant, "then you can go."

The two men sat and sipped their coffee, Eddie smoking, the old man talking. The servants had all left the room, no one else entered they were entirely alone.

As all old men are apt to do, Sediki began to reminisce. He talked in his musically educated voice about his childhood and Eddie smoked and sipped his coffee, now accompanied by a liqueur, and his thoughts wandered, he caught the word alcohol and was brought back to the present.

"It is the cause of the country's downfall and it will have to change."

The Englishman was slightly alarmed and began to listen to Sediki carefully.

"When I was young, Hamra was a good place, the people prayed five times a day and the mosques were always full. We lived our life completely by the Koran as we have been instructed to do and Western influence was kept out of the Sheikdom. Of course it was a Sheikdom in those days, my great uncle Yusef Bahktar Kadar was the ruler.

Eddie nodded his head recognising the name.

"Yes, you have remembered my name, Kadar."

"It's my job to remember names," Eddie murmured "you belong to the ruling family then?" he prodded, impressed that he was sitting with a member of the Royal House

He was surprised that he was so interested, but in spite of himself he had been enthralled by the evening's events.

"Yes, I am almost the only survivor of that part of the family. The Princes' family name is of course the same, but when Sheik Yusef's five sons overthrew him, they changed the name." Sediki looked up and gazed sadly at the far wall. When a son is ashamed of his father's name it is a terrible thing."

"What happened to Sheik Yusef?" Eddie asked.

"His throat was cut and his body left to the carrion hunters in the desert, it was a very bad day for our family, and even worse for the country."

"But the country has expanded, it is very wealthy now, and all the people seem to be living well." the Englishman said in a placatory manner. Sediki looked at the salesman and sighed

"You are a Westerner, how can you understand?"

"Try me" Eddie said eagerly, he had begun to feel great respect for Sediki and wanted him to return the feeling.

"It is a matter of quality, what matter quantity when you have that?"

Sediki moved his stiff leg a little and rubbed his knee. "Yes, there is quantity now, plenty of goods in the shops—from the West. Plenty of everything, money, gold, silver, jewels----power. Even plenty of land, Yusef's sons saw to that, but think of how these riches have been obtained, at what expense." he paused and looked directly at Eddie. "You are still interested?"

"Yes, yes of course, go on" he urged.

At that moment a sound came from outside the room that had them sitting bolt upright in their seats, it was a shrill strangling sound, not a scream and not a groan, somewhere between the two.

"Wha------?"

Sediki waved his hand at the Englishman "Take no notice, take no notice, it's nothing to do with us." he said.

Eddie looked towards the velvet screened door from where the noise came, but no one entered and no other sound could be heard. he settled back into his seat for Sediki was continuing.

"It started with the land, the five sons knew that if one of them should inherit Hamra—and it isn't always the eldest son you know, that is a Norman practice.- yes, they felt that if one should inherit, then there would be little left for the others. They were all very ambitious, there was only one way in which all of them could have land and power, and that was by taking it from their neighbours."

"Surely, excuse me if I'm wrong," Eddie said cautiously "Haven't the Bedu been fighting each other for land since way back? I read that somewhere."

"Quite right, there is even an Arabic saying about it. 'My neighbour is my enemy, my neighbour's neighbour is my friend.' You think about it, neighbours have always been enemies in this part of the world." he thought for a moment " also in your world, what about France and England? Yes you are quite correct, the Bedu have always been at war with their neighbours, Mr Miller."

"Eddie, please, call me Eddie."

"Yes, Eddie." the old man complied, "but we are talking not of desert skirmishes, but of invasion on a grand scale. They

176

imported from Turkey and Syria, the best fighting men they could find as mercenaries, spending the last penny that Hamra could afford to pay for them. The five sons had no intention of leading the fight, oh no- they waited at home, while their people were sent to fight with foreigners until all surrounding sheikdoms had been drawn into their net. But God is not mocked, Edward." Sediki rejected the familiar version of the name. "Edward is a much nicer name than Eddie." he explained and went on. "They sat in their desert towns, each ruling a portion of land, a very large portion of land in fact, which was the new country of Hamra. They married, some even had the four wives allowed by the Koran, but they could not produce sons. One of them could produce no children at all. It was a punishment."

"What happened to you at the time?" the story was pure Arabian Nights, thought Eddie.

"I was in England, my cousin sent a message to stay where I was until everything had settled down. I stayed until the five sons were all dead. While I was away they found oil in Hamra, people started to become wealthy on the dead bones of their old ruler. Western influence has come and will stay unless something is done about it. The Princes are all Westernised and only pay lip service to the Koran, but they find it useful in keeping the country in order. That is why I say the price has been too high for the quantity that is in the country."

"Were you afraid to come home?" Eddie was conscious of the privilege of talking to a figure out of history.

"I didn't come until I was assured that I wouldn't be executed." Sediki laughed showing perfect teeth. He waggled his beard with a wrinkled hand. "My cousin made sure I'd be safe."

"Your cousin, another member of Yusef's house."

"Ahmed." Sediki nodded in the direction of the entrance hall. Ahmed is my cousin. His full name is Ahmed Bin Hauz Al Bahktir, his mother was my mother's sister."

Eddie though for a moment and then said with a grin "Yes, now I remember where I've seen you before, you were talking to Ahmed outside the Grand Mosque the other day, I recognise your stick, it was you wasn't it?"

The old man frowned, "I suppose it could have been." he said cautiously.

The Englishman looked round at the curtained door as a thud resounded against it, then the sound of music began, not the Arabic music that might have been expected but raucous popular music from the British charts, a disco beat and loud singing.

"You see what has happened?" Sediki said disgustedly "Western morality" and added quickly "It's all right for those who come from Europe, but it is not right for Hamra. I'm not insulting you Edward, I am just saying that East is East and West is West and the two can never be one."

Eddie felt that he was being held responsible for all the evil that had come out of the West and he began to feel a little resentful. He forgot that he had been so interested in talking to the man and became impatient. He had been asked to a party had a couple of drinks, a plateful of food and been stuck with the old man who had talked to him about religion. he liked the old man and had been flattered that Sediki had told him his story, but enough was enough. he looked at his watch ostentatiously

Sediki smiled at the younger man, "I'm keeping you from the party." he said apologetically. "I have to say that it has been nice talking to you and I had forgotten that you would wish to be on your way."

"No!" protested the Englishman guiltily "not at all."

"Well, then, seeing you are so interested in our history, let me take some more of your time and show you something." the old man got up from his seat slowly and painfully, supporting himself on his stick. Eddie groaned inside, perhaps he had been too accommodating, too pleasant. It happened everywhere he went. Arabs were always taking him to meet someone, or inviting him to eat, or spend time with their relatives. That was supposed to be his work though, he thought sourly, this is supposed to be a night out.

Although Eddie was longing to find the party and have another drink, he could not refuse to go with Sediki, he really liked him and considering the man's connections, he was not about to be rude to him.

"Fine, fine." he assented and followed the tall figure back into the large hall with the chandeliers.

24

EDDIE followed closely behind as Sediki stumped across the Persian carpets.

The chandeliers had been switched off and the only light in the hall came from strategically placed lamps on low tables. Briefly he caught sight of a coloured garment as a woman ran laughing out of the hall through the ornamental arch by the dais. Twinkling in the pools of light on the tables were glasses, some bottles fallen over and laying in patches of liquid on the floor glinted coldly. The nearer they got to the dais, the more Eddie could pick out items of clothing lying scattered about. A dish dash lay draped across the dais steps, a great pile of transparent blue sari material had been abandoned on one of the couches along with a camel rope. Eddie could hardly believe that he was in the same place that had seen the sedate progress of honoured guests earlier in the evening. They had certainly been having a high old time of it in here. He took a look around, where was everybody? Where was the owner of the dish dash and what did he have left on? Eddie grinned at that, more to the point what did the Indian lady have left on after taking off such a pile of material. Pity about the drinks he thought.

Sediki walked heavily across the hall ignoring the debris as though it was quite usual and stopped as they came to the long line of velvet clad boxes. He raised his stick and pointed to one of them, "Here we are, this is what I wanted to show you." From his pocket he took a silver key with an ornate handle. He inserted it in the carved door of the box and stepped inside. "come on." he urged. The interior of the box was velvety black with only a chink of light coming from the wooden panel that he had supposed was a window.

"There's a bench by the wall, sit on it for a moment." the old man instructed. There was a scraping sound and light flooded into the box, Sediki had removed the panel of wood and behind it was a fretwork grill which allowed those inside to see out, without themselves being seen. The box had luxuriously cushioned benches around the walls and a small table of ivory and rosewood in the centre with a brass coffee pot and cups set on it.

"I wanted to ask someone about these boxes," Eddie said "I wondered what they could possibly be when I first came into the hall."

Surprisingly Sediki laughed, "They are the result of family squabbles," he said "there were so many females in the family during the five son's time that they were always squabbling."

"Were they locked up in here? Eddie was willing to believe anything about the bad old times.

"No, no" the old man laughed again. "females are very curious creatures," he said nodding his head wisely "they always want to know what is going on outside their quarters. The daughters of so many wives—must have numbered about seventy" Eddie whistled in amazement."yes, quite a number isn't it?"

Sediki eased himself down onto the bench beside the wooden grill, "It was difficult to keep them all in order, as you may imagine. They would keep poking their noses into their fathers' business, so they came up with a brilliant compromise."

Eddie looked through the grill as a wave of rock music blasted through a door and subsided again, he could see nothing.

"Compromise?" he prompted Sediki.

"Yes," the man chuckled to himself again "it was quite good really. If they behaved themselves the women would be allowed to attend the Majlis in these boxes, if they didn't well--- they would just have to stay in their quarters, seems it worked very well."

The thought of seventy women from the harem boxed up and peeping through the grills was intriguing.

"Did the men know they were there?"

"Eventually they did, and they would all turn up at the Majlis looking handsome in special clothes and fancy headresses." Sediki waggled his head to illustrate the young men's ostentation. "the perfume from their clothes apparently used to make the rulers sick." he burst into laughter at the thought, but it worked." his face saddened a little as he went on.

"Then when the Princes came to rule the women lost interest. They had their Western toys by that time, and preferred to stay in their own quarters watching television and smoking cigarettes."

"So the boxes are museum pieces now?"

"I'm afraid so," Sediki peered through the grill and said suddenly "I must have a word with someone over there." he straightened up and took his stick, walking to the door. "I'll be back in a moment, don't worry."

Eddie stood up and made towards him. he was going to ask where he should go now, but Sediki, surprisingly nimble had started to stump across the hall.

"Damn!" Eddie said loudly and thumped the velvet upholstery, "I always get myself into these messes, what am I supposed to do now?"

He peered through the grill, but there was no movement, although the music was playing in a room very near. Doors slammed on occasions but apart from a servant carrying a tray on the other side of the hall, he saw no one.

"Damn and blast!" he bit his finger in vexation, he may as well go home as sit here in semi darkness on velvet cushions in the middle of a Palace that was to all intents and purposes empty.

He waited a short while then stood at the door of the box, there was no sign of Sediki and he had been expected to stay put, but irritation was gaining on him. The old man may have forgotten all about him, so he started to stroll across the room in the direction of the music. In such a large place he felt exposed, rather like walking along in the middle of an empty football pitch. He stopped and looked around him giving Sediki a chance to return. Whistling silently he looked up at the great chandeliers that even now sparkled and reflected distant light. Then the door opened and a blast of music burst into the room. Along with it an Arab, his head bare and dish dash flapping as he tugged at a girl by his side. It was obvious he was drunk, he was lurching badly and in danger of falling over. The girl, as sober as her companion was drunk almost fell over him as he dragged her along.

"Here, steady on," Eddie ran towards them and then stopped. There was blood trickling from a gash in the girl's neck and her cheek bone was swollen. Eddie noticed that she was shielding an exposed breast with her arm, her dress was badly torn. She turned large frightened eyes towards the Englishman and sobbed.

The Arab caught sight of Eddie, and still clutching the arm of the girl he held up his other arm in greeting.

"My friend, my friend," he called loudly "you have come to the party!" and he staggered towards him.

Eddie had experience with drunks and knew that he would have to handle this one very carefully if he were to help the girl, so he went towards him smiling.

"Hello, yes, it's a great party isn't it? Come on let's sit down over there."

he took the arm of the man and pointed to a low couch. At the same time he made meaningful nods to the young girl who was vainly trying to wrench herself out of the Arab's grasp.

"Hey,hey! Not that way, my lishle dove, thish way." and with one huge effort the man swung his captive in the direction of the couch and let go. She landed fortunately on the soft cushions and lay imobile, stunned, while her captor staggered to her side. Eddie sat down with them and took out his cigarettes.

"Have a smoke?" he offered.

"Thatsh right," the man said "'ave a smoke." and with Eddie guiding his hand he took a cigarette and lit it. The girl moved and like a cat, the Arab pounced on her again.

"Oh no!" he waggled a finger at her "No, no, no."

Eddie tried again "You seem a nice man." he said with a smile.

The man turned to him and answered holding his cigarette at arms length as though he were going to catch fire.

"Yesh, I- I'm a very nice 'an I am." he sighed and gazed into the Englishman's face "A very nishe 'an."

"I don't think you would like to see anyone hurt would you?" Eddie went on. The Arab looked amazed, his eyes trying to focus on the face in front of him, but the lids drooped constantly. "I don't hurt anybody." he pointed to himself and dug himself in the chest "I don't hurt anybody, nishe 'an." he wobbled slightly and his head flopped but he recovered instantly "nishe!" he grinned fatuously.

"Your friend has hurt herself." Eddie felt it was make or break time.

"My friend?"

"Yes, this young girl, she's hurt." the girl's head had sunk onto her chest and her dark hair was soaked in blood from her neck. Tears poured down her face, but she made no sound as though frightened of reminding the man that she was still there.

"She needs help."

"Help?" The Arab looked around, "where's my friend?"

"No", Eddie was being very patient "No, this young girl is hurt."

Once again the man turned on the girl and grabbed her arm, she cried out softly and moaned through her tears.

"Sheesh mine." the man said trying to get to his feet and dropping his cigarette. "mine not yours." he stood swaying and pointing to Eddie's chest "you can't 'ave 'er."

"No, of course not." Eddie soothed putting his hands on the man's shoulders "no, but she's hurt." he tried to bore his eyes into the man's drooping lids.

"Naa—she likes it." and he shrugged the salesman's hands off "she likes it," he repeated, they all like it, give 'em some gold, they go home 'appy."

Eddie had been as patient as he would ever be up to now, but the sight of this drunk in front of him and the girl obviously needing attention for the wound in her neck, had made him so angry that it was about to spill over. He never noticed the gold embroidery on the man's collar as he went to grab him.

"Now just listen to me, you half baked oriental-----" but he never finished what he was about to say for there was a touch on the arm and Sediki was at his elbow, his eyes flashing a message that he was about to ignore, but the old man squeezed his arm tightly and drew him away.

"But---"

"Quiet!" Sediki hissed.

"Ah Sediki, my friend, good ole Sediki." the drunken man lurched towards him and wound his arms round his neck. Across the top of the dark head the old man hissed "go---now!" Eddie hesitated "quickly!" he urged

There was nothing else to do, he would have to leave the girl and hope that the old man would look after her. Crossing the great hall and looking over his shoulder as he went, he still could not believe what he had just seen. That drunken bum would be thrown out if Sediki had his way, he would have liked to stay and help him.

It was all spoiled for him of course. The party had not been his sort of party, he was grateful now that the old man had kept him talking. The splendour of the earlier ceremony and the wonderful thoughts and warm feelings towards the Royal house had vanished like melting ice, it left him cold.

He knew now what went on at the Palace, he'd experienced it at first hand, no wonder there were tales of girls disappearing and being sent home in air ambulances. The gossip was true and it was not at all amusing, it was horrible.

Then he remembered the gold embroidery on the drunk's dish dash. He stopped in his stride and gaped "Ye gods and little fishes!" Was he? He must have been, that's why Sediki got him out of there so quickly.

Eddie made a dash for the courtyard and went swiftly to his car, his one thought to get home. The only thing he could hope for was that the drunken prince would never remember who he was, or even what had happened at all. Driving into Abdul Aziz Street he looked back at the shimmering Palace with its fairy tale structure and pulled a face. It had been like looking under a stone and finding slugs. Eddie shivered and turned the air conditioning off.

25

FOR a time after the visit to the Summer Palace, Eddie was morose. he had started to think and it was dangerous, for his temper, ever close to the surface, erupted for no reason at all. He remembered Martha's chat in the car that night going to David's party- something about a hairdresser swinging from the chandeliers. He remembered how they all laughed and accused the women of gossiping. Now he began to suspect that all the parties at the Palace were drunken riots. He tried to get the vision of the young girl out of his mind, but it stuck there and he still wanted to batter that drunken bum into mincemeat. Then again Eddie remembered that he was the one that was helping to import the stuff.

"Wonderful!" he breathed to himself staring into space "I'm creating monsters."

He wondered why people could not enjoy their drinks like he did, get happy, laugh, sing, tell jokes and go to bed happy. What was wrong with them. Sediki's words came to mind and he was depressed. he had liked Sediki and hated the thought that if the old man had known what he was involved in, he would never have wanted to speak to him.

Eddie thinking was Eddie quiet and people began to notice.

"He's different." Martha said to her husband sitting in his easy chair hidden behind his newspaper. "he is, he's different, listen love, I'm talking to you." she nudged him.

Don lowered his paper with a loud rustle "What is it?" he asked impatiently.

"Eddie—something's happened to him, he's different."

"He's busy." her husband replied lifting the newsprint to his face.

"Not that." Martha persisted "he's lost his bounce."

"Rubbish! the voice came from behind the newspaper. Martha grasped it and put it behind her back "listen to me will you?" she said pushing her face into her husband's. He folded his hands into his lap and looked her in the eye.

"All right, what is it?"

"Eddie."

"You said that."

"He's lost his bounce."

"You said that as well."

"Well?" she shouted "all I want to know is why?"

"How should I know?" the round man shouted back, his face red and his eyes staring.

"Oh go back to your paper, you're more handsome that way." she said shoving the newsprint in front of his face rudely

She tried again with Jenny.

"What's the matter with Eddie?" she asked directly, Jenny pretended not to understand.

"Eddie?"

"Yes, you know, your husband, the one with the large eyes and sandy hair."

"Nothing as far as I know." Jenny answered "do you want a coffee?"

"No, I don't want to be put off the scent." Martha said triumphantly.

"All right Martha, what's this all about?"

"You of all people must know what's wrong with Eddie, he's different."

"Yes." Jenny was non comittal, if she had noticed it herself she was not about to admit it to the eyes and ears of the world.

"Come on Jenny, what's up?"

"Nothing as far as I know, really." Martha opened her mouth and Jenny said quickly "Oh I know what you're going to say again, he's different, right?"

"Right."

"He's quieter that's all."

"I know, I just want to know why, has the business not been doing well?"

"Ah!" Jenny smiled at her friend, "now I get it."

"Well, it was just an idea." Martha looked at her defensively.

"No Martha, business is fine, I think he's just a little tired."

"Eddie tired?" Martha fell into the settee and bounced against the cushions, "I've never known him tired before." she said.

"No, well he's been working pretty hard you know, I expect he's ready for his leave."

"Another three months isn't it?"

"'fraid so." Jenny sat down beside her "still not too long now, he needs a rest I think."

"Not upset about you and him?" Martha pointed her head in the direction of Bill Jolly's flat. Jenny caught her meaning.

"Of course not," she said indignantly "there's nothing for him to get upset about.

She sprang up and went to the percolator on the sideboard.

"OK I'll have one." Martha said not at all abashed. "does he know?" she persisted.

"Know what Martha?" Jenny put the percolator down with a bang.

"Well, you know, about you and Bill"

"What about me and Bill?"Jenny asked dangerously.

"Oh you know"

"Now come on Martha," Jenny carried a cup and saucer to the middle aged woman "you had a go at me the other week at David's party, what are you insinuating."

Martha opened her mouth and said slowly " I didn't did I?" she was shocked.

"Yes, you jolly well did." Jenny said and then burst into laughter.

"Yeah, yeah!" Martha waved her hand about "jolly well, Bill Jolly, funny!"

Jenny looked at her friend seriously.

"There's nothing wrong between Bill and me." she said deliberately.

"Oh yes!" Martha said rudely.

"No!" Jenny was emphatic "we just enjoy each other's company." she said primly.

"That must be a great comfort to Eddie." Martha said nastily.

Jenny had noticed the difference in her husband of course, but had put it down to the extra work and the change that had come about between them. If he was so different that Martha had started to notice, she began to wonder if she ought to be worried about it.

Eddie stayed at home on Thursday night. It was a wonder to everyone who began to think that he had been taken ill. He sat looking out of the lounge window into the darkness and sipping at his gin. At one point he almost decided to throw the towel in, get out of the partnership and get back to normal living. It was no good thinking that way, he knew, he realised that now he was in the business he had to stay in. He knew too much, the partner knew him, there were loads of people who knew him and what he was up to, even if he had no idea of who they were. He was trapped and he hated it, he felt that his life was being manipulated. Up to now he had always been in control of his life, and the situations he created for himself were ultimately for him to handle. Now he had no control over his own business. Even if he refused to sell the bathroom equipment, the booze would still come in and be distributed, the only person who would suffer would be himself, he would stop making money. He shook his head, drank deeply and stopped thinking.

Friday morning he went for a walk, It was so unusual that the occupants of the flats who were not suffering from hangovers, peeped at him through their windows in disbelief. It seemed to Eddie that for the first time he was really seeing Hamra. Things he had never bothered to notice before, he stopped to look at. The cart of vegetables drawn by a thin old Pakistani and some young boys, the goatskins sweating outside a modern apartment building. The small donkeys supporting fat Arabs with sticks, the coffee seller with his chink, chink of tiny cups and tin kettle. He was looking for the word, the right word to describe the place and found himself outside the Grand Mosque.

As it was Friday, the faithful had already gathered for the sermon that was being broadcast over the louspeakers. In his new frame of mind and curious, Eddie slipped off his shoes and stood inside the doorway. The worshippers stared at him for a moment and turned away. Within a few moments the sermon was over and the crowds started spilling into the street, shuffling into their shoes. Eddie realised his mistake too late, and was forced to wait until the place was nearly empty to find his own. Relieved he darted out of the doorway and into the street. There, parked nearby was a large Rolls Royce and about to step into it—an old man with a grey beard and a stick— Sediki. Eddie darted forward and tapped on the window.

"Good morning, Sediki."

The old man rolled down the window "Ah Edward! How are you?" he asked courteously

"What happened to that----" Sediki intervened by opening the door of the car.

"Get in Edward."

"Eddie scrambled into the sumptuous saloon "This is nice." he heard himself say. The old man tapped the driver on the shoulder and pressed a button to close the communicating window, then the car drove off.

"Now then we can speak freely." Sediki turned to his passenger.

"What happened the other night to that girl?"

"Nothing at all." the old man said " shall we take you home?"

"Oh—yes please down Khadair St.---"

"The driver knows the way."

"Oh!" Eddie was taken aback, the world and his wife seemed to know where he lived, "yes, well, the girl." he prompted.

"She was all right, not to worry, Edward. She was patched up and sent home. "

"Just like that?"

"Just like that." Sediki answered.

"It was disgusting." Eddie pressured.

"Of course."

"Is that all you can say?"

The old man turned to him. "Edward, you know my views on such things, I told you clearly that night, but you must also know that I am powerless to change them. We all have to accept these things until they can be changed, and if young women are greedy enough to be drawn into events over which they have no control, then there is nothing we can do except hope they aren't hurt too badly."

"Sorry, I understand." Eddie said, then "Who was that drunk? I thought----"

"Think nothing." the old man snapped, "and that's an end to the matter Edward, you must not tackle me again on this subject, it is too dangerous."

The Rolls drew up at the steps of the flats and as he

stepped out Eddie was aware of the audience peeping at him from the windows. He waved to them cheerily and bounded up to the door, as he went to unlock it he felt someone at his elbow. It was Aziz.

"Hi!" he said "open up quickly."

Eddie seized the Lebanese by the arm and he said roughly "Just the chap I want to see." and pushed him into the entrance hall.

"Not here." Aziz urged and started running up the stairs, Eddie followed, suddenly invigorated.

Jenny was preparing lunch for herself having decided that the trip to the hotel was off for that day, but she gladly made the two men coffee and just as happily received the flattering looks of admiration that Aziz sent in her direction.

"Your wife is very good looking." he said admiringly.

"You've said that before." Eddie snapped at him.

Aziz cleared his throat, he evidently thought it best to come to straight to the point.

"You're needed at the godown today, they are stocktaking and we need to get the orders together for a new consignment. This afternoon would be all right about three o'clock."

"God!" Eddie exclaimed "Why does it have to be mid afternoon everytime we go anywhere? Don't you ever have a zizz?"

Aziz waggled his head and his curls danced "Best time of day to avoid unwelcome curiosity, Eddie you know that."

"I'm damned well fed up with all this secrecy." the Englishman said throwing himself down into an easy chair.

The Lebanese looked a little taken aback, "Can't be helped, part of the business I'm afraid." he picked up his coffee cup and stirred the liquid gracefully, replacing the spoon without a sound.

"Three o'clock?" Aziz asked again.

"Oh all right!" Eddie was ungracious and sipped at his coffee noisily.

"You wanted me for something?" Aziz pressed him.

Eddie looked up to see where his wife was and looked back at the Lebanese and frowned "Hang on." he said quietly.

"Jenny?" he yelled to her. She came out of the kitchen wiping her hands. "listen, are we going out for lunch?"

190

She looked at him and said indignantly, "Now isn't that just like a husband, here I am making myself something to eat because he's been out all morning, not having said a word to me, mind" she addressed Aziz " and now just as it's ready he asks me out to lunch."

The Lebanese laughed politely and took out his cigarette case to cover his embarrassment he offered it to her.

"No thanks." she said and managed a smile.

"Well?" Eddie pursued "shall we?"

"All right," she answered "I'll put it in the fridge and have it tomorrow."

"That's a girl!" Eddie said patronisingly "tell you what" he said as though it were an afterthought "pop down and ask Martha and Don if they want to come with us."

"OK!" his wife called as she went through the door into the kitchen.

Eddie gave a pointed look at Aziz and the Lebanese interpreted it by waiting until she had left the flat before he asked again.

"Now then, what was it?

"That ruddy party I had to go to."

"Oh yes, I'd forgotten about that. How was it?" he leaned back against the cushions and drew on his cigarette.

"Terrible." Eddie said at once "Do you have any idea what goes on up there?"

"Some." Aziz nodded, his face not changing expression.

"Why the hell I had to go there I don't know. I got lumbered by an old man, a nice old man" he conceded " but he said he belonged to the ruling family and read me a lecture on the evils of alcohol."

Aziz grinned" Is that all?" he said

"No, it damned well isn't. Those bloody hypocrites, the princes, all starch and Koran one minute and well---" he stopped, searching for the right word "animals, that's the only word for it, animals the next."

"Yes, " Aziz said "it is known."

"And then there was Ahmed."

"Ahmed?" Aziz stubbed out his cigarette and looked up interested.

"That bloody beady eyed chap that we saw in Al Jalawi and you said you hadn't seen him, then you said you'd find out about him. Seems he's a cousin of the old man I was with.

Eddie was not prepared for the expression on his companion's face. It could have been one of horror. "What was the old man's name?" he asked almost in a whisper.

Eddie looked at him curiously.

"Sediki, he said his name was, like the drink. In fact he had just given me a lift home before I saw you."

Aziz looked stunned and his swarthy skin paled a little.

"Why? Do you know him?" Eddie was puzzled by the reaction. There was a pause and the Lebanese seemed to collect himself.

"Ah yes! Sediki. Ahmed's cousin, yes I know them both."

"You said you didn't know that one with the hooked nose and beady eyes." the Englishman accused him.

"I know, I know." Aziz waved a hand in the air "I said I'd find out and I did."

"Well, so have I now, he's the Princes' Major Domo."

"Not quite." Aziz smiled recovering quickly from the effect of Eddie's words.

"What then?"

"More I suppose like their god father, you might call it in your country."

"Go on."

"Ahmed would have been Sheik today if the princes had never been born, he was the only possible male to inherit, but when the princes were born, he was the only person that could be trusted to look after them, too many women interfering. He more or less brought them up and saw to their education, almost a father to them, their own father was so old. The princes were regarded as a miracle after waiting so long for sons."

"That's a miracle that went sour all right." Eddie remarked morosely.

"Well, anyway Ahmed more or less brought them up and guided them and has watched over them ever since." Aziz sighed, "there's very little that goes on in this country without Ahmed knowing about it, and if it's going to hurt his precious princes, someone had better watch his step."

"Quite a story! If I wasn't involved in all this, I'd still feel it was Arabian Nights." Eddie scratched at his chin. "What about Sediki?"

Aziz ignored the question "you said he was Ahmed's cousin."

"He is, his mother married into another branch of the family though, and he's spent many years away from Hamra."

"That makes sense" Eddie said remembering the old man's story, then he thought again of Ahmed and snorted, "you can never tell with these Hamrans can you?"

"What do you mean?" Aziz asked.

"There he was, as stately as any king, playing the part of the elder statesman all gold beads and camel sticks, and then that drunken bum--- Why does he allow those burkes to carry on like that?"

The small man took out his cigarette case and offered it to Eddie. "Ahmed has no control these days over the Princes, he has to do what he is told. He still has a great deal of power though, for they are the only ones who can give him orders, and in any case they depend on him a lot, but even he has to be careful.."

The Lebanese stood up and stretched, blowing smoke at the ceiling.

Eddie said "I think Sediki would like to have the country return to Yusef's day, he talked a lot about it being better then."

Aziz said abruptly "That was dangerous."

"Ok, ok, I didn't say it, he did."

"Then don't repeat it, it's dangerous talk." Aziz frowned.

"All right, but I'm not likely to am I?" Eddie grinned into the sallow face.

Jenny came back into the flat with Martha at her heels.

Oh Jenny!" Eddie remembered what she had gone downstairs for. "right you are Aziz, three o'clock it is."

The small man greeted Martha and walked swiftly to the door, he bent his head to Eddie's "Meet you at the same place." he said in a low voice.

"Do we have to walk in the heat?" Eddie asked whispering.

"No, this time I'll direct you with the car."

"Thank goodness for that!" Eddie said as he waved him down the stairs.

26

THE street outside the warehouse was empty and deserted, the residents of the Souk were resting in air conditioned rooms or behind open windows. Inside the yard behind a locked gate there was intense bustle. The labourers, a mixture of Pakistanis and Yeminis, their Shiva Kamis overwashed into a uniform grey colour, were moving boxes and crates. The fork lift travelled in and out of the godown doors at a speed that seemed reckless. Inside the building, quite cool, a partitioned office had been constructed in the corner. A typewriter, some files and a desk appeared to be the only equipment necessary to run the business.

Aziz conscientiously introduced Eddie to all the workers and he shook a dozen hands and received many greetings before he was allowed to start the stock taking. An old man in white, with a gold trimmed pill box hat, handed him a clipboard, returning from the office with a printed list. Eddie took it without looking up and started to read the figures. He began to walk towards a pile of boxes at the other end of the godown.

"Come!" he said half turning to the man and then "Shafique?" he said in wonder "what the hell are you doing here?"

The older man bowed slightly "I work here, Mr Miller when I am not in the office."

"Bloody hell Aziz!" I didn't know you'd pinched our office staff, how many others are there?"

The Lebanese laughed delightedly "Only Shafique's son, look, over there." he pointed to the pickup "he's our driver."

"How long has this been going on?" Eddie asked the old man.

Aziz answered for him "Before you started, Shafique is one of our best men, I told you I only have men that I can trust." The Pakistani bowed slightly at the compliment.

"Is this all the staff?" Eddie asked waving a hand in the direction of the labourers

"Nearly" the small man said evasively, walking off to a pile of stock, "Come on, there isn't much time before the Souk opens again, I want to be finished by then."

It took barely an hour to complete the reordering and the stock taking, Shafique was evidently in charge of all the paperwork and Eddie smiled to see the old man had organised himself so well that there was no need for any other clerk. At the company he would have needed at least two extra hands to deal with it. It was clear to him now how Aziz knew his whereabouts when away from Hamra, clear also how the gin got to him. Shafique had obviously been the one who had told Aziz about the salesman's record. Eddie did not know whether to be grateful or not.

The days and weeks passed in much the same way as before, the sales figures increased and Eddie was in no danger of having the new contract implemented. he was still away for most of the week travelling around the country and Jenny happily painted and talked, played Bridge and went shopping. Now and again they heard from Bobby, but mostly the news came from his grandmother.

Eddie's bank balance was growing healthily every week and soon they would need to plan where they would spend their leave. It was one month before the end of the company contract when the bombshell came.

"Can't go?" Eddie shouted, his eyes protruding dangerously.

"Sorry" Aziz said backing away as though from a wild beast.

"Sorry?" Eddie shouted again.

"Sh, sh" Aziz placed a placatory hand on the Englishman's arm, he shrugged it off impatiently.

"Come on Aziz, I've worked like a dog for this, I need the break."

"Yes, yes, I know, but you can't go yet, it's impossible."

"Why not? Why not in a month's time?" Eddie's suspicions were aroused, was the partner going to refuse to let him go now he was making so much money?

"Sit down." the Lebanese pointed to the chair.

"No- tell me, why not? Surely the partner can manage for a month or two until I get back, he's made plenty of money. I must have put enough money in his pockets in the last few months." he pulled out a packet of cigarettes that threatened to become squashed in his angry hands.

Aziz flicked his lighter and lit the cigarette that was bobbing up and down in Eddie's lips.

"Listen to me will you? We have containers arriving the very week you want to go on leave, and we need you here."

"I don't see why." Eddie said reasonably "I've already sold the stuff all you have to do is to deliver it."

"You don't understand." Aziz said sitting down carefully and crossing one leg over the other elegantly.

"You're damned right I don't. Aziz old chum, I don't understand."

"There's an order in the containers you don't know about." he said nervously.

"What? Bathroom stuff?"

"Yes, one for the Palace."

"Oh great, that's great!" You take an order for the Palace and don't tell me--- just a minute, just a minute." Eddie perched himself on the arm of a chair "the Summer Palace? Who gave the order- and who took it?"

"It isn't the one in Abdul Aziz Street, it's the Winter Palace.

"Yes, go on, who gave it?"

"The princes, or rather Ahmed."

"Oh nice! Good old Ahmed again." Eddie said sarcastically "go on, who to?"

"Sediki." Aziz said.

"Oh! I'd forgotten Sediki, I suppose he gave it to Shafique, who just happened to be up at the Palace for a wing ding!"

Eddie felt continually threatened by the palace and the Terrible Three, which is how he thought of the princes. He had been looking forward to clean green grass, tall trees in cool woodlands, he had been longing to go home and be his own man for a time.

"I still don't see why I have to be here." Eddie said. "You could deliver it couldn't you?"

"No, sorry, they want you to deliver it and explain how to install the equipment to the maintenance men."

The Englishman opened his eyes in surprise. "What on earth for? It's simplicity itself. If my Bedu up country can manage it, then it ought to be easy as pie for the plumbers."

"Not to these fellows." Aziz smiled, feeling a little more confident, Eddie had stopped shouting. "They don't know much."

"Well, if I stay until then, can I go afterwards?" Eddie asked meekly.

The Lebanese darted a glance at him suspecting sarcasm.

"Of course."

"Of course!" mimicked the salesman, "how nice of you, I shall tell my wife that you've ruined her holiday." he said nastily.

Aziz was crestfallen, he leaned forward in his chair "It isn't my fault, believe me, we all have to do what we are told."

"Yes," Eddie sighed deeply "I'm beginning to see that."

"Cheer up!" the Lebanese stood up briskly, "Party tomorrow night at David's"

Eddie glared at the man until he had wiped the smile off his face.

"I shan't be there, parties aren't in my line lately." he said.

"Corinth has been asking about you." Aziz said innocently flicking at a piece of fluff with his finger nail.

Eddie started at the name, he had tried to put all thoughts of the girl completely out of his mind. He had regretted ever trying to become acquainted with her, it had been a mad fancy. Now he recalled the picture of her sitting in the library, her hair shining in the soft light, her dark eyes smiling. Then he pulled himself together, Corinth had never smiled at him much. "I might pop in." he said sullenly.

"You do that." Aziz said slapping the man on the back "Can't let you get down in the mouth, must keep your spirits up."

"Especially as I can't go on leave."

"Only a week or two, Eddie." Aziz reminded him.

They walked to the door and the Englishman paused. "You can have no idea what two weeks can mean to someone who had planned to be home before that."

"Oh I can, I assure you." Aziz said seriously "I know it will be difficult for you, but in the end you will be glad that you stayed."

For the first time in their brief association Aziz was wrong, very wrong indeed.

That Thursday night the Millers stayed at home. A message had reached them saying that the party had been cancelled due to illness. Eddie hoped that Corinth was all right and had only caught a cold or something harmless, but he was not upset.

197

He was quite content to stay at home, he had never really wanted to go to the party in the first place.

During the next couple of weeks, a feeling of gloom began to descend on the capital. The activities of the Religious Police became intensified, and rumours of arrests and violent beatings ran round the city like fire. Small stores, cafes and restaurants had their windows broken and the owners taken away and imprisoned. Any store caught open after the call to prayer had been sounded was demolished, the walls beaten down by the police themselves.

Gradually the Ex Pats began to show such caution that they started living on their nerves. Front doors, sometimes left open through forgetfulness were now checked and double checked so that no one could enter unless the catch was released from inside.

Wine was dug up out of villa gardens and poured down drains. Sediki became unavailable and no amount of money could purchase imported alcohol. The embassies sent urgent messages to their countries not to send anything incriminating in their diplomatic bags, and yeast disappeared from the supermarket shelves.

The Ex Pat community assumed that the lead up to Ramadan was being taken a lot more seriously that year and acted accordingly. Parties were cancelled and groups that were used to gathering for mutual enjoyment disbanded. The Dramatic club, The Operatic Club and the National Societies decided not to meet again until Eid, the holiday that signified the end of the fast. The Welsh Society stopped singing, The Scottish Society stopped dancing and the Irish stopped doing both. Now that friends were hesitating to meet as often as they were used to, a nervous peace descended on the capital. Jenny and Eddie spent their weekends packing and planning for their holiday, their flat an island where strangers were not welcome. Martha and Don had already left for their leave and there was no one else in the block of flats that the Millers wished to befriend. Bill Jolly had been abandoned immediately and Jenny used the telephone constantly instead. No one was going to take any risks.

The week before Ramadan the atmosphere in Hamra became worse. Gun fire was heard at various times throughout the day and night. News came that a compound had been entered and the walls of a house battered down, the occupants taken away. It was enough to make the Ex Pat community stay as close to home as they could. It was said that the bachelors in the house had been drinking, no one doubted it, but it was the first time that a compound had been entered and nerves were shaken.

Eddie returned to Hamra and looked for Aziz, he was nowhere to be found. Shafique and his son were also absent from the firm. Reggie thought they must be preparing for the fast.

A message came in the mail to the effect that the Palace would be expecting him on Sunday, the consignment was already there. Eddie looked again for the Lebanese to confirm his departure the following week, he wandered about the Souk for quite a time until he found the warehouse, but it was padlocked and deserted.

The bright flood lights that normally beamed out around the perimeter were switched off, and although the salesman waited until all the cafes and restaurants had emptied, they remained that way. He looked for Aziz at the juice seller's, but it was closed and the place in darkness.

Eddie made up his mind that he would go to Khofar, install the bathroom equipment and return the same day, travelling through the night. That way they could get the plane home the next day. He would leave a message for Shafique.

"Damn it all!" he said to himself "if they are going to be away when I need to confirm arrangements, then I'll make my own arrangements and to hell with them."

It was on the Friday, after a good lunch at the hotel, that the police came for Eddie.

27

The man in charge had threatened to break the door down unless Edward Miller himself came down to them. Puzzled as to why he had been singled out, Eddie willingly agreed to go down. Jenny followed behind anxiously.

"Be careful, someone might have been telling tales, watch what you say." she urged.

"They must have the wrong person, it can't be me they want," he said hopefully. He blanched when he saw how many police were outside the door, they seemed to fill the street. A pickup of men brandishing sticks was parked in the road, more on foot jostled each other around the door.

"Open!" the leader mouthed through the glass door.

Eddie did as he was told and was instantly grabbed by two of the men, cleanly dressed in white shirt and blue trousers. Along with the beret, the uniform singled them out as religious police.

"Just a minute---" Eddie struggled with his captors, "hang on!" they took no notice but bundled him into the pickup beside the driver, squeezing in beside him. Over his shoulder he could see Jenny pleading with the man who had demanded that the door should be opened. Without answering her he had turned and taken his place in the back of the pickup with his men.

Eddie could see no more for the vehicle had started to pull away and his view was obscured by the bodies of those in the back.

"Where are you taking me?" The Englishman's voice sounded strangled even to himself. There was no reply.

"Where are you taking me?" he repeated into the face of the man next to him. There was no answer, the man fixing his eyes directly through the windscreen.

"You speak English?" Eddie asked in despair.

The policeman shook his head.

"Do you speak English?" he addressed the driver.

There was no response.

'Hell!' Eddie said to himself 'What am I being arrested for? I haven't had a drink for a fortnight. I don't have any booze and

I've been out of the capital for the last week, what the hell is all this about?'

He racked his brains to think of some reason that would make these madmen want to arrest him, but apart from his activities with Aziz, there seemed to be no answer. Then he swallowed quickly, thinking that Aziz had been nowhere to be found, further, Shafique and his son had disappeared as well perhaps they had all been arrested. Someone had evidently talked.

That was it, he told himself, now he was for it, how on earth was he going to get out of this? A flash of yellow material caught his eye and he noticed an Indian girl in a Sari walk down the street. It reminded him of the Palace.

'That was it!' he thought to himself 'I've got immunity, the Princes. I have to be in Khofar on Sunday for the Palace job. If necessary get hold of Ahmed and he'll sort it out.' Eddie began to feel more confident and visibly relaxed.

His captor noticed it and stared at him curiously. He began to reach into his pocket for a cigarette, but catching the eye of his guard thought better of it.

'Never mind' he thought, 'this won't take long to sort out, I shall be home again in no time. 'The pickup stopped outside a building in the centre of Hamra. There was nothing written on the exterior to indicate that it was anything but another block of flats. Eddie soon found otherwise, however, for he was pushed up the steps, through a door into a room, and through another door until he fell against a bench. The door slammed behind him and he was alone.

The Englishman cursed softly and thoroughly to himself and brushed himself down. He took a handkerchief from his pocket and wiped his forehead looking around him. There were no windows in the room, just the four walls, a bench he had already made acquaintance with and a table. He walked around for a while, mulling over in his mind what he would say. He thought naively that all he had done was sell bathroom fittings, the booze had never been part of his activities, he could deny all knowledge of it. What had he done apart from sell good merchandise for his partner?

His partner! Had he been arrested? 'Damn!' he said to himself, if he only knew who he was., he should be here helping me out.' he thought angrily.

After about thirty minutes Eddie sat down, he was beginning to get very nervous. No one had been near him, the sounds of activity outside the room were minimal, what was going to happen to him? His confidence started to ebb and he thought back over the time he had been in Hamra. Could someone have told them about the parties, the expensive drinks? He had only been to Ex Pat parties, never been near Arabs unless he was selling them genuine goods—or the time he had been to the Palace. His confidence surged again, mention the princes, or Ahmed and the job on Sunday, they've got to let me go then. "Come on, come on" he said to the closed door.

Eventually impatience overtook him and after that anger. What a bloody cheek to leave him here like this! He sprang up from the bench and went to the door, he was about to bang on it but he tried the handle first, and surprisingly it turned.

The door opened inwards and he could see before him a high desk and a man behind it writing diligently. The Englishman went forward,

"Hey you!" he said belligerently, the man looked up "yes you! What the hell have you got me here for?"

"Mr Miller?" the man said in a perfect English accent.

"Yes, you speak English?"

"Of course." the man said.

"Of course." Eddie repeated thinking of Aziz. "What am I here for? That's what I want to know, I've been shoved around, stuck in that room and generally made a monkey of, what's it all about?"

"Mr Miller, you are here because we have been requested to arrest you."

"That's no answer! Eddie said astounded by the logic.

The man looked at him mildly "Please to return to that room." he pointed with his pen.

"Why? What are you arresting me for?"

"All in good time Mr Miller." the policeman said starting to write again.

"Now look here." the salesman took a step forward and the man laid down his pen with a sigh.

"You have someone coming to see you, it will take a little time for him to get here, but you must be patient and wait."

"Well, why on earth didn't you say so? Who?" he demanded "Who's coming to see me?"

"Your business partner, I thought you would have known that."

Eddie felt a wave of relief wash over him. His partner, obviously coming to bail him out of trouble, pay a hefty bribe and he would be out of the place and heading back to his flat, he turned on heel and went to sit down in the small room. "Hurry! hurry!" he breathed.

The afternoon wore on, the mezzerin sounded for evening prayers and Eddie began to despair of ever being rescued from the Police Station. Soon after Salah, a young policeman in a badly fitting uniform brought him perfumed tea. Trying to talk to him had produced no result, for whether anyone could speak English or no, the only person who seemed prepared to speak to him was the man on the desk. Eddie smoked cigarette after cigarette stubbing them out on the terrazo floor. he had looked at his watch constantly and like prisoners before him had found that time went very slowly. Unconsciously he played a game with himself and restricted checking his watch to what he thought was fifteen minute intervals.

At about seven o'clock the door opened and the young policeman came to fetch him. For a time Eddie's hopes rose, but then he was led down a corridor and down some steps into the basement and the hair started to stand up on the back of his neck. There seemed to be no one about, just the policeman and himself. Their footsteps echoed back to them off the cement walls and when he cleared his throat, the sound vibrated around the corridor loudly. The policeman was leading him to the cells, the Englishman was pushed through an iron grilled door into a small space and the lock was turned.

Eddie leaned his head against the grill in despair. 'What am I doing here?' he thought bleakly, 'what possible offence have I committed that they would know about. Has Aziz been arrested and tortured so that he's talked? Was Shafique tortured? He was an old man, maybe he was the first to talk. Am I to be tortured?' Sweat broke out on his forehead and he sighed heavily.

The sound of a laugh made him turn quickly, behind him on the floor sat three men, Arabs. Their clothes were filthy and one of them was wiping his nose on his gutrah. They looked up at him, their crooked teeth gleaming in the light from the corridor.

"English" one of them said and pointed to the floor.

"God! What have I come to, sitting on the floor with this lot." he shook his head violently and turned his back on them. The men gabbled amongst themselves and then laughed loudly. The Englishman wondered if he was to spend the night in the cell, and the thought made him shudder. The men smelled pretty bad, as though they had spent their days amongst camels without washing. Eddie's temper got the better of him and he grabbed the bars of the grill and rattled them violently.

"Hey!" he shouted, "someone come here, hey!" he stopped when he realised that the men behind him were laughing at him. No one appeared in the corridor outside the grill, and although he twisted his head as best he could, there seemed to be no one at the end of it. For a moment the Arabs stopped laughing, waiting for the Englishman to perform again to add to their amusement. The place was in total silence.

Eventually Eddie had to give up all hope that he would be rescued that night. Slowly at first he levered himself down to the floor, squatting so that he need not show that he was capitulating. Later, his spirits completely deflated, he sat down on the tiled floor. He noticed a bucket in the corner and with considerable relief used it and returned to the space he had taken for his own. The Arabs set about making themselves comfortable for the night and Eddie, thinking he would need his wits about him on the following day prepared to do the same. The floor was warm but it was hard, his elbow of little use as a pillow, but gradually he succumbed to his weariness and fell into sleep. It could only have been a short while later that he awoke with a start.

The Arab nearest to him had moved nearer and had a hand on the Englishman's leg. Eddie jumped up as though a scorpion had stung him.

"Get off me, you bloody Wog!" he yelled throwing the hand off his leg and pushing the man away from him "get away!" he kicked out.

The Arab grinned displaying two rotten front teeth and

shrugging his shoulders, he turned over. The other two grunted in their sleep but breathed evenly. Eddie sat down again, his fists ready to punish any of the men who might approach him, none of them did, they slept soundly, if noisily for the rest of the night. Eddie sat slumped against the wall, his eyes heavy, unwilling to allow himself to be taken by surprise.

Morning found him still sitting against the wall, his hair wet and sticky with sweat, his clothes rumpled and dirty. Inside his head a throbbing had started that was to remain with him for the rest of the day, he felt completely exhausted.

At seven o'clock a Pakistani with a great bunch of keys on his hip, brought a bowl of rice and some water. Without a word he pushed the bowl under the grill on the floor and the jug through the bars, returning later he brought four paper cups. Immediately the Arab prisoners swooped on the rice, balling it in their fingers and throwing it into their mouths. Genially they made signs to invite Eddie to do the same, but he shook his head and poured some water.

Steps approaching later alerted the Salesman, already tuned to the sounds of his prison, that someone new was walking down the corridor, he almost refused to believe that they were coming for him. A tall Arab dressed in a navy blue dish dash and a red and white check headdress, a shumag, stepped in front of the grill. He called the Pakistani to unlock the cell and with a clang the door was pushed aside. With more signs the man invited Eddie to follow him.

Eddie longed to ask to be allowed to wash, he felt extremely dirty and very uncomfortable. He knew as well that he was at a disadvantage looking as crumpled as he felt. Maybe a cool wash would do something for the headache that was engulfing him. It made matter worse to see that the Arab he was following was as smart as paint. His clothes were spotless and creased in the right places as though they had come straight from the laundry. The man's beard was shiny, black and bushy and he smelled of perfumed after shave.

"I need a wash." Eddie said, his voice sounding strangled in the echoes of the corridor. The man glanced over his shoulder but said nothing. "Please!" he begged " I must have a wash." he tried to gain a step on the man to look into his face, but there was still no response.

"Hell! Eddie's temper was rising again, but it made his head ache more, so he said nothing.

The man led him to another room and stood back for the Englishman to enter. With relief he saw that it was a bathroom, and although he heard the door being locked behind him, he was so grateful at that moment for being there that he would have been happy to stay all day. His spirits rose again and he thought that maybe this time he was going to be able to get to the bottom of all this and extricate himself.

Refreshed and hopeful, Eddie was led once again down another corridor lined with wooden benches. He noticed that for each door he passed there were two benches. Evidently these were interrogation rooms, there were people of all nationalities coming and going in the corridor. The noise was incessant with groups of men talking and shouting, and some demonstrating angrily to the officials in their navy blue dish dashes.

The guard indicated a bench for Eddie to sit down and was soon swallowed up in the crowd as he turned away. He watched the crowd of people for a time and looked at the other prisoners being brought to sit outside other rooms. No one came for him, or to tell him what to do, he assumed he would simply have to stay there until his name was called. It reminded him of an outpatients department at a hospital, except he though grimly, there he would be allowed to go home. For a moment he wondered what might happen if he were to walk up the corridor and out of the front door. It would do no good though, he decided, they would soon pick him up again. If he got to the airport he had to have his exit visa otherwise he would not be free to go. No, better to sit it out and get the whole thing sorted out now.

He had been sitting on his bench for some time when something drew his attention to the room at the end of the corridor. His view was unclear, it wavered as men passed backwards and forwards in front of it, but he felt drawn to stand up and look over their heads. There in front of the high desk was a man looking as crumpled as Eddie was himself and incredibly he was shouting and dancing around, slapping his forehead and staggering about the room, first out of sight and then back again in view. Eddie recognised the black curls straight away, it was Aziz and he was obviously complaining in high tones to the man behind the desk. It seemed to be more than a complaint for he continually slapped at his head in accompaniment to a string of Arabic. The policeman answered mildly enough, but it only served to provoke more shouting from the Lebanese, he walked round the room in circles, returning to the desk and pushing open palms at the officer. His hair danced and he was evidently in a frenzy, finally he pulled a handkerchief out of his pocket to blow his nose, and a guard came from behind the desk and took him firmly by the arm.

"Aziz!" Eddie stretched to make himself seen, "Aziz!" he shouted, but the noise in the corridor was too great for his voice to carry. He tried again but gave it up as he saw that the Lebanese was being brought down the corridor towards him.

So the little man had been arrested after all, Eddie thought. He wondered where he had spent the night, by the look of his clothes it had been on the floor as well. His heart warmed to the man in spite of the fact that they were both in trouble and Aziz would not be able to help him. At least it was a friendly face, and maybe together they could sort things out. Where was the partner? he wondered for the umpteenth time.

28

AZIZ flopped down on the bench beside Eddie, his face was pale, an almost dark yellow. His eyes flashed, alighting on nothing in particular, but indicating the tumult in his mind. He sat, his breath coming in gasps from the exertions in the entrance room, he was completely unaware of the Englishman until he spoke.

"You too?" Eddie said.

The Lebanese was about to unleash another spate of Arabic when he stopped with his mouth open "Eddie! Allah Humdalila." he exclaimed raising his hand in the air. "I didn't know what had happened to you."

"I still don't know what has happened to me, what are we doing here?"

"We have been tricked, my friend" Aziz answered at once. " I have to tell you we are in serious trouble, we have been tricked, I tried to tell them-----"

"Just a minute, what do you mean tricked? Eddie broke in "is it to do with the business?"

The small man looked at him in surprise "Yes, of course, don't you know?"

Eddie was exasperated again "No, I don't know. I was brought here last night, thrown into a mucky cell with three Bedu, had nothing to eat and here I am. How am I to know what's going on?"

"Huh!" Aziz said disgustedly "Hamra! I thought I had been so careful, huh!"

The Englishman felt like hitting Aziz "For goodness sake tell me what has happened. Is it the booze?" he darted a look over his shoulder, no one had heard him.

"Aziz laughed bitterly "Yes, it was the booze----"

"Surely Ahmed can get us out of this, I've been thinking ----" Aziz laughed again and this time it sounded light headed.

"Eddie, there's no help there, they're all dead."

"What?" Eddie almost screamed. The man in the blue robes reappeared at that moment and pointed to the door in front of them. Aziz said something in Arabic to him and the man nodded.

"Come on." he signalled to the Englishman, we have to go in here."

The two men entered the room and were surprised to find it empty.

Eddie closed the door quickly behind them and grabbed the Lebanese by the arm.

"Who in the blue blazes is dead?" he asked, his eyes bulging and his head thrusting forward into the small man's face.

"The Princes, all three of them, shot dead." Aziz flopped into a chair by the desk in front of them. "I thought you must have heard, that's why we're here." The adrenalin that had produced the pantomime in the entrance room had all but evaporated and the Lebanese rested his chin on his chest.

"Good God!" Eddie shook the man's shoulder "What's that to do with us?"

He stalked off round the room "I only went there for a party and that was over a month ago."

"They used us, my friend, we've been tricked, framed as you say in your country." Aziz looked up at the angry man and shrugged hopelessly.

"Tricked, how? Who for goodness sake?"

"It was that last consignment, the one with the Winter Palace fittings." he broke off as the Englishman began looking under the desk and examining the telephone. "what are you doing?"

"Might be bugged, we'd better watch what we say, they can all speak English when they need to."

Aziz laughed without humour "Don't bother, they know all they want to about us."

"How? Who talked? Shafique?"

"No, they knew right from the beginning because they planned it that way."

"God!" Eddie threw his hands up "I don't get all this, give me a fag Aziz, I've smoked all mine."

The Lebanese took out the familiar turquoise case from his pocket and they both lit a cigarette. Eddie looked towards the door hearing a noise outside. "Tell me everything before someone comes in, quick."

"The last container didn't have alcohol in it, I suppose you can guess what it really had hidden there." the man ran his fingers through his curls.

"Go on, what?"

"Guns," he said, "a consignment of rifles, small arms and hand grenades, all neatly packed in the secret space." he drew on his cigarette and narrowed his eyes in the smoke as Eddie's mouth sagged open.

"Good God Almighty!" he gasped "Guns?" he began to think he was going mad. "I've never had anything to do with guns." he said indignantly. Then he thought, "who found them?"

"The Police."

"How did they know? Who told them?." he paused "Who ordered those anyway?"

"I keep telling you Eddie, we were tricked." Aziz despaired of making him understand.

Eddie's face was beginning to turn an ugly red, his headache had returned and felt as though a road drill was operating inside his skull.

"For goodness sake Aziz, who tricked us?"

"The partner."

"Our partner?"

"Yes, our rich influential partner." Aziz ground out his cigarette with the heel of his shoe and sagged back into the chair.

Eddie sat down in the other one, he knew he was experiencing a nightmare and no one was going to walk him up. Then he remembered that Aziz knew who the partner was. He was about to ask him when the door opened and a well dressed Arab walked in with a notepad in his hand.

He ignored the two men until he had settled himself behind the desk and carefully headed a sheet of paper.

He said "Mr Edward Miller, Mr Aziz Hilu."

The two men stared at him and waited silently for what might come.

"You have been brought here on very serious charges." the man shook his head so that a corner of his headdress fell forward onto the desk, he lifted and tucked it at the back of his head. "The rulers are dead, they were murdered by men who were supplied with arms from outside the country. The insurrection was short lived however, and the situation is now under control, so although for a time a few rabble rousers thought to undermine the peace of the country, they failed."

The speech of the man was educated, his manner mild, but Eddie caught the glint in his eye and hesitated before saying " What has this to do with me? I'm just a salesman."

"A salesman only, Mr Miller?" he asked gently "more than that I think." he said "You have been operating illegally as a business owner in this country."

Eddie was puzzled.

"Illegally?" he echoed "what do you mean by that?

The Arab sighed "In Hamra a business needs a licence to operate, you did not have one."

Eddie looked from Aziz to the man behind the desk and suddenly erupted into a laugh. "Good God man! Three Princes have been murdered and you're sitting there telling me I need a licence for my business, I don't believe it." he crossed one leg over the other and laughed hysterically.

The man ignored the outburst and continued calmly.

"It is important that you understand the facts Mr Miller, I assure you that the questions I ask are all related to this terrible tragedy." he fiddled with his pen and laid it down in front of him.

"Now, you were operating without a licence at a warehouse in Nehar Street, in fact no papers have come to light anywhere about your business, except the orders found inside the building and the wayleave documents."

Eddie wished Aziz had told him who the partner was, he wanted to tell the man about the agreement and the arrangements that had been made, but to mention a partner and admit that he had no idea what his name was, merely confirmed his guilt. He had no option but to say nothing about it.

"In a secret compartment at the back of the containers you imported alcohol."

"Ah yes! But I had nothing to do with that."

Aziz looked at him and looked away again.

"So you don't know anything about that?" the Arab persisted.

"No-yes, well not really," Eddie floundered.

"Yes, I believe Mr Miller, you knew only too well what was coming into the country."

"I didn't sell it." Eddie protested throwing a glance at Aziz.

"No, that is true, the alcohol was dealt with by someone else." Aziz shifted in his chair "but you know what was happening in your name."

The salesman could not help himself "And in my partner's" he said suddenly "don't forget him, he's an Arab."

"But Mr Miller we have already established the fact that you have no partner, there is no agreement or record that you have one."

"Balls!" Eddie said coarsely. The man ignored the expression. "tell him about the partner Aziz, go on, what's his name? Maybe we can get some sense out of all this."

"Shut up!" Aziz said into his companion's astounded face "just be quiet and let them get on with it." he said in a low voice.

Eddie closed his mouth, he was thoroughly bewildered. He felt as though he were walking through a room filled with string that crossed and recrossed itself until whichever way he went, he would be caught up in it.

"Eventually," the Arab went on as though uninterrupted "you were drawn into a group of people who wished to overthrow our rulers. Terrorism is something that many countries have to deal with these days. You helped them by bringing in not alcohol, but arms." the man sat back in his seat and picked up his pen, examining it from end to end closely. "Unfortunately for you, they were not discovered until the damage had already been done. Our rulers, the Princes were shot."

There was silence in the room as the Arab watched the Englishman. Eddie was frantic, how could he defend himself? By admitting to knowing about the secret compartment, how could he deny that he knew anything about the guns?

"You are in what may be described as a sticky situation Mr Miller, the men who murdered the Princes have already been executed." Eddie gave a start and sat up "It is the only way to make sure that it never happens again. The punishment for murder is death, Mr Miller, you must know that."

What was he saying? Eddie's head was pounding as though someone had used it for a punch bag. He looked at Aziz, amazed that he was sitting so quietly, as though a threat of execution was an everyday affair. He swallowed noisily and looked at the man behind the desk

"You will be taken to another place under guard until further enquiries are made. Mr Hilu" the Arab turned to Aziz " I believe we understand each other?

"Perfectly." he said bitterly.

"You will accompany Mr Miller and interpret for him if need be."

Aziz made no reply.

"But I don't understand—" Eddie started to say. The Arab looked at him quizzically, "I just don't understand any of this." he sunk his head into his hands, of a sudden he looked up at Aziz, "I wish I'd never listened to you, never even met you." he said "everything will be fine Eddie'" he mimicked the Lebanese "'no need to worry', now look at this mess."

"Shut your mouth." Aziz said urgently "just be quiet."

The Arab stood up and adjusted his headdress, he picked up his notepad and went to the door. He turned and looked at the two men. "A guard will come for you in a moment." and he left the room.

As soon as they were alone Eddie exploded "Aziz, you'd better explain all this, leaving nothing out or- or you'll find the Princes aren't the only ones dead!"

The Lebanese held up his hands "All right, no problem!"

"Never mind the 'no problem', speak for God's sake."

"The whole operation was a set up---"

"Who's the partner? Come on, who is he?"

"Sediki." Aziz glared at the desk "Sediki has tricked both of us."

Eddie whistled "My Sediki at the Palace?" Aziz nodded glumly.

The Englishman scratched his head bewildered "But why? he thought for a moment about the old man and felt saddened. He had liked and respected him "why would he do this to us?"

The Lebanese sat up in the chair and looked at the salesman.

"You're not using your brains Eddie, can't you see? It was a wonderful way of getting the Princes out of the way. Blame it on someone else and take over clean as clean."

Eddie stared at the small man everything immediately starting to fall into place.

"Take an English idiot, promise him money and booze, let him work his socks off and then when everything is running smoothly bring in the arms."

"That's about it." Aziz said "and a Lebanese idiot as well."

"What?"

"Me, I fell for it as much as you, Ahmed knew I was always into a deal. They weren't always legal."

"Oh yes! Ahmed! Where does he fit in? I thought he protected the Terrible Three?"

"I don't really know, but I expect those two thought it all up, Sediki could never have managed it alone."

Eddie strode around the room, his stomach empty and churning, his head aching and his blood pressure rising. "This is bloody terrible!" he spluttered and then stopped and swung on Aziz "We started a revolution, you heard him, he called us terrorists. They've been executed, is it our turn now? Hells Bloody Bells Aziz! We're going to be executed."

Aziz clamped his eyes together and opened them wide and shook his head, there were tears. forming. He nervously twitched at his trousers and tried to dust some sand off his knees. He could not trust himself to speak, he kept shaking his head.

Eddie, seeing the small man's collapse allowed his own anger to cool and sat down beside him again. "What a bloody pair!" he attempted to provoke a grin from the Lebanese. "Come on Aziz, we're in a jam, but we're still in one piece so far. What can we do, come on you have the brains."

Aziz sniffed and blew his nose strenuously, trying to regain his dignity.

"I don't know what to do, I really do not. I think we are in their hands, and they can do what they wish with us, it's hopeless."

Eddie was outraged "What kind of attitude is that? Now listen to me, there's got to be a British Consul in Hamra that can do something, if we can get word ou---"

"They won't let you get word out." Aziz broke in "you heard him we are being treated as terrorists, they aren't going to let anyone know where we are."

"Sediki and Ahmed know darned well we're not terrorists, I don't know what they're playing at having these bods bring us here and start reading the riot act."

"Think Eddie, they have to, it's all part of the plan. The Police were tipped off to find the arms, there must have been some left in the container," he thought suddenly "the Police found them, they had to then find the people who brought them in. They were tipped off to find us and the case is closed, no suspicion falls on the ruling house. A couple of foreigners. Very neat, very clean." Aziz said admiringly.

"Yes, chop us and it's all over, Hamra can get on with the next lot of Yusef's relatives."

"There's only one thing," Aziz turned to Eddie looking hopeful "I think we'd be dead by now if they were going to execute us." The salesman caught onto the idea with some relief, "You know you've got a point there Aziz, my little fella." and he thought for the first time in two days of his wife.

"Jenny! Oh my God! What's happened to her?"

"They won't touch her, don't worry." Aziz was reassuring "Worst thing they'll do is send her home."

"What if we could get in touch with her, she could get the consul---"

"Forget it, there's no one here that will take any messages, Jenny won't know where you are and if she did, they wouldn't let her see you, forget it. It's no good trying to work something out that way.

The two men fell silent still trying to think round the problem, and realising that whatever happened to them now, they were in the hands of men who had ruthlessly used them for their own ends already.

Suddenly the door was flung open and two men in Religious Police uniform strode in. They spoke to Aziz and he turned to Eddie and said "Come on, we're going somewhere."

29

Eddie and Aziz were half pushed, half escorted to a landrover outside the building. Curious onlookers pressed forward yammering to each other and gesticulating at the unlikely sight of a European being manhandled by Police.

The vehicle was enclosed with a hard exterior allowing for a measure of air conditioning, and no chance of escape. The Englishman asked where they were going, and what was to happen to them, but the short answer of "It is not known" from Aziz cut short any other questions and he gazed gloomily out of the window and across the desert into which they were now passing. At first he recognised the way, the road that had been an integral part of his life in Hamra, he recognised the wrecks and rusting hulks strewn along the way. A sand storm threatened at midday and the wind blew in twisters over their heads and out into the desert.

The heat was oppressive, the air around them was laden with fine grains of sand, creating a cocoon inside the vehicle that was claustrophobic. The two policemen threw their berets under the dashboard and mopped their foreheads continuously with pieces of cloth. Aziz asked for water and one of them turned and said something in Arabic that sounded to Eddie like 'wait'. Late in the afternoon they reached Abdul Aziz crossroads.

The usual cacophony could be heard clearly inside the Landrover. Lorries, pickups and cars were jostling for position at the pumps just as they always did. Eddie wished ardently that he was among them.

The vehicle slowed as it joined the queue approaching the filling station, and as the engine reduced power, the air conditioning faded and the heat became unbearable. Aziz groaned and edged away from Eddie, trying to create a gap between them, and for Eddie the heat was almost past bearing. His face was colouring dangerously, the blood pumping through his body sounding like drums, and then he became angry.

"God in heaven!" his voice rasped over his dry tongue "get us out of here before you kill us both". The Landrover jerked to a stop and the two policemen turned round in surprise "come on, you half baked gorillas, get us out." The Englishman was desperately trying to get the rear door open. Aziz looked as though he were about to faint, he attempted to speak but gave up, the effort too great. His hand ready with a gesture flopped to his side.

"Ok, Ok!" the driver opened his door and a blast of hot air belched into the vehicle. The other Arab, taking one look at the passengers, jumped out of the Landrover and ran to the small house at the side of the station. Within a moment he was running back with a colourful pot filled with water. Aziz and Eddie were out of the landrover, leaning with their backs against the vehicle panting, their heads back and mouths open taking in great gulps of hot desert air.

No one seemed to notice the drama taking place, drivers and passengers alike were only too anxious to be on their way along the road. After a few minutes, the Police driver taking first in the queue, filled the landrover with fuel and gestured to his passengers to get back into their seats.

"No way, Sweetheart!" Eddie said angrily, his eyes large and bulbous.

"Be careful!" Aziz warned in an undertone.

"Bugger that for a lark!" Eddie responded crudely "I'm not going anywhere without water, what kind of Arab goes into the desert without water?" he asked Aziz reasonably "tell em!"

The Lebanese used his charm to great effect and within moment a goatskin of water was carried from the house and placed into the back of the Landrover. Eddie looked at it distastefully, but made no comment. At least it was water. whatever it would taste like out of a skin. Aziz grinned at him knowing his thoughts and in spite of everything Eddie's spirits were lifting. He slapped the small man on the shoulder and smiled cheerfully. "Oh well, where the hell are we off to now?"

Aziz shrugged "They won't say."

They clambered back into the vehicle and it swiftly pulled away from the cross roads in a direction which Eddie had never taken.

"Where does this go" he asked his companion.

Aziz took a good look around but there was nothing to see except banks of sand eroding softly in the late afternoon breeze.

"I'm not sure," he said cautiously "but I believe this must be the Royal Road."

Eddie looked puzzled "I didn't know there was one."

"It's little used." Aziz looked solemn "that's if I'm right, I've only heard rumours about it. There's supposed to be a gate somewhere along the way with guards, and if a foreigner gets that far he is turned back, not always in one piece either."

"That's ridiculous!" the Englishman exclaimed "How is anyone to know if they don't sign post it?"

"Ah! That's Arabic thinking." Aziz touched his nose and blinked "you should not be going anywhere unless you know where you are going."

Eddie looked long and hard at the small man. "I think the sun has finally got to you, Aziz old buddy! You're talking gibberish."

"What?"

"Rubbish"

Aziz grinned. "Not at all my friend, what right has anyone to go somewhere unless he is invited? If he knows that he is going to Al Jalawi or Waddi Ben Bakar, then he would not be going up a road that did not lead there." He paused and cocked an eyebrow at the Englishman "would he?"

The interior of the landrover was becoming stuffy again and Eddie wiped at his forehead and ran his thick fingers through his hair "I give in, I haven't got the brain power to work it out any more.

The two Policemen exchanged remarks and the vehicle slowed down again. There in front of them was an enormous wrought iron gate with two sentry boxes on either side. A man dressed like a Bedu stood before it, his rifle cradled in his arms, his curved dagger at his waist shining in the dying sun. "The Royal Road," said Aziz in wonder.

The driver jumped out and showed some papers to the Bedu, the gate opened and they were on their way again.

"Did you see that?" Eddie said looking back towards the gate. "A dirty great gate and nothing on either side of it except sand, anyone could get past that." "Not if I know these people, "Aziz answered him "there will be traps in the sand, no vehicle would get across and you can be sure that there'll be something unpleasant for anyone trying it.

"Mm hey what now?" Eddie peered through the window into the darkening landscape. "You said you'd heard about this road, where does it go?"

"I'm not sure, I can only say what I've heard."

"Which is?"

"Either a Palace or a Prison."

"Well, we know which it will be for us don't we, at least we won't be chopped." and he drew a finger across his throat.

Aziz looked pained "I don't think so now, they are taking a great deal of trouble to get us away from Hamra."

They both looked out of the window into the dark, there was nothing to be seen, no lights except from the pale moon pinpointing mounds of sand and the few bushes, scrubby thorn and an odd palm tree. They appeared to be travelling through a different landscape now.

The two men had not eaten since the day before, and their stomachs were empty, Eddie started to gnaw at his fingers. He had nothing in his pockets, not even one of Bobby's sweets. The appalling rice and water he had refused earlier in the day now seemed most attractive he was so hungry.

The journey had been long, hot and uncomfortable, the events of the last two days felt as though they had taken place months ago. They were both beginning to feel that they were on a journey that would last for ever. Their minds had become numb, and if there was anything they wished for, it was that whatever was to happen to them would happen quickly. Gradually their thoughts turning in on themselves, the two men closed their eyes and fell asleep, their heads nodding gently on their chest.

They awoke with a start when the driver applied the hand brake and opened his door. Through heavy eyes they peered through the window. The moon cast light over a low roofed villa set amongst Palm trees, a light shone from the porch illuminating a pathway lined by flowering bushes.

"Palace or Prison?" Aziz murmured,

The passenger doors were opened and the two men

climbed out carefully, their limbs stiff and sore from sitting in a cramped position all day.

They stretched, their captors waiting patiently beside them. Aziz vainly tried to smooth his clothes into shape and pulled at his collar. Eddie merely ran his stubby fingers through his hair. He was looking forward to a shower, surely, he reasoned, there'd be a shower in a place like this?

Someone in the house had heard them arrive for the front door opened. The two guards urged their charges along the path. Framed in the doorway was a figure that seemed familiar to the two men.

"Shafique!" Aziz said in amazement and ran forward to shake the old man's hand

"Good God!" Eddie stumbled towards the door, "we wondered what had happened to you, they got you as well then?"

The two men were overjoyed to see the Pakistani, they laughed and patted him on the shoulder, Shafique's eyes filled and he brushed at them with his boney hands

"It is good to see you," he said to both of them, "please to come in I shall look after you."

"Is this a house?" Aziz asked in the Entrance Hall noting the good furniture, the lamps, the Persian carpet.

"Of course" Shafique said and led the way into a large room. It was comfortably furnished and with modern décor, European lamps and furniture.

"Is it a prison?" Aziz asked again.

"Of course." Shafique answered.

"Damn it all man, what kind of answer is that?" Eddie caught sight of himself in the mirror and he had to admit he looked like a wild man. he rounded on Shafique, who was signalling to the Policemen to wait outside.

The old man grinned "Oh Mr Miller, you do not change, it is good to see you."

The Salesman was slightly mollified and a little ashamed.

"What's he on about?" he asked Aziz who was sitting down in an easy chair and pulling out his turquoise cigarette case. The Lebanese made his companion sit down.

"It is the prison and Palace that I've heard about in rumour." he said "we shall have to ask Shafique to tell us more about it, I'm beginning to see what it means."

"That's more than I am" Eddie said resentfully "I'm dying for a shower, a good drink and a huge meal." he looked as the old Pakistani came through the door.

"It is coming Mr Miller." he said and softly closed the door.

"What are we supposed to be doing here? It's all very nice and all that, but so far away from Hamra, it has to be a prison."

"That's right my friend, a prison in a Palace" Aziz waved his arm, taking in the expensive furnishings.

"I wonder when someone will come and tell us what we have to do?"

"Patience Eddie, I think we shall have to stay here for quite a while in our prison/palace, but if Shafique is here and the food is good, maybe it won't be so bad. Maybe we have been given a very light sentence."

The Englishman looked around him and threw himself into the cushions of a sofa. Aziz was right, it was comfortable, certainly most unexpected and wonderful after the night he had spent in that terrible cell.

He asked suddenly "What about David?"

"David?"

"Yes, was he arrested, do you know?"

"Why should he be?"

"I thought he was the agent for the containers."

"Only at first, later someone else was involved."

"Who?" Eddie shouted "for goodness sake you can't keep things to yourself anymore, there's no point."

Aziz was mildly surprised "It was no one important, so why are you so upset?"

"Oh" The Englishman thought for a moment that there would be another mystery, another secret he knew nothing about.

The old Pakistani came back with a tray on which there was an assortment of hot food and coffee. The two men almost ran to the table and piled their plates.

"Eat slowly!" Aziz said "starving people should eat slowly."

"I'm not starving." Eddie said, a fork halfway to his mouth.

"I am." Aziz said and giggled. They both laughed with delight. The aside was not funny, but they were eating at last in a civilised place however far it was from civilisation itself.

For a brief time they were almost happy.

"I've got to have a shower, "Eddie said later as they sat in the comfortable room. their feet resting on the coffee table. "I've just got to have a shower, but better than that would be a whole bottle of gin and several bottles of tonic." the two men laughed at the absurdity.

"What? After all the trouble that stuff has got us into?"

"I've got to have a shower though." Eddie said seriously,

"Shafique!" Eddie bellowed at the top of his lungs.

Aziz dropped his feet to the floor in alarm.

"Don't worry, old chum, I don't suppose there's anyone else around, and we have to know what the form is don't we?"

Aziz said hastily "At this moment I don't care, not at all."

"Shafique!" Eddie called again.

The door opened almost immediately and the old man came in for the tray.

"Can we have a shower? Do you know how long we are to stay here?" the Englishman asked. The old man picked up the tray and smiled "come on Shafique, we have to know what's going on."

"Someone is coming," the man said "They will tell you everything." and he went to the door.

"Here! Eddie called "you can't get away with that, come back here" but the old man had gone again.

The Englishman stood up "Come on, let's follow him and see what's in the rest of the place."

Aziz grabbed his arm "No, sit down Eddie, we can't be sure of anything yet," he said nervously "let's just wait a little longer."

Eddie hesitated, he had regained his confidence, but it was still apt to desert him at moments. He sat down again, suddenly unsure of himself again.

"Someone's coming!" Aziz warned "that's not Shafique."

The two men sprang involuntarily to their feet as the door opened, Standing silhouetted in the hall light was an Arab woman, her black Abbaya closed and tucked under her chin. As she moved into the lamplight her face was revealed.

"Corinth!" Eddie's mouth was open, his eyes bulbous "What on earth?"

Aziz fell back into his chair and started to laugh, he laughed until the tears rolled down his cheeks and Eddie still gawped in astonishment.

Irritated the Englishman turned on the small man "For God's sake shut up,----what's so funny?"

Corinth moved into the room as though on castors "Hello you two." she said.

Aziz subsided and wiped his eyes, coughing and giggling.

Eddie sank into his chair and said in a subdued voice "Corinth, are you mixed up in all this?"

The girls slipped off the black cloak and let her long hair free over a long blue dress, quietly she opened a small cupboard and took out a bottle marked Export and three glasses.

Eddie said to the Lebanese, "I don't believe any of this." and then, "Is she involved?"

Aziz had regained his composure and nodded, waiting for the girl to speak. She was pouring gin into the glasses, returning to the cupboard for the tonic water.

"The only thing I know is that Corinth has been doing her woman's' liberation thing. When she came back to Hamra she knew she wouldn't be allowed to work, so she helped David with his Clearing and Forwarding. David, not being what people might call a man's man, she felt safe living in the same house. That's all I know really, I was sworn to secrecy and I kept it to myself. Right?" he looked at Corinth "I'm beginning to think now that there is a lot more she didn't tell me." The girl smiled and handed the men their glasses.

Eddie took his absentmindedly "Just a minute! hang on, you said living at David's. He's gay?" he looked up at the girl "I thought you were his wife!"

Aziz giggled again infuriating his companion. "That was what people were supposed to believe, no one bothered her then."

Eddie gulped at his drink and swung round on Aziz "You didn't tell me, why didn't you?"

The small man looked at him surprised "What for? It wasn't important to the business."

Corinth sat down and sipped at her drink, it looked odd, a woman in Arab dress sipping gin. Eddie bent forward to her "Then when we tried to meet----" he left the rest of the

223

sentence hanging in the air.

"I'm sorry Eddie," Corinth looked embarrassed "I had no wish to hurt your feelings, but I had to make sure that you came in on the plan."

Aziz picked up his ears "You seduced him?" he giggled.

The girl was indignant "Of course not, I just tried to interest him."

"You did that all right." Eddie muttered " I wondered why you disappeared off the scene after the business started." he slapped at his knee as though slapping away all the disappointments and hopes he had experienced. Corinth placed her glass on the table.

"Well, don't you want to know what you are doing here?"

The two men were taken aback.

"I thought we were being imprisoned as terrorists." Eddie said glumly.

"Is that why you're here? Aziz asked "do you know what's going to happen to us?

Corinth smiled and nodded, leaning back in her chair.

30

Eddie suddenly realised he was drinking gin. He looked at his glass and a smile spread across his face. "I'll have another of those." he said and went to the table and poured himself a large one.

Aziz was impatient, "Go on Corinth, let us know the whole story, we have been through a terrible couple of days."

The girl sank deeper into her chair, resting her arms on the cushions

"You must know by now that the Princes are dead." The men nodded "and that Sediki and Ahmed are now in control. My grandfather will be the ruler, Sediki is helping him."

"Ahmed? You mean Ahmed is your grandfather?" Eddie whistled, he slapped his forehead suddenly, the eyes, he should have known. He shook his head wondering how he had missed the connection, then reminded himself that there had never been a connection between the two for him to guess at. Corinth smiled and continued.

"You must have worked out by now that the whole business of the bathroom equipment and the booze, was planned so that arms could be brought into the country under someone else's name"

"Yes, mine" Eddie said in disgust.

"Mine as well, remember." Aziz looked at the girl "We have worked most of it out." he said.

"Never mind." Eddie interrupted, "I want to hear it from the horse's mouth."

"Thank you Eddie." Corinth's eyes sparkled.

"You know what I mean," he said sullenly.

"We had to find a salesman with the right character and the best record, it was important because he would have to be ambitious enough not to want to be in the warehouse all the time, he had to be out on the road. Shafique recommended you Eddie."

"I guessed that, but that means that Shafique knew what was going on all the time."

"No he didn't. Shafique and his son were family servants to my grandfather years ago and he was asked to recommend someone because he was working in an European firm. He knew as much as he was allowed to."

"Go on, I suppose you needed a thick salesman that didn't look further than the money in the bank when a secret partner was suggested, as well." Eddie said bitterly.

Corinth nodded, "I'm afraid so, we were banking on your greed,"

"Great!" he looked at Aziz "I love me too!"

Aziz grinned at him "They needed a greedy Lebanese as well, one who did deals that weren't always-well- legal."

Corinth smiled at the small man and nodded.

"You see, both bad characters Eddie, we suit each other."

"So we now have the operation working" Corinth continued "then we brought in the arms."

"Just a minute," Eddie interrupted again. "What about those poor buggers who did the deed, they were shot weren't they? Were they tricked as well?

Corinth was indignant "No they weren't tricked. They knew exactly what would happen to them, they volunteered for Islam."

"Holy war" Aziz nodded to the Englishman.

"God!" Eddie breathed "Is that why we weren't chopped?"

"No Eddie you weren't chopped as you so elegantly call it, because Sediki was most specific that you were to be imprisoned instead. You must understand Eddie, that Sediki and my grandfather are good men, they weren't happy about what they had to do, but it had to be done. They know that they have used your instincts against you, but they are also very grateful. Without you both the result might have been very different. In any case, I think Sediki liked you Eddie."

"I liked him."

"What is to happen now?" Aziz asked prompting the girl.

"What about Jenny?" Eddie asked and then racked his brains for all the other questions he had been asking himself since he had been arrested. Maybe this would be the last chance to get to the bottom of everything.

"Jenny was put on a plane this morning. The situation was explained to her and she seemed to understand everything. She knows that she will have to keep it all to herself whilst you are our hostage."

"Hostage?"

"That's what you are really, you will be staying here, it's my villa by the way, and you can't really call it a prison."

"What about the company, they are going to want to know where I am."

"You went on leave with Jenny this morning if anyone asks, you were due anyway, you simply went without saying goodbye—and you won't be returning, but they won't know that for a few months."

"You've forgotten the way I was taken from my flat, loads of people saw that."

"Oh?" Corinth asked coolly "who particularly?"

The salesman thought quickly, Martha and Don were already away on leave, the rest of the company had flats up the street. There was no one he could think of that would care. "You've got it all sewn up haven't you?" he said.

"I hope so," the girl replied.

Aziz broke in on them "How long are we staying here?"

"As long as it takes." Corinth answered raising her palms to the ceiling.

"Aw, come on!" Eddie pleaded "even a condemned man knows how long his sentence is."

"Put it this way then," the girl said "as long as it takes Sediki and my grandfather to become established in Hamra, not just with the people in this country, but with the world. Then you will be put on a plane home. By that time whatever tale you have to tell will be too late, unimportant, you understand?"

"Quite!"

Aziz said hopefully " I don't think it will take very long."

"It might not." Corinth agreed "In the meantime you have a Hindu heaven."

Eddie's ebullience was returning, staying in this villa did not seem so bad when he thought of what might have happened to him. "What's that?" he grinned at the girl.

Aziz explained "Hindus believe that what you treasure most, you have in heaven."

"So?"

Corinth laughed at him, "You have all the gin you can drink, and the money you worked for is yours to keep. Sediki wanted you to have that."

The Englishman scratched at his head, he'd forgotten that he needed a wash

"What are we supposed to do while we are here?"

"Whatever you wish," Corinth said lightly "drink, eat, walk, sleep, play cards." She walked to the window and pointed into the dark "Over there there's a tennis court. You can live a life of luxury."

The salesman thought of the holiday he had been due to have and smiled to himself. 'Not too bad, Eddie boy. A nice holiday, plenty to drink, plenty of money in the bank and company to talk to, even if it is old Aziz.' he looked at the girl and then at Aziz "It could be OK. Is Shafique staying?

"Yes, and his son, they'll be looking after you both."

"Great!" Never one to make the worst of any situation Eddie was returning to his normal high spirits. "Right then, Aziz old buddy, you and me starting tomorrow will plan what we are going to do. Sport, walks-walks!" he groaned "could even take up some kind of hobby. Then on Thursdays we'll have a party." he looked at Corinth, "You'll come and see us?"

"Of course, sometimes."

"Of course!" Eddie mimicked "Well, just you make it on Thursdays, party night, eh Aziz old man?"

"Of course." said Aziz.

For a moment Eddie lost his bounce and looked down at his feet. He felt enormously relieved to have been given a reprieve. Even though it had all been a fix, he knew they could have dragged him off to Chop Chop Square. He thought briefly of Jenny and Bobby and knew they would be all right. They had money and a home in the UK. He would miss his trips into the various parts of Hamra and the buzz he earned from being the top salesman, but here he was with no responsibilities, money in the bank plenty to drink and servants to wait on him. 'Not bad Eddie, old Bunion' he said to himself and raised his head to grin at Corinth.

"How about another one?"

"Of course." she said and laughed.

Finis

228

Printed in the United Kingdom
by Lightning Source UK Ltd.
119913UK00001BA/32